Skywriting

Also by the Same Author

Singing to Cuba

Skywriting

A NOVEL
OF CUBA

Margarita Engle

BANTAM BOOKS

New York   Toronto   London
Sydney   Auckland

Skywriting is a work of fiction. With the exception of
historical figures, all characters are completely
imaginary. Any resemblance to real people in
the U.S., Cuba, or elsewhere is entirely unintentional
and coincidental.

SKYWRITING

A Bantam Book / July 1995

BOOK DESIGN BY GLEN M. EDELSTEIN

Library of Congress Cataloging-in-Publication Data
Engle, Margarita.
Skywriting : a novel of Cuba / Margarita Engle.
p.   cm.
ISBN 0-553-09987-6
1. Cuba—Fiction.   I. Title.
PS3555.N4254S59   1995
813'.54—dc20   94-42478
                                                         CIP

Published simultaneously in the United States and Canada

Bantam Books are published by Bantam Books, a division
of Bantam Doubleday Dell Publishing Group, Inc. Its
trademark, consisting of the words "Bantam Books" and
the portrayal of a rooster, is Registered in U.S. Patent
and Trademark Office and in other countries. Marca
Registrada. Bantam Books, 1540 Broadway, New York,
New York 10036.

PRINTED IN THE UNITED STATES OF AMERICA
BVG   0 9 8 7 6 5 4 3 2 1

para familia

and

in memory of the uncounted tens of thousands of Cuban raft people who have perished at sea while seeking freedom

A despot easily forgives his subjects for not loving him, provided they do not love each other.

ALEXIS DE TOCQUEVILLE

Con letras de astros el horror que he visto
En el espacio azul grabar querría

With astral letters I would carve
In blue space the horror I have seen

JOSÉ MARTÍ

CONTENTS

INTRODUCTION

During the summer of 1992, I was in the home of relatives in Cuba when suddenly, secretly, after a brief visit, two distant cousins *"se tiraron al mar."* They "threw themselves into the sea" on a makeshift raft, at a time when such flights to freedom were strictly prohibited.

I waited, along with many other relatives, including the two *balseros'* parents and wives, for news of a safe arrival in Key West. In public, we had to pretend nothing had happened. In private, there was the recurrent agony of waiting for the daily Radio Martí broadcast listing the names of *balseros* who'd survived their ordeal at sea.

I returned to the U.S., still waiting. Later, news finally arrived: My cousins had been arrested by a Cuban patrol boat before reaching international waters. During our excruciating vigil, the *balseros* were already prisoners at secret police headquarters in La Víbora, but as punishment for the entire family, no one had been informed. Instead, we were allowed to imagine the worst: sharks, storms, waves, the depths . . .

Skywriting is the flight my imagination took while waiting. The pain of that personal vigil was combined with an endless series of absurd attempts to communicate through censored mail and through all the other barriers of fear imposed by tyranny.

Finally, on December 27, 1993, exactly two hours after I completed the final draft of the manuscript of *Skywriting*, I received an unexpected call from my *balsero* cousins. They had just arrived in South America, after eighteen months of elaborate diplomatic proceedings that combined the emotions and efforts of exiled cousins in Venezuela, Miami, New Jersey, California, and Sweden.

My joy was beyond description, yet I continued to think of those left behind in Cuba, and those still adrift at sea. By late 1993, tens of thousands of desperate men, women, and children had attempted to flee the Commander's Cuba on rafts and small boats. Perhaps one out of four survived. In August 1994, the stream of refugees became a flood.

Margarita Engle
August 31, 1994
CALIFORNIA

1
A Sigh Across the Sea

Oigo un suspiro, a través
De las tierras y la mar

I hear a sigh across
The lands and the sea

JOSÉ MARTÍ

I KNEW MY HALF BROTHER CAMILO FOR EXACTLY TWO HOURS BEFORE HE climbed onto a raft of inner tubes and tried to cross the sea.

When we were little, I believed we shared a secret language. I imagined we knew each other so well that our memories became intertwined. I thought I could remember his dreams.

We dreamed of bearded demons floating in torrid air and of luminous four-winged angels cradling our sun-scorched heads. We dreamed we were just about to arrive at our home, a place we could not remember, a feral, peaceful, primitive home in a place we had never seen.

In real life, all we ever shared was a handful of postcards sent across the sea occasionally, one or two each year, and the same father, a father we never knew. Our father was a bigamist and a hero. He had two wives, one an islander who dwelled on the fringe of the Commander's inner circle, and the other, my own mother, an expatriate North American, a rebel until, like so many other rebels, she found that her rebellion swelled and surged and outgrew her, and she had to flee from the boots of a giant who now stomped across the land.

Camilo was born in Cuba soon after the mysterious disappearance of our shared father. I was given to the light a few months after my half brother. I was born homesick. I have always been homesick. I have always yearned for a wild place where I once belonged and for lost memories, for memories which are not my own.

Although I was born in the barren California desert, I was conceived in the Cuban jungle, hot, green, rainy, dripping with orchids and angel hair. The heart of the island is a magnet, enormous and powerful, pulling me back through time and space, pulling me in and down, swirling, *el ojo del huracán*, the eye of the hurricane.

I was born in a hospital surrounded by windswept sand dunes, by date palms, dust devils, and the charred seashells of ancient waters. I was very young when I noticed that I had an invisible half brother hidden by a mythical sea. When I was eight Camilo sent me a postcard of the cathedral in Old Havana. When I was nine he sent me a picture of carnival dancers wearing glittering headdresses and ruffled skirts. At ten it was a picture of stuffed and mounted big game fish at the Hemingway Museum near Havana, and at eleven an image of José Martí's quaint birthplace.

On each postcard my half brother jotted a friendly note, saying, "Hope to meet you someday" or "Wishing you a joyful New Year." Once he sent a photo of himself in his bright flag-waving Young Pioneer uniform. Later it was a militia uniform, and finally, a fur hat and wool coat, standing on the steps of the Linguistics Institute in the U.S.S.R., his breath condensed in white streaks. He never smiled in these pictures, yet he always included a joke at the end of each note, something brief and enigmatic.

I answered with postcards from Disneyland (castles, roller coasters, people dressed like Mickey Mouse), the San Diego Zoo (elephants, giraffes, a giant Galapagos tortoise), and the beaches of southern California (surfers, the world's largest sand castle, a labrador retriever posed on a lawn chair, wearing sunglasses).

I sent Camilo a picture of myself flying through the air during a gymnastics tournament in Palm Springs. I wrote quick sloppy notes in my carefully studied Spanish: Hope you are well, regards to your mother, wishes for a very happy birthday.

Camilo wrote that he was specializing in simultaneous translation, and had already mastered several foreign languages, Russian, French, Japanese, German, Swahili, English, Mandarin, even the enigmatic clicks of Zulu. He learned languages easily, he said, without effort, the way other people sigh or breathe. All this while I was still rooted in the sand dunes, struggling to decide whether I should study at all, or simply become a trader of tribal antiquities, like my expatriate mother.

The father I shared with Camilo was assassinated before our births, but while he lived, he studied history. He traced the lineage of our Peregrín family from Conqueror and Conquered to Communist and exile. He traced the ancestry of censorship from the Inquisition to State Security. Then he vanished into thin air, carried off by the implications of his study.

My half brother was named not for our father, but for Camilo

Cienfuegos, a handsome young revolutionary whose surname meant Hundredfires, and who, just like our mysterious father, had disappeared into thin air while flying across Cuba.

For a long time everyone in Cuba said that Camilo Cienfuegos was not killed, but simply disappeared, glided away into the sky, a bearded symbol of betrayed innocence, vanished along with the dreams of youth. They also said that my father was assassinated by the CIA. Now, so many years later, nearly everyone admits that both were murdered by the envious Commander, that man who couldn't stand the thought of anyone more valiant or more revered, a man who liked to think of himself as Atlas, bearing the weight of the world on gargantuan shoulders, or a stone imitation of Christ, bearing our sorrows and hopes, commanding love.

Throughout our childhoods, Camilo and I called out to each other across the sea which still separates us from each other.

Perhaps the air is not really thin at all. Perhaps those who vanish "into thin air" are simply obscured, as if by mountain fog or jungle mist or a curtain of silk, a veil of clouds and lace . . .

I knew my half brother for exactly two hours before he floated away, the two hours between 11:00 P.M. on August 31 and 1:00 A.M. on September 1, 1992. It was a night of fireflies and heat, a night in hurricane season, humid and electric, pulsing, windy, incandescent, the kind of night that always brings rain and sends Cuban women scurrying for the Chinese fans they still use in place of air-conditioning. The fans are old, inherited arcs of silk decorated with colorful embroideries of songbirds and bell-shaped flowers.

I met Camilo at his home in Old Havana, a medieval walled city of cobblestone streets and marble staircases, where stone gargoyles still blow rainwater through ancient grotesque smiles.

I imagined that our secret childhood language consisted of syllables added to confuse the adult ear, or of words spoken backward, or disguised as drumbeats, or polished sticks rhythmically clicked against each other, or bird calls.

After my half brother vanished, I imagined he was held in a castle dungeon, entombed inside a wall that faced the sea. I imagined the wall was endless, interrupted by a single high window, tiny but always open, so that through it Camilo would know when the earth was passing through a shower of meteors. Through that small stone-framed opening he would be able to see a full lunar eclipse, the umbral shadow passing slowly across the face of a strawberry moon . . .

Sometimes he could see the new moon in the old moon's arms, or a flock of pink flamingos pointing their long necks, like arrows, aiming at the sky. I imagined Camilo as he studied the flaming birds, wondering how many shrimp they had eaten and whether their intensity of color came from the sun or from minerals in the hard shells of the crustaceans.

He watched as iridescent blue dragonflies, *libélulas,* zigzagged across his walled fragment of sky. Pale luna moths, *las mariposas nocturnas,* rested on the walls of Camilo's dungeon cell, their wings flashing spots the size of owl eyes, glowing.

Camilo saw one brief spurt of a vast migration as a lone tern journeyed past his window, traveling between Arctic and Antarctic.

During storms, waves rose from the sea and poured in through Camilo's high window, drowning him. He was revived by an angel, who breathed fire into his ear.

Food was shoved through a slit in the cell door. A one-eyed giant peered in, pressing his single eye against the opening. The food he gave Camilo smelled like urine.

My half brother climbed onto the outstretched hand of God and was lifted to His shoulder. From there, Camilo could see how tiny the castle was, with its one-eyed giants the size of fleas.

Camilo returned to the dungeon. Rats crawled across the wet stone floor, demons, roaches, centipedes, serpents, flame-colored crabs.

I imagined that my half brother cursed the one-eyed giants in our secret childhood language, and they, excluded from our memory, understood nothing and lumbered away, perplexed.

Or perhaps we had no secret language, no language at all, just a few postcards and photographs, a few notes and wishes and jokes.

Camilo was not held in the dungeon of a medieval castle, although he was held captive, for nearly one full year, within the entrails of a viper.

ON THE NIGHT OF AUGUST 31, 1992, I ARRIVED AT JOSÉ MARTÍ International Airport in Havana, prepared (or so I believed) to meet my half brother. I had spent six months reading magazine articles and library books about Cuba. I had learned and memorized many facts of nature and history. Cuba, for instance, harbors a bird as small as a bee, the world's smallest humming-bird (*Mellisaga helevae*) and the world's largest cactus (*Dendroureus nundiflorus*), along with the world's smallest bat (*Nycteceius lepidus*, commonly known as the butterfly bat) and the world's smallest amphibian (*Sminthillus limbatus*).

So I felt prepared for Cuba's nature, an island surrounded by sea, where endemic creatures have been created, existing no-where else.

To prepare for my journey I read about Option Zero. The Commander had ordered his people to prepare for life without

Soviet fuel. The future would consist of horse-drawn ambulances, candle-lit office buildings, fields plowed by oxen, and sugarcane chopped the old way, one machete stroke at a time, by slaves who slept in barracoons at night, listening to the sounds of distant drums and night-flying birds.

So I felt prepared for Cuba's movement through time.

I READ ABOUT A BRITISH ATTACK AGAINST HAVANA IN 1762: THE aggressors saw so many lights in the trees of a nearby forest that, believing they were being ambushed by an army with torches, they fled, terrified.

The lights, of course, were fireflies. So I felt prepared for Cuba's illusions.

BEFORE DECIDING TO MEET MY HALF BROTHER, I HAD GONE TO MIAMI AND talked with my father's exiled relatives. They told me that *cocuyos*, fireflies, were simply *estrellas*, stars brought to earth, or *almas*, souls from purgatory, or *prendas*, decorations for the hair of beautiful women, or *faroles*, lanterns for fugitives hiding in caves.

They told me that in 1959, when the Commander first seized power, many women were so frightened that they lost all their hair, even the eyebrows. Cuban doctors (or so my father's exiled relatives still vowed more than three decades after their initial moment of terror) had all prescribed the same remedy, emigration to Miami.

Of course, I knew this was true, because it eventually happened to my mother, and she wasn't even a real Cuban, just an imaginary one, an expatriate who'd married my real-Cuban father without believing that he was already married. Shortly before my father was assassinated in midair, my mother fled the island, arriving home bald with fear. She chose, instead of Miami, the desert, which like her own head, was bare and stark.

Eventually her hair grew back, but she'd left me prepared for Cuba's fears.

IN MIAMI, MY FATHER'S EXILED RELATIVES SPOKE TO ME IN THE MOST incredibly rapid-fire Spanish I'd ever heard. They talked about emotions as if they were geographic locations, islands or peninsulas. "I put myself happy, *me pongo alegre*," they would say, or "I put myself sad, *me pongo triste. I wounded myself. Me lastimé.*"

They spoke to me in folk sayings and fables. "To bad times, a good face. *Al mal tiempo, buena cara.* The cat has four feet, but it can only choose one path. *El gato tiene cuatro patas y sólo puede coger un camino.* Don't try to plow the sea. *No se puede arar el mar.*"

So I felt prepared for Cuba's parables.

They fed me codes, told me that in the Commander's Cuba, "volunteer work" meant forced labor in the sugarcane fields, and "resolving a problem" meant paying a bribe or completing a black market transaction.

They gave me volumes of Hemingway and José Martí. I read about an old man floating in a frail boat off the coast of Cuba, battling the devil disguised as a shark, the old man's faith encased in the form of a big fish. The old man said, "It is silly not to hope . . . besides, I believe it is a sin."

I read that Hemingway's third wife wrote to him from abroad, to his tranquil haven on Cuba's coast, explaining why she hated the land he'd chosen as home, complaining that she detested the island, that in Cuba she felt she was being strangled by beautiful tropical flowers big enough to swallow cows.

I read that Longfellow and Richard Henry Dana had compared Cuba to the Garden of Eden.

So I believed I was prepared for Cuba's beauty.

I READ THE POETRY OF JOSÉ MARTÍ:

> *A un banquete se sientan los tiranos.*
> *Pero cuando la mano ensangrentada*
> *Hunden en el manjar, del mártir muerto*
> *Surge una luz que les aterra, flores.*

> At a banquet the tyrants sit down.
> But when a bloody hand
> Is immersed in food, from the dead martyr
> Surges a light which frightens them, flowers.

I READ ABOUT THE LITTLE MOORISH PRINCESS WHO TOSSES HER FAVORITE pink pearl into the sea, and then asks the sea to give it back. "*¡Oh mar! ¡Oh mar! ¡Devuélveme mi perla!*"

I read about the heart that carries its home as a broken anchor, then wanders like a lost boat that doesn't know its destination:

> *Corazón que lleva rota*
> *El ancla fiel del hogar*
> *Va como barca perdida*
> *Que no sabe a dónde va.*

SO I FELT PREPARED FOR CUBA'S LONELINESS.

*   *

I LISTENED AS EXILED RELATIVES BEWAILED THE ALTERATION OF SPACE AND time. They said in the old days the world was simple, there were only five continents (Europe, Asia, America, Africa, and Oceania). And time lasted longer. A proper period of mourning endured five years. "Now," the old women moaned, "if you're sad for more than six months, the American doctors call it patholog-ical, deranged, self-destructive, no matter how many relatives you've lost, one, ten, twenty, a hundred. For one hundred rela-tives left behind, the proper mourning should last five hundred years, no?"

My father's exiled relatives always said *sueño con*, "I dream with" instead of "I dream of." They said *tormenta*, "torment" when they referred to a storm.

They drew upside-down question marks before their ques-tions, and they put inverted exclamation marks in front of their passionate affirmations. "¿Why wait until after?" they would de-mand, baffled by the arbitrary logic of English punctuation. "¡Af-ter, it's too late! You need to see the punctuation before the statement, not after. Otherwise, how will you know what to do with your voice when you reach a question? You must say, '¡No!' or '¡Yes!' not just 'No!' or 'Yes!' You must say, '¿Really?' not just 'Really?' "

I found that my father's exiled relatives came in two varieties, those who mourned for Cuba day and night, and those who kept themselves from mourning by never mentioning Cuba at all. Of the aloof ones, the mourners would say, "Despite his misfor-tunes, he's like the tango." And when I didn't understand, they elaborated: "Hand to hand, like the tango, *mano a mano, como el tango*, hand to hand, like a prayer, *mano a mano, como una oración*." Or they would say, "To keep from crying, he sings. *Para no llorar, canta.*"

They said they were better survivors than the astronauts. They said everything would someday turn out exquisite, as if dreamed by Martí.

THEY PREPARED ME FOR A TROPICAL AUGUST, HURRICANE SEASON, 1992, José Martí International Airport: soldiers, policemen, Canadian and European tourists, *cocuyos*, fireflies illuminating the runways.

BUT I WASN'T PREPARED FOR MY REAL HALF BROTHER. I HAD GROWN SO accustomed to the imaginary one that now, facing my first encounter with the real one, I felt like all was a dream, all a fantasy, everything fluid and light, nothing solid, everything animate, mobile, translucent.

I was led to a hotel near the sea, walls decorated with metallic sculptured fish and coral-hued plaster casts of mermaids and sea fans. I raced out into the night, anxious to meet the only sibling I would ever have, the one I had imagined all my life.

Havana's streetlights had been turned off to conserve the last remnants of Soviet fuel. Black marketeers prowled the sea wall. Soldiers watched them, and secret policemen watched the soldiers, and desperate young men carrying inner tubes watched the secret police, and prostitutes watched stray bands of European tourists, and children watched fireflies, and a sorcerer watched me.

I asked a soldier for directions to Camilo's street. He pointed the way with his gun. The sorcerer followed. His eyes were wild, his hair disarrayed. He was as lean as a skeleton and as hollow-cheeked. He caught up with me and berated me, claiming to see something in my eyes, something he didn't like. He asked if I wanted to know what it was. I answered, "¡No!" then shouted, "*¡Basta!* ¡Enough!" and he spun away, an intruder sent reeling, as if he were the stranger in that ancient city and I the guardian who belonged.

My flight toward Camilo continued, through a downpour, down the corridors of Old Havana's dark narrow cobblestone streets, beneath the spitting grimaces of crouched gargoyles.

At Camilo's door, I found a key descending from above, from an open window on the second floor of a sixteenth-century building carved entirely of marble and mahogany. The huge brass key, dangling from one end of a twisted ball of twine, looked more like a spider than a key. It danced in the air above my head until I reached up and clasped it then guided it toward its goal, toward the mahogany-framed keyhole that matched its coded shape.

The key allowed me into an unlit entryway, then it lifted away, retrieved by its coil of twine held in an unseen hand. A dark marble staircase led me up into a house shaped like a chimney, where people dwelled inside the bricks, and plants thrived in a courtyard, the center of the house open to face the sky.

I was on the second floor. Neighbors looked down from above and up from below. The house might as well have been built of glass or crystal. Curious eyes followed me, while fireflies and luna moths flickered in and out of the sky.

Thunder bellowed. Slices of pale lightning. Heat moved down through the carved walls, one shadow passing across another. My half brother smiled. It was a smile I had never seen, a smile never captured by any camera.

LATER, WHEN CAMILO HAD VANISHED AT SEA, I IMAGINED THAT AN ANGEL hovered beneath his dungeon window. The angel had four faces, four wings, a body of flame and light. I imagined the angel comforting my half brother by gazing out the high window, describing the view. "Today," the angel would offer, "the sky is shiny like the glaze on a blue Chinese vase, Ming Dynasty, at its center a single blossom of light, the sun."

Leaping dolphins, the shimmering sea, waves reflecting amber and jade. I imagined Camilo must have known that thirty-five species of sharks inhabit Cuban waters. I imagined he knew about the sharks before he decided to build a raft by attaching a few inner tubes with strands of rope (yes, it was just rubber and rope, but I always think of Camilo's raft as something made of inner tubes and hope).

I IMAGINED HE ASKED THE ANGEL TO CARRY HIM AWAY ON FIERY WINGS and received, as answer, *un suspiro,* a sigh.

2

Option Zero

En un dulce estupor soñando estaba
Con las bellezas de la tierra mía

In a sweet stupor I was dreaming
With the beauty of my land

JOSÉ MARTÍ

I WAS NOT PREPARED FOR CUBAN HUMOR. WHEN I FINALLY MET MY HALF brother for the first time, he didn't tell me he'd always longed for this moment, or he could hardly wait to get to know me, or he'd imagined me taller, or brown-eyed instead of blue, or shriveled by the desert sun instead of toasted in patches (raccoon eyes where my sunglasses produced a mask the color of almonds, surrounded by shades of nutmeg and cinnamon-tea). He didn't treat me like a long-lost sibling, but like the kid sister who'd been there all along, pestering him, asking too many questions, getting in the way.

CAMILO WAS TALL, WHEAT-HUED, BLACK-EYED, LEAN (ACTUALLY HALF-starved), with a smile like whitewashed adobe bathed by a

shower of brilliant sun. He looked happy. He looked like someone who had always been happy, someone who could never be
any other way than happy. He said, "I would offer you a Free
Cuba, but we're out of rum and there are no sodas here, and we
don't have limes."

Then he added, to explain the joke, "In the old days they
called rum and coke with lime *'Cuba Libre,'* but now we just say,
'Cuba Libre, ha ha.' You understand?"

Numb, I nodded yes, I understood. The drink was now called
Free Cuba, ha ha, and no one had it. There was nothing funny
about the sound of ha ha in Camilo's street joke, yet he looked
delighted.

"Water is fine," I said. I wondered whether we could ever
really get to know each other after spending our childhoods in
such different states of mind. I was ready to be serious, dead
serious. I had flown to this island called sad by my father's exiled
relatives, and I expected sorrow.

Of course, all of these expectations pre-dated my immersion
in love. They came to me long before God pushed Camilo into
my solitary life, and later a giant puppy and a strong sweet
botanist, and so much love that I could actually swim in it, splash
it onto the rocky slopes of desert peaks, drink from its pools and
rivers. Perhaps if I'd known I was going to be adopted by a
wolfhound and embraced by Alec, I might not have ventured to
Cuba at all. I might have stayed alone on the sand dunes, waiting
for love, and if that had happened, chances are I would have
been incapable of recognizing the fragrance of love's flash flood
as it approached.

Recognition was something I had to learn through torment,
like putting pasty raw dough into a fire, and taking out something edible, baked bread or a scone or spice cake.

If I had already known about love before meeting my half brother, I might have stayed home, afraid of the only liquid in my trail of solidified years, afraid of the burdens and blessings.

MY HALF BROTHER WAS GIVEN TO THE LIGHT IN A PLACE AND TIME WHERE no one could overlook poetry or politics, the two sides of every Cuban coin, on one surface Martí's cry for "Homeland and Liberty," and on the other surface some invisible feudal warlord dressing himself as a symbol of the future.

Later, I would constantly feel uprooted by Camilo's cheerful desperation. On that first night in Cuba, I would have hugged him if he'd seemed a little less lighthearted. His mother came out of the kitchen to embrace me. She was small, dark-eyed, lovely, delicate, and fierce. She carried herself with the air of a panther in its nocturnal forest, ready to pounce. She was one of the old guard, a revolutionary in the physical sense. She had fought, like my own mother, aiming guns and firing, hiding in caves, ambushing enemies. Exultant at first, triumph, victory, parades. And then her husband disappeared into "thin air." Now I looked at her and thought that maybe thin air was like a dance of seven veils, revealing more than it concealed.

Camilo brought me tap water in a big ceramic cup. The cup was shaped like a pirate's scowling face, one eye patched. "An heirloom," he said.

I longed to ask ten million piercing questions about our shared isolation. Instead, I waited, gazed out the window (the one through which Camilo had sent me the key to his door) at lightning drifting out to sea, shadowy figures zigzagging their way across the old walled city.

If I had been alone I would have closed my eyes and reinvented Cuba. I imagined saying, "Please excuse me while I dream," as I'd heard my father's exiled old-lady relatives say. Dreaming, I would surround the island with mermaids instead of sharks. I would take the alligators out of its rivers and the scorpions out of its soil, replacing them with butterflies and unicorns.

WE TALKED ABOUT THE WEATHER, ABOUT THE FLASHES OF LIGHTNING, hurricane season, the houses crumbling all over Havana as downpours dissolved their unpainted walls. Camilo asked me about snow. I answered that I lived in the desert, where it was always hot, even in winter, always hot and dry, even five minutes after a rain, even during flash floods, even on the floor of an ancient sea.

My half brother said he had been surprised by snow. "When I went to the Soviet Union to study," he reminisced, "I expected to find that snow would be as soft and smooth and sweet as ice cream. I thought it would be something I could eat. Instead, it was slush beneath my boots."

Tricks of the imagination, we agreed. "A couple of weeks ago," I said, "when Hurricane Andrew hit Miami, I was visiting one of our cousins there. We had been watching television in her living room, news of course, weather reports. Then suddenly we noticed that we were swimming and all the furniture was floating around us. That's how abruptly everything changed."

Camilo told jokes about eating dog meat and cat meat purchased from *La Bolsa Negra,* the "Black Bag," Cuba's nickname for its prolific black market, the ubiquitous roving throngs of illicit street vendors. I could see that his jokes were not meant to be funny. Cuban housewives really were hungry enough to cook their cats and dogs.

Camilo told one joke after another:

" '¿What do you think of the government?' a soldier asks his friend. 'I think the same as you,' the friend responds cautiously. 'In that case,' says the first man, 'I will have to arrest you as a subversive.' " Camilo told this joke in a whisper, as if he and I were the two friends in the forbidden joke.

" '¡SOCIALISM OR DEATH!' IS THE COMMANDER'S NEW SLOGAN." CAMILO laughed. "*Socialismo o muerte.* So we say: 'Socialism for the Commander, and death for the rest of us. *Para el Comandante socialismo, y muerte para los demás.*' "

"THIS," MY HALF BROTHER SAID, "IS THE MOST TYPICAL OF CUBAN STREET jokes." He made a show of glancing upstairs and downstairs, waving at the neighbors, smiling, then lowering his voice. His mother suppressed a giggle. "She won't understand those jokes," Camilo's mother warned, but he persisted.

"THE COMMANDER CALLS A MEETING OF THE CENTRAL COMMITTEE OF THE Communist Party and says, '*Compañeros,* Comrades, I have two pieces of news to share with you: one good and one bad. The first is that next year we will have nothing to eat but rocks.'

" '*Está bien, Comandante.* That's fine, Commander, we'll adjust to the situation, we'll eat rocks,' the Party officials answer. 'Now tell us the good news.'

" 'That *was* the good news,' fumes the Commander, 'the bad news is there won't be enough rocks to go around. *Lo malo es que no alcanzan para todos.*' "

"¿What do hungry housewives call the Commander?"
It was a riddle. I said, "I give up."
"Onion," said Camilo. "They call him '*cebolla*' because he makes them cry every time they go into the kitchen."

*   *

WE WENT ON LIKE THAT FOR MUCH OF THE TWO HOURS. I HAD envisioned my real-life half brother as the quiet type like my imaginary one, serious, pensive, burdened by the weight of his island's plight. My imaginary half brother would have suffered in silence. He would have volunteered to cut sugarcane on holidays and Sundays, never complaining, always secretly planning some valiant act of defiance. He would volunteer with one of the work brigades digging a beehive of mysterious tunnels beneath the city of Havana. He would pretend he believed that the tunnels would serve as bomb shelters when the North finally attacked. He would carve faces into the tunnels, leave messages hidden in stone niches, organize a resistance of poetic intellectuals who knew they might someday have to trade their pens for swords and slay the giant.

My real half brother now seemed more like a cheerful six-foot pixie, a mischievous Charlie Chaplin kicking the Commander's backside when no one was looking.

His black eyes literally twinkled like Christmas tree lights or the flashing on-and-off signal lights on the wings of airplanes. I couldn't imagine why Camilo found my presence so amusing, so pleasing. We were finally united after so many years of separation, a long-lost brother and sister. Wasn't this supposed to be a hushed emotional moment? Shouldn't we reminisce, recover our shared nostalgia for the father we'd never known and the intricate family ties we'd never developed, and the betrayals of a history we couldn't fathom?

A BLAZE OF LIGHTNING HELD THE SKY HOSTAGE. I LOOKED OUT. TURKISH moon, stars, planets, meteors, and yet it was raining from invisible clouds. In the courtyard the upstairs neighbors were scurrying about, sweeping, mopping, dusting, even though it was past midnight. "They spy on us," Camilo's mother said. "They know I am a high-level official in the Ministry of Sugar, and they think if they catch me doing or saying something which is prohibited, they might be able to advance themselves by reporting me to the Commander.

"Everyone is so scared," Marisol continued. I loved her name, a graceful name, sonorous, meaning Sea-and-Sun, a name that sounded like a swan on a quiet lake, gliding. I tried to picture her aiming a gun, firing, stealing the boots off a dead soldier. I struggled to figure out why we were sharing these jokes and fears in the same breath.

LATER, AFTER CAMILO DISAPPEARED, I IMAGINED HIM SKETCHING cartoons of bearded giants stomping across the palm trees, the green countryside, the old walled city, crushing crowds of tiny people who looked like ants or mites or gnats.

I had been inside the real dungeons of real medieval castles in Spain and France. On her antiquity-collecting journeys, my mother always took me along, steering me through catacombs and the basements of museums, through Roman aqueducts and Gothic cathedrals and Moroccan bazaars.

The cells of real dungeons had no high windows. They didn't face the sea. They were barely large enough for a grown man to crawl in and curl up in the fetal position. They were underground. They smelled like the dens of predatory beasts, like the lairs of pregnant wolves and hibernating bears.

"ALL OVER CUBA," MARISOL NOW WHISPERED, "EVERYONE WAITS FOR THE attack of the enemy."

"She means *you*," Camilo interpreted, chuckling, "you in the North, you are the enemy we are supposed to fear. Those are our instructions. That's what the tunnels are for, and the wartime shortages, the sacrifices, Option Zero. We're waiting for you to attack us so we can become martyrs for a holy cause, martyrs who died defending the Commander. We have been ordered to die for love."

A lone firefly dived into the room as Camilo spoke. Marisol waved her silk fan in its direction, as if to show its design to the glowing insect. The fan portrayed a peacock with green and blue feathers spread across the silk like some flamboyant other-worldly setting sun, or a rising blue and green moon, or a blue-fire volcano dropped onto flat ground.

"They tell us you are two-headed cannibals with sharp fangs and venomous claws," Camilo said, quite seriously. "They tell us you will capture our children and fatten them for the table, just as they used to say South American cannibals once did with the children of our peaceful Cuban tribes. You see how it is to live on the only island where people have always been truly innocent and harmless, just and free and generous and kind, yet surrounded by so many other lands where no one has ever held a benevolent thought or believed in the mythical future or imagined an improved past?"

"Oh, Camilo." His mother laughed. "You always carry things too far, always take it a little beyond the boundary. Carmen, all he's trying to say is we're supposed to believe we're good and you're bad, and if we look you in the eye you'll probably spit poison, like a cobra. It's a myth we live with, like any other myth, created for a very obvious purpose, to teach us something, to warn us, and motivate us."

"It helps take our minds off the hungers," Camilo said, "our many hungers." He leaned toward me, falcon eyes glittering, keen smile, grim tone of voice. "Our rations are down to nothing but rice and a single piece of bread each day, hardly any beans at all, sometimes an egg or two, no meat, no chicken, few vegetables, a little coffee, some sugar, no flour, no oil, no milk, not even for the children. Just a little powdered milk for the smallest babies and diabetics. ¡No fish! But you will argue, 'This is an island,' and yet you will be wrong. Because if we enter the sea and catch a fish, we have to turn it over to the government. Soldiers patrol the beaches, waiting for our fish, ¿you see?

"¿What would *you* do, Carmen? Stay or flee, hide or run, fight or starve. Consider the options when you live on an island, when you finally realize that your king on that island has gone mad, and you are at his mercy. You have no weapons, you're tired and weak and hungry, and most of all you're scared, petrified, paralyzed."

I considered, as Camilo spoke, but I did not consider options, only illusions. This was not the reunion I had planned. I was neither wise nor brave. I wasn't clever. I couldn't think of a way out. I couldn't answer Camilo's questions. I didn't understand that he was leading me toward a view of his own way out.

"¡Lunacy!" Marisol whispered. "No more of this crazy talk. It's too dangerous."

I WAS GLAD MY MOTHER HAD ALLOWED ME TO SHARE THE SAME SURNAME as my half brother. Camilo was my only connection to the father I'd always wanted to meet, dead or living, ghost or corpse. Our surname was Peregrín, meaning pilgrim. It meant that some ancestor had committed a sin centuries earlier, and had offered penance in the form of a pilgrimage, sacrificing a long arduous journey and gaining a humble nickname. It meant that we were not alone in our struggle to understand and correct our errors. I loved our surname. It made me feel linked to Camilo, chained like his brass key and his ball of twine and his open window and locked door.

In some odd, fantastic sense, I loved my half brother even though I didn't know him. I didn't know him at all.

Our two hours passed with jests and warnings, and then, as I realized how late it was, how thin and distant the streaks of lightning had grown, how dark and frightening the streets would be, I said, "I have to go now."

Marisol tried to talk me into staying in their house. They had plenty of room, just the two of them. "Look at this place," Marisol gestured, "we live surrounded by this clutter left behind by those who fled a long time ago, by all the cousins in Miami. Someday, we think, they might come back to claim it, so we keep everything intact, just in case. Many people used to live here, maiden aunts, migratory uncles moving back and forth between the ranch at the heart of the island and the markets of Havana. Now, of course, there are no family ranches, and no markets, and the relatives in Miami never write or call. They went away, and never looked back. They forgot us."

The house was cluttered with extra furniture, crockery, old leatherbound books, clothes, bedspreads, knicknacks (clowns, poodles, pirates, angels, elephants) clocks, fans, shoes, mountains of photographs stashed in open cardboard boxes, the relics of exiles, left behind as a sign of hope.

Of course, the exiles had not, as Marisol suspected, forgotten anyone or anything. They had simply changed the people and things they took with them in place of photographs, which were carried as remnants of memory wrapped up and tucked inside their imaginations. They had only changed people a little in their minds, but when they told their children, and their children told their grandchildren, and their grandchildren told friends and neighbors in Coral Gables and Hialeah and Homestead, they found that their descriptions had grown mythical, fabulous, enchanted. Cuba became a land of Pegasus and Perseus, flying horses and winged sandals, the towering wheel-eyed Cyclopes, and the evil father Uranus, and Night, Doom, Fate, Death, Sleep, Dreams, Nemesis, all the children of Chaos and Erebus, of Chaos and the darkness of the unseen netherworld hidden beneath our feet.

I would have liked to stay in that cluttered home with Camilo and Marisol. I could have learned to ignore the prying upstairs neighbors (a turbaned woman was still sweeping and mopping and snooping, peering down from the courtyard ledge into the half-open rooms of Marisol's home, hoping to catch her in some treacherous act that could turn the Commander against her, push her aside and open a niche at the edge of the coveted inner circle) and the black marketeers on the street below, and the darkness, and lightning, and insects buzzing in and out of the house, and the prowling of secret police, and the translucence of angels whirring their wings in the courtyard.

I wandered around the house, inspecting photographs of ancestors and heroes. The Commander dominated each wall, his massive bearded image flanked by the gentler ones of Ché and Camilo Cienfuegos, both martyred in myth and murdered in reality, sacrificed, secretly, as offerings.

In the kitchen I noticed a poster of the three revolutionary heroes (Ché, Camilo, and the Commander) costumed as the Three Kings, bearing gifts in the form of slogans: land reform, Marxism-Leninism, solidarity.

There were papers from Marisol's job scattered across various desks and tables. She worked at the Ministry of Sugar, and her high-level bureaucratic position was an important one. Sugar kept Cuba alive. Without sugar there would be no rum, only cigars, a few European tourists, and the memory of dances that had once been the island's most familiar export, *rumba, conga, mambo, cha-cha-cha*.

I noticed an old snapshot of Hemingway on his famous Cuban beach, posing with a trophy marlin, smiling and showing off, surrounded by admiring friends. Camilo, hovering behind me, said, "I suppose you already know that your mother came to Cuba at Hemingway's invitation." He moved to my side, and studied the portrait of the man whose books had immortalized Cuba's shark-infested waters.

"Here's our father," Camilo indicated, singling out a tall, grinning rogue who looked so much like the young man standing next to me that I would have believed Camilo if he'd said he'd been alive at the time of the photograph and had known Hemingway himself.

"And that's your mother." I peered into the eyes of a woman my own age, carefree, inebriated by sun and daiquiris, ignorant of her future. She looked delighted. I was surprised that Marisol allowed my mother's picture to rest on her wall.

It was the first time I'd seen a photograph of my father. As a child I had often wondered what he looked like, whether the handful of words my mother had used to describe him would turn out to be true: headstrong, arrogant, selfish-shellfish. She'd used the words abruptly, resentfully, slamming them shut whenever my demands for information grew too persistent.

Shellfish was her way of describing a combination of selfishness and reticence. Men, my mother had often told me, were shellfish in general, closed, withdrawn, protected, and Latin men, she emphasized, were even more shellfish than others, even though they liked to dress for a masquerade of emotion and eloquence. You couldn't pry them open with a chisel, she'd insisted, and wouldn't want to, because inside lurked a shapeless mass, a creature who didn't know what it wanted. Men, my mother vowed, weren't sure who they should be, El Cid the gallant knight or José Martí the poetic martyr. They put themselves inside a hard shell, she said, and hid from the liquid world all around them, everything flowing, changing, passing them by. She said all of this with the intense disdain of a wounded knight, the loser in a battle of lance and shield.

I was brought up thinking that my father must have been something like a clam or an oyster, impenetrable, glued to a rock, washed by waves. But now, seeing his photograph for the first time, I saw that he was just like any other rebel—enthusiastic, hopeful, doomed.

"I CAN'T STAY," I APOLOGIZED TO CAMILO AND MARISOL. ALTHOUGH I longed to fall asleep beneath my father's picture, wrapped in one of the many heirloom bedspreads folded and stacked in Marisol's extra bedrooms, I didn't feel ready for this much of the past flooding me all at once. I wanted to slow time. I thought that maybe, by force of will, I could accomplish that slow motion replay I'd dreamed, let the past drift into me, floating and humming. The folded bedspreads of Marisol's house were all white cotton lace, painstakingly crocheted by myriad female ancestors, the delicate shapes of birds, flowers, leaves, and stars all linked together with loops and twists of thread. I longed to wrap myself in one of those pale hallucinations, and wake up connected to the ancestors' hands, a child whose forehead is stroked by the fingers of old women.

Instead, I promised to return at ten o'clock the next morning. Marisol said she would contact all of my father's relatives in Havana, invite them all to a reunion in my honor.

"They're not *all* in exile," she assured me. "In fact, many of us still believe that no one living in exile can ever be happy. The exiles may have plenty of food, and nice clothes, and nightclubs, cars, good jobs, relaxing vacations at pleasant resorts, but that's not the same as being happy, ¿no?"

"Well," Camilo interceded, "happy or not, at least you've been introduced to the dead."

He led me away from the photograph of my murdered father standing beside my dead mother and her famous suicidal friend and his enormous sacrificed fish.

I RETURNED TO THE HOTEL WITH ITS FLOCKS OF MERMAIDS AND TRITONS and moray eels and floating stingrays. I dreamed with death and smiling ghosts.

In the morning the elevator was broken, and the stairway door was locked. I couldn't leave the hallway of the eighteenth floor. I found myself standing next to a window, looking down. There was no screen, no glass, just a gap in the wall, low enough for someone to step out of the building easily, and float or plummet eighteen stories to a patio where statues of mermaids were partially hidden by tropical foliage. A maid came ambling by, patting her stack of towels and washcloths. She noticed me leaning out of the dangerous window. "We have a lot of suicides in Cuba," she said, laughing at her own dark humor, "so we try to make it easier for them."

She unlocked a metal door, and I glided down eighteen flights of stairs, bought a bottle of rum to celebrate my reunion with the only long-lost brother I would ever have, and sailed along the cobblestones to Marisol's curious medieval house.

Remnants of the night's rain still dripped from the curled lips of stone gargoyles. The key reached me as before, dancing on its string, teasing my hand as it swayed just out of reach.

"¡Grab it!" came Marisol's voice from the window above. She sounded hysterical as she shouted down to me, "¡Hurry! *¡Apúrate!*"

I seized the key. Clinging to my bottle of rum, I struggled with the keyhole, the stubborn door, the dark staircase, slippery marble, the glare of an upstairs neighbor's eyes, hooded beneath her coiled turban of vermilion cloth. I waved. The neighbor grinned. Marisol pulled me away, out of sight, into the kitchen, an enclosed back room where we couldn't be seen and where, if we whispered, we couldn't be overheard.

"¡Gone!" Marisol uttered. "¡Vanished!" She looked like she had been attacked by drooling, venomous demons. Her face was on fire, volcanic. I couldn't begin to imagine what had gone wrong.

"¡My son is *gone!*" She said this with such vehemence that it sounded like a shout, a cry of agony, even though she was actually whispering. *"Se fué mi hijo.*

"¡A boat person!" she said, "a *lanchero*. He left on a boat." Ominously, she added, "or a raft, a raft person, a *balsero*. There are hardly any boats left these days, so they leave on rafts, the young people, the men. They all want to leave. They want to float away. *Se tiran al mar.* They throw themselves into the sea."

She sounded dazed now. "He floated away," she repeated, "in the dead of night. He left me only this note and a verse by Martí. Look, the note says he's sorry he couldn't say good-bye, but this was his chance and he had to take it, and maybe some-day I would understand or at least forgive. And here's the verse."

Mírame madre, y por tu amor no llores:
Si esclavo de mi edad y mis doctrinas,
Tu mártir corazón llené de espinas,
Piensa que nacen entre espinas flores.

Look at me mother, and for your love don't cry:
If, slave of my age and my doctrines,
Your martyred heart I've filled with spines,
Think that between spines are born flowers.

I RECOGNIZED IT AS A POEM WRITTEN WHILE MARTÍ WAS STILL A TEENAGER and already in prison, arrested by Imperial Spain for founding a newspaper called *The Free Fatherland*. I wondered how Martí's mother felt when she read the verse. I wondered whether Marisol now, reading it, feared that her son had said good-bye forever.

"Look." Marisol rattled the note under my nose. "He says he left *now* because he needs *your* help. Now what do you suppose that means?"

I shook my head. I knew nothing of boats or rafts or notes or help or verse or prison or spines or even flowers. I knew nothing of fatherlands, free or captive. I had a bottle of rum in my hand, and I was prepared for a celebration, nothing more.

"It's lucky I didn't invite any of the cousins yet," Marisol fretted. "I was going to start inviting them this morning, but now . . . well, now, if anyone finds out . . ." She didn't finish. I already knew what she meant. If anyone found out that Camilo had left Cuba without permission, it would create a scandal. The son of a Sugar Ministry official, the child of privilege. An inner circle prodigy, the recipient of a coveted Soviet education, the master of numerous foreign tongues, one of the Commander's

best examples of the system's reputed success, a role model for
los Pioneros, for "Young Pioneers" all over the island.

"*¡And* it's hurricane season!" Marisol added. She was angry
now, vexed, infuriated, seething. If her son had been there in the
room, she might have spanked him, no matter how high he
towered over her.

"I got up this morning," Marisol went on. She seemed desperate for a listening ear, for some semblance of understanding. "I
came into the kitchen and started throwing together whatever I
could come up with, a few crusts of bread, some rice, a pudding
of flour and fruit from the Black Bag. I'm good at this. I have lots
of practice. I know how to make a pudding stick together even
when I can't find eggs or milk or butter. Camilo calls them my
miracle puddings. He says I hold them together with energy
instead of ingredients.

"Now," Marisol lamented, "my son is gone, just like that,
gone." After a thoughtful pause, she asked, "¿How long would it
take to reach Florida on a strong boat? ¿A few hours? ¡Surely not
more than one day! Let's not even think about rafts, not yet. Let's
wait, and hope the boat has a good motor. And if by chance it
runs out of fuel . . ."

Suddenly all the possibilities struck her. "¿What if they catch
him? ¡Three years in prison! But no, they won't, he'll arrive in just
a few hours. The Miami cousins will find him. They'll take care
of him. He'll be fine. We must have faith.

"We . . . must . . . have . . . faith," Marisol repeated,
separating the words from each other, spacing them evenly, like
shrubs on a desert sand, giving each word its room to grow,
space to respire and come to life. I could hear the words breathing, feel their breeze. *Hay . . . que . . . tener . . . fe.*

"You brought rum," Marisol said, suddenly noticing me,

abruptly remembering that she was not alone, that an inconvenient and naïve guest had showed up just as she was about to become insane with fright and fury, just when she needed the freedom to panic and rage.

"We'll celebrate with your rum and my pudding," she proposed, "just as soon as we hear that he's arrived safely in Key West. The winds will take him there. Hurricane season, yes, but sometimes that's good, if the motor fails, there's plenty of wind. ¿He would have a sail as backup, no? He's intelligent, he's educated, he would think of all these things, ¿no? And when he arrives, the Miami cousins will take care of him. They'll help him get settled, file for asylum, find a job, ¿no?"

I nodded yes. Of course our cousins would help Camilo. He would be a hero if he made it across the Caribbean on a small boat. If he made it on a raft, he would be a superhero, a culture-hero, a knight who'd survived impossible odds, a poet whose dreams were strong enough to carry him across the sea. He would be a hero blessed by God, carried by angels, blown by a fiery wind. He would arrive in Miami like Jonas, a reluctant prophet. Each of his words would be regarded as revelation. He would tell the Miami cousins what had happened to their homeland since the onset of their exile. He would predict an explosive future. But I didn't really believe that Camilo would have a sail as backup, or a good motor and plenty of fuel, or enough fresh water. *Balseros* usually fled with whatever they could find, a few inner tubes, some rope, a buoyant palm log.

The Miami cousins had talked a lot about *balseros*. So many were arriving on the Key of Bones these days that whenever Cuban-Americans gathered to form *conga* lines or to celebrate the birthdays of Catholic saints, or to eat nostalgic foods no longer available in the Commander's Cuba (crab fritters, roast pork, manioc drenched in garlic sauce, *paella* with clams and mussels and chicken and spiced sausage, an astonishing array of puddings crafted from coconut, yams, plantains, condensed milk . . .) the Miami cousins, instead of simply celebrating, would mourn the *balseros* found dead and the rafts found empty, and rejoice for those found alive.

Many facets of the *balsero* mystery were discussed at these Northern family gatherings. How did any *balseros* at all manage to survive? Unlike Haitian boat people, unlike Chinese refugees and Vietnamese boat people, the Cubans rarely had boats. They left their island alone, or in groups of two or three or four, on a handful of inner tubes bound together with twine and wishes. They left at night, slipping past soldiers with submachine guns. They left without much chance of surviving, and they knew it. They knew the risks, the one-in-three or one-in-four survival estimates. They knew that whenever a raft with three or four brothers set sail, only one was likely to arrive on the Key of Bones.

The Miami cousins said they wondered whether those killed by sharks or Cuban patrol boats would come back as ghosts to haunt the Commander. They wondered whether the *balseros* who shriveled up from thirst (dried like slices of mango laid out in the sun) would find their families in heaven, or simply float on the surface of the sea forever, invisible as humans, easily mistaken for shreds of seaweed nibbled by fish.

Now, thinking of her son, Marisol said softly, "Miami is not the promised land, is it. He'll have problems, won't he. But at least he'll be free to speak. That's all he ever wanted, even as a child. All he wanted was freedom. He hardly seemed to care about toys, just adventure, the freedom to run and shout." Marisol put no question marks into her voice this time. She was studying the label of my rum, a Cuban bottle packaged for the foreign tourist, a pretty label showing the statue of a woman perched on a castle tower, overlooking the sea.

"This woman on the rum label is waiting for her husband," Marisol told me. "See, she's called *La Giraldilla*, the weathervane. Her name was Doña Inés. She was married to Hernando de Soto, a governor of Cuba. He went off to search for the Fountain of Youth, left her waiting.

"She lived in the Royal Force Castle, Havana's oldest fortress. Every day she climbed the tower to scan the horizon looking for ships. Every day"—Marisol sighed deeply—"poor little Doña Inés, she gazed out to sea and hoped for her husband's return, and he never came. He found Florida and died there. No Fountain of Youth after all. Just another piece of ordinary earth with ordinary people and trees and rivers of ordinary water that couldn't change the path of time at all, not one bit.

"Doña Inés took her husband's place as governor of Cuba, the first, the only woman governor. They made a bronze statue of her in 1631, see, holding a cross in her left hand. They put her on the tower as a weathervane to guide ships into the harbor. And of course, we put her on our Havana Club rum also, so we can sell it to tourists and tell them the legend and find it lovely and wistful and sad. But I don't know if any of the foreigners who drink this rum ever really think about Doña Inés, what it was like for her, waiting, and for her husband, searching for some mythical land he'd dreamed or imagined."

Marisol looked at me as if she'd momentarily forgotten who she was, as if she'd become Doña Inés the Weathervane.

"She's still there, of course, bronze, two meters high, fastened to the castle tower, waiting. ¡How many hurricanes she's survived!"

MARISOL AND I STAYED TOGETHER, WAITING FOR NEWS OF CAMILO, HOUR after hour, evening after evening, not as weathervanes, but bronzed and immobilized nonetheless, obsessed.

"Every day," she said, "we have a crisis in Cuba. The economy, the sugar harvest, the loss of Soviet aid, the war in Angola, the wars in Central America, the war in Grenada, the impending attack from your cruel North, the need for bomb shelters beneath our city, all these ridiculous tunnels being constructed even though this island is so riddled by caves that one day it will simply collapse, the earth will give way, we'll sink into whatever lies beneath our feet. The food shortage, the fuel shortage, the soap shortage, the medicine shortage, the rising crime rate as people grow desperate and steal anything they can sell to the Black Bag.

"But this," Marisol's eyes grew round, alarmed, "*this* is a crisis of the family . . . this . . . is different . . . a personal crisis." *Una crisis personal.* Again she separated her words from each other, gave them each a wide, respectful border of anticipation. "Now," she added, "we have the agony of waiting."

She fell silent, staring at her pudding, my rum, at Doña Inés glued to the bottle, waiting for her husband while he searched his legendary North.

I thought of all the horrible *balsero* fates described by the cousins in Miami. Washed off their rafts by wind or waves, toppled by exhaustion, consumed by sharks. I pictured Camilo beneath a dazzling blue sky, landing on a white-hot sandy coast, floating onto one of the Florida Keys, probably the one called, by refugees, the Key of Bones. I imagined Camilo's rescue, saw him being welcomed, fed, comforted, his raft of inner tubes left behind in the fangs of the sea.

I admired Marisol's optimism, her certainty that soon we would celebrate. She never allowed herself to think of a flesh roasted by sun or a brain cooked by salt, of insanity, or sharks with their multiple rows of spiny teeth, or seagulls plucking eyes from the faces of the dead.

"He left you something," Marisol finally murmured, shaking herself out of her reverie of hope. She handed me a bulky package wrapped in cloth and tied with straps of old leather and moldy linen. "I don't know what it is, but there's a note."

The note said the package was for me. It instructed me to smuggle the parcel out of Cuba and then wait awhile before opening it. There was no indication of the length of time one could designate "awhile." The note said that if I failed, Camilo's survival, or his death, would be equally meaningless. *Un rato,* "awhile." Within my bilingual mind, the phrase became "a rat of time," a rodent gnawing at the root of my serenity.

"It's not a suicide note," Marisol said. I agreed. Yet it was nearly as unpleasant as a suicide note. I wasn't sure I wanted to become responsible for the meaning of my long-lost brother's life.

"At seven o'clock," Marisol said, turning away from me and this enigmatic package Camilo had put in my care. "At seven o'clock, over Radio Martí, they will read the names. Every evening they list the names of all the rafters found on Northern beaches or at sea.

"So there's nothing to do but wait. Seven o'clock, then we'll know." Marisol appeared to be struggling with acceptance of her predetermined schedule. She closed her eyes and prepared herself for the vigil. She had not yet shed a single tear.

I looked at my watch. It was exactly ten-thirty, barely midmorning. How would we get through the long, tormenting hours until seven o'clock?

"Tomorrow is Monday. I'll have to go back to work." Marisol groaned, her eyes suddenly flying open. "¡I'll have to pretend nothing's wrong! Please, God, let them find him today, because I don't know how I can go through with it, go to work and pretend, hide my feelings. You know if they find out he's gone . . . they persecute the whole family. I have much to consider. They'll ask me to disown him, to abandon his memory, say he's no longer my son.

"¡And the concert! *Ay*, Carmen, last year I joined a choir, just for fun, just to please the Commander, and now I have to sing, tomorrow night, in front of all the big shots. How will I do it, stand up there in front of everyone, singing all those happy songs.

"But by then, we'll know, won't we, by then everything will be finished, settled, he'll be in Miami with the cousins, safe and free, starting his life all over without me, without Cuba."

Marisol looked like she was fighting off demons. I imagined claw marks on the skin of her neck. She seemed to be defining the future, outlining a plan of attack for the approaching hours. Desperation, instead of overpowering her, was making her stronger.

3

Vigil

Si me pedís un símbolo del mundo
En estos tiempos, vedlo: un ala rota.

If you ask me for a symbol of the world
In these times, look at it: a broken wing.

JOSÉ MARTÍ

SEVEN O'CLOCK CAME. WE HEARD A BRIEF LIST OF THE NAMES OF strangers. We sat facing each other across the kitchen table, between us a prohibited shortwave radio. In the kitchen, with its four walls, we were invisible to the turbaned upstairs neighbors (most of the other rooms had only three walls, with an open side facing the courtyard). Marisol adjusted the antennae, as if by doing so she could force the radio to disgorge her son's name. She kept the volume very low, inaudible to prying neighbors. She said she guarded Radio Martí very carefully, like buried treasure.

Listening to the names of strangers, I imagined the joyful reunions of each surviving *balsero* with relatives in Miami, and the simultaneous hidden celebrations going on somewhere in Cuba at that very moment, as those names were announced. I imagined the secret joy of mothers left behind. At least they knew that their sons had survived the crossing to my mythical Northern homeland. At least the mothers knew that even though they might never see their sons again, the young men were safe from harm and someday, when the Commander was dead or overthrown, travel bans might be lifted, and families reunited, and the sea might become nothing more than a memory separating generations.

"He's ripped us apart, torn our families in half," Marisol grumbled. There was never any need to ask who. "He" meant the Commander. "The crazy one" meant the Commander. "The onion," "the Count of Meat," "that guy," all of these epithets referred to one man. Stroking the chin with the fingers (to create an imaginary beard) meant the same. When that silent signal grew too familiar, it was replaced with an inverted beard drawn from the top of the head, forming a cone of fingers, making the speaker look like a swaying Balinese dancer or a Hindu guru bowing before a shrine.

At any rate, I would have known who Marisol meant just by watching her eyes. She was glaring at the Commander's smiling portrait on the kitchen wall as she sighed, "Tomorrow, at seven o'clock."

WE FACED THE NEXT TWENTY-FOUR HOURS. SEATED AT THAT KITCHEN table across from each other, Radio Martí between us, Marisol and I knew we were facing eternity. Marisol would have to show up at the Ministry of Sugar and pretend nothing was wrong, dissimulate, smile, make small talk, conduct her bureaucratic routine with apparent serenity. While she was at work, I would have to drift through Havana alone, wondering about waves and sharks and the effects of drinking salt water, and the durability of inner tubes. Suddenly I found significance in the term inner, *interior, lo de adentro*, thinking how appropriate it was for these secretive departures from island shores.

When seven o'clock returned the next evening, we would either hear good news and be relieved and celebrate with pudding and rum, accompanied by the tiny paper figure of Doña Inés, or we would continue on again, devastated, for one more day. Each set of twenty-four hours, I suspected, would be more sinuous than the last, more labyrinthine. We would meander through rooms and hallways, knowing we might encounter a Minotaur at any turn.

If two weeks passed, and we still didn't know, Camilo would be presumed dead, "lost at sea," a euphemism for drowning or being chewed by sharks. Lost at sea sounded like floating forever, becoming invisible. It sounded peaceful. It sounded like vanishing into thin air.

We thought of a possible means of helping Camilo. We thought of it at exactly the same moment. Our eyes met, and Marisol, never forgetting her neighbors, shout-whispered "¡Call the Rescue Brothers!" Shout-whispering was a technique the Cubans had perfected for communicating with emphasis, while keeping their voices low enough never to be overheard by neighbors or bus drivers or mailmen or children. *"¡Llama a los Hermanos al Rescate!"* Even their own children were instructed daily, at school, that parents should be turned in to the secret police if they ever said anything rebellious.

Marisol's eyes had been wearied by anxiety and dread. Now they surged back to life, as she shout-whispered, "Go to your hotel and use the phone and call your cousins in Miami and tell them to call the Rescue Brothers and tell them to search . . . search . . . search!" *¡Busca! ¡Busca! ¡Busca!*

Marisol said she had never wanted a phone of her own because Ministry officials were plagued by horrible anonymous prank calls, insults, threats, even Santería voodoo curses. She said *santeros* were always trying to turn her into a loathsome beast with their maledictions and black magic.

So I literally flew to the hotel. I ran so fast, over so many cobblestones (with flocks of black marketeers pursuing me, shaking jewelry in my face and rat meat and homemade shoes and hair dye concocted from kerosene and herbs) that my knapsack, containing Camilo's enigmatic package, bounced against my shoulders, like a single broken, useless wing.

The knapsack haunted me. Camilo's escape infuriated me. I realized that if I ran into my half brother now, I'd be more likely to berate him than to greet him with a rush of relief. My anger disturbed me. Why was my rage directed at Camilo, who had no other way to leave the island, no way out unless he floated away on a raft in the dead of night? Why not rage at the Commander or the soldiers patrolling the beaches or the United Nations for allowing tyrants to imprison entire islands?

I imagined that if Camilo had asked me for help, if he had said, "You're my sister and I want to leave, help me get out," I would have gone back to the prosperous North, raised money from the Miami cousins, returned to Cuba, paid massive bribes, and we would have left together, the two of us, siblings, seated on an airplane, while smiling Cuban government stewardesses offered us candy and espresso with too much sugar.

I imagined that it could have been that simple, a diplomatic arrangement, a pirate's ransom paid, a safe exit, Camilo's mysterious packet tucked under his airplane seat.

It was virtually impossible for any Cuban to escape the Commander's island unless relatives in the outside world became dedicated to the long, arduous, and expensive process of negotiating ransom. The Miami cousins, with their hundreds of captive relations, couldn't be expected to pay for so many hostages, but in Camilo's case, if they knew his desperation, if they knew he would set out on a raft, challenging the sharks and the sea and the hurricane season sky, certainly they would have tried. We would have managed.

Running along the cobblestones, imagining the chance to scold Camilo for choosing the more dangerous of two paths, I ignored the reality of his concealed package as it plopped against my back with each furious step. I forgot that it made my own path dangerous. I forgot that I had been assigned the role of smuggler.

Black marketeers pursued me with Cuban cigars arrayed in cedar boxes, and old gold coins bearing the image of José Martí on one side, and the Cuban heraldic shield on the other. When these Black Bag merchants finally gave up on me, they would turn aside, ensconce the offerings they carried for tourists, and pull out the ones reserved for Cubans, plastic bags filled with powdered milk, bars of soap sold at a quarter of the average monthly salary, cans of meat pilfered from dwindling hoards of Soviet supplies.

"Sugar pizza," one man offered, switching his sales pitch from gold coins to Option Zero food staple. He showed me a mangled slice of bread topped with ketchup and brown sugar, and offered it at an outrageous price. I laughed, then realized it was the first time I had experienced genuine mirth since arriving in Cuba. Camilo's clever street jokes had brought me, instead of hilarity, a sinking feeling, a nauseous dread.

THE LOBBY OF MY HOTEL WAS DRENCHED WITH HORIZONTAL RAIN AND the spray from big waves carried by wind. "Hurricane season," a bellboy greeted me. "Not a good day for the beach."

I pictured Camilo slapped by waves and tossed by wind. I wondered whether he had taken along enough fresh water, or was he depending on rain? How would he catch it, in a cup or a pot, or in his open, upturned mouth, like a baby bird? Was he supplied with sugar pizza from the Black Bag, or did he plan to snare fish with makeshift hooks and eat the creatures raw? Could he catch a hungry seagull with his bare hands if one landed on his raft, if it eyed his toes greedily, planning to eat him bit by bit?

I raced to a phone stall, called a cousin in Miami and shout-whispered, "¡Call the Rescue Brothers!" I pronounced the words, rapidly, in English, hoping it would create havoc in Miami, total chaos, a stampede of cousins joining together to figure out who had left Cuba, and when, how far out to sea the boat or raft might be at this moment, in which portion of the big triangular sea it languished, a triangle framed by Cuba on the south, Florida on the north, and the Bahamas to the east. I returned the old-fashioned black phone to its cradle, letting my words sink in, letting them create an image of Rescue Brothers searching the waves.

The currents should carry Camilo to the Key of Bones, where most of the surviving *balseros* landed, along with many of the dead. But hurricane season could mean shifting winds, an unforeseen tug of waves toward George Town, or Andros Island, or the

Dry Tortugas, or into one of the vast empty spaces between islands, the spaces where raft people simply disappeared. Spaces that, on a map, looked so tiny and harmless, peaceful blue spaces fading to white as they approached the outlines of a mapmaker's clearly delineated shore.

I wondered how many inner tubes Camilo had managed to find or buy from the Black Bag, how strong was the rope he'd bound them with, making them a cohesive unit. Could he lie down, or did his legs have to dangle over the edge, a lure for sharks?

I imagined the Miami cousins calling each other frantically by phone or getting into their cars in pajamas or half-dressed, racing to warn each other, to collect money for the Rescue Brothers' fuel.

The Rescue Brothers, *Los Hermanos al Rescate*, were simply refugees who hadn't been able to forget the friends and family left behind. They flew out of South Florida, in small private planes, scanning the surface of blue depths for *balseros* to rescue. When they spotted a raft or boat from the air, they would radio the U.S. Coast Guard, reporting the position of the helpless, hopeful rafters. Sometimes the Coast Guard would find survivors on a small boat or raft, sometimes dehydrated corpses, or nothing at all, just empty floating inner tubes whipped by shredded remnants of rope, the legacy of a failed attempt to escape something I could barely bring myself to imagine, even though I'd seen it all around me, all over Havana, the weary, sorrowful eyes, the silent gestures and whispered conversations, the hunger, the stoic dreams hidden beneath slogans and parables and jests.

Two years later, when the vigil was all over, I learned that with the fuel purchased by a horde of hopeful Peregrín cousins in

Miami after my cryptic phone call from Havana, ten *balseros* were rescued. All were strangers. None was even remotely related to our family, but we would all feel, decades later, that at least the fuel had been put to good use, ten desperate half-starved men and women plucked from the yawning sea, the Rescue Brothers rejoicing each night for a week, as they managed to accomplish what they'd set out to do, money for fuel being their only limitation.

At the time of my phone call, we, Marisol and I, only cared about Camilo. We had no way of knowing that Camilo was already in the jaws of a viper.

ON THAT FIRST NIGHT WE DIDN'T SLEEP. WE PACED THE SEA WALL FROM end to end. Then we set out in Marisol's Ministry of Sugar car. It was a small blue Soviet Lada with official license plates. Marisol drove along the White Way Road, to the beaches known as Havana's Blue Circuit, to Bacuranao, Mégano, Santa María del Mar, Boca Ciega, Guanabo, Jibacoa, and Trópico. We had no way of guessing which of these beaches had launched Camilo's raft (motorboat, Marisol still insisted, convincing herself in one last desperate campaign to retain her ability to feign composure while passing through public places). Marisol, as a mother (a creature by definition optimistic, I later realized, when I finally gave my own children to the light) could not bring herself to picture a raft of black rubber tubes bound together by strands of dream.

I, on the other hand, imagined the worst. I paced the serene beaches (coconut palms, sea grapes, quiet shallow coves, the open sea, a maze of mangrove-lined canals) while music floated over the sands from remote huts and government hotels, *son montuno, bolero, guaguancó, mambo, cha-cha-cha, conga* . . .

We had left my rum untouched, the picture of Doña Inés vigilant on its glossy label, still waiting for good news from the Fountain of Youth. We had tasted a few bites of Marisol's miracle pudding, knowing it would spoil if we didn't consume it soon, because every time the electricity was turned off to conserve fuel, Cuba's refrigerators grew torrid, and scant rations were buried beneath swelling waves of hot blue mold.

As we paced the sands, Marisol poured an emotional salt into her wounds, reminiscing about Camilo's childhood, the Varadero carnival where he'd watched Papa Sun and the Butter-fly, a trip to Hemingway's museum-house, where little Camilo had once studied the old man's sea, concluding that it would be easy to catch a big fish and haul it to shore, as long as you had a good enough boat, big and strong and motorized, with plenty of harpoons to fight off the sharks, and plenty of spare food, and a friendly invisible angel to urge you along.

Camilo's mother told me that when he was very young Camilo often begged to visit the statue of the Indian Maiden on Dragon Street, a white marble statue of a lovely girl said to have met the Spanish sailors when the Spaniards first landed on Cuba's coast, a mythical girl who was said to have waved her arms in a generous circle, showing how large the island was, how beautiful and bounteous and safe.

She said Camilo liked to stand very close to the monument, waiting for it to come to life and speak. She said he often did the same with the bronze lions on the Prado promenade, and the monolithic statue of José Martí in Revolution Square, and the iron and wire image of a naked, sad-faced knight in Don Qui-xote Park (stripped of everything but hope, Marisol said, describing the lonely knight) and the two bronze statues at the top of the steps of the Academy of Sciences (representing the

Virtue of the People and the Progress of Mankind) and the white marble figures of Faith, Hope, and Charity on the portico of an archway at Cristóbal Colón Cemetery.

I knew that Marisol paced those beaches without understanding what she hoped to find. I did the same. What could we possibly expect? A message scrawled in sand? Camilo lolling in a homemade dugout canoe after changing his mind about fleeing? Camilo, filled with regret, waiting for a chance to hitchhike back to Havana and resume his life of secrecy and hope?

No, he was gone, plain and simple. There could be no changing of minds, no revisions of plans, not now. This was a life-and-death situation, life or death, life against death, life following death. This was the kind of decision one could never revoke. *Balseros* were at the mercy of wind. They could never change direction.

Soldiers pacing the beaches held their weapons poised for attack. Their guard against escape attempts was perpetual, night and day. No one was allowed to leave the island. Young men with inner tubes floated idly, close to shore, swimming, or fishing, or pretending to fish.

I compared Camilo's plight to that of Hemingway's old man, tired and weak, pulled along by strands of hope, pursued by evil. But Camilo was young; he could not die like the old man might have died, remembering the games of lions on a distant shore. No, Camilo would have to die in a storm cloud of fury, knowing he was young and hadn't yet had his chance to live.

"If he wanted to leave, he should have just defected when he had the chance," Marisol shout-whispered. Her voice held a bitter residue. "He should have gone with his girlfriend Alina when they were on their way back from Moscow. He should have just stepped off the plane somewhere in Europe, and told some official he wanted political asylum. Instead, he came back, acted like he was happy to be home, went to work every day, bundled up that package he gave you, and waited. I don't know what's in the package, but if it's so important to him, he could have written and asked me to send it. I could have found a way to smuggle it out. There is always a way. When one door closes, another opens. When one light goes out, another comes on. *Cuando una luz se apaga, otra se enciende.*"

Marisol sighed and mourned, while I, watching the soldiers, began to imagine Camilo under arrest, the humpbacked gibbous moon sailing freely beyond a high dungeon window. The serenade of a fiery angel, music of flame and wind.

In our galaxy are probably one billion hospitable planets. God is big enough to tend them all at the same time. Why, I now wondered, of all those worlds, and of all the islands in every sea, had God chosen my half brother to sail away from these shores, trading everything he'd ever known for a speck of hope and a glow of trust?

These things didn't happen by accident. They were planned. A raft doesn't float away without a push. I imagined Camilo in a dungeon, gazing up beyond an angel's wings, seeing the shimmer of Venus at dawn, cradled by a crescent moon.

"How insignificant all other problems have become," Marisol stated. She said this with awe, a kind of scientific curiosity, as if she had just noticed an unusual cloud formation, or a red sheen on the waves, or a soldier with only one eye. She sounded like the Miami cousins during Hurricane Andrew, shocked and reverent, saving hysteria for after the winds passed.

Just before dawn we drove slowly back to the old city. Marisol dressed herself for work. We each swallowed a taste of strong coffee and half a crusty roll of bread.

"You can eat his rations," Marisol said with a matter-of-fact tone, acceptance, a pragmatic masquerade. Of course I did decide to eat Camilo's rations. He wouldn't need them at sea, or in Miami, or in prison. We couldn't predict where he would end up, but we couldn't report his absence either. Marisol would be held responsible if she admitted knowing that her son, an ostensibly loyal mouthpiece of the Commander's reign, had tied his dreams in a bundle and fled. Besides, they (the one-eyed soldiers) might take Camilo's packet from my knapsack, and shred it, or burn it, or bring it to trial. . . .

I could be accused of smuggling or of aiding and abetting an illegal attempt to flee the island. They could assume it was not a coincidence that I arrived in Cuba right before the moment of Camilo's departure. They could say I helped him prepare his raft, gave him dried food and fishing gear, a filter for converting sea water to fresh. They could say I had brought such a filter from abroad, the kind every well-equipped sailboat carries with its emergency supplies. They could say I filled my brother with tales of Northern riches and dazzling technology, computers that translate books, insect-shaped robots sent to collect rock samples from distant planets, virtual-reality screens strapped onto faces like the masks of primeval dancers. Yes, they could say I'd helped Camilo. They might read my mind, see how much I *wished* that I had thought to help, that I had thought to bring along a filter and a box of freeze-dried astronaut's meals, the kind carried by mountaineers and white-water rafters.

Yes, I could have helped, should have. I longed to reverse time, go back and start over at eleven o'clock on the night I met my long-lost sibling for the first time. I would ask pertinent questions, find a way to perceive what Camilo kept hidden, a way to help him plan.

I thought of his boat (Marisol's dream) or raft (my nightmare) as some sort of sea monster swallowing my brother. I was angry with the sea. I remembered that José Martí had once written a poem about hating the sea because, *"entre música y flores,"* amid flowers and music, it brought tyrants from Spain (and yet the poet's own parents were born in Spain) and now I found that I, who had always loved the seashore with its shining ribbons of blue space above and below, I who had always longed to escape from desert to beach, I was enraged by the sea because it hadn't warned me that my brother would have to cross it alone if he wanted the things I'd had all my life (freedom to speak and to cross borders, and to go sailing by day instead of night), the birthrights handed to me along with my U.S. passport.

I ACCOMPANIED MARISOL TO HER PRESTIGIOUS OFFICE AT THE MINISTRY OF Sugar. She showed me off, delighted (a pretense) to be hosting the visit of a long-lost relative who had finally obtained all the permits needed to meet the Cuban half of her family (actually I was a stowaway on the island, I had no permits, but Marisol was influential enough to ignore such formalities).

I smiled a lot, shook a lot of hands, agreed to attend various gatherings of the privileged few. If I was lucky, everyone advised me, I might even get to see the Commander waving to the audience of a baseball game later that week. He had just returned from the Olympics in Barcelona, and he'd had a chance to meet his own long-lost cousins in Galicia (his father, like the father of José Martí, was Spanish-born), so he was in a good mood despite the economic free-fall, and if I was truly lucky, I might get to meet him and shake his hand. My own half brother was, after all, in line for the nation's top simultaneous translation position. Camilo could someday be an important person in

Cuba, a Sugar Ministry secretary advised me greedily, if he played his cards right (this was said with a wink and the familiar gesture of sketching a beard on the chin).

I heard these predictions with a fixed grin, while Marisol explained that unfortunately her son had just caught a virulent strain of *el gripe*, Thailand flu, and would probably miss work for at least a week, maybe two. She glanced at me, and I nodded sympathetically, saying that all over the world this year's flu season had been predicted to start early and hit hard.

Marisol's eyes told me that if our vigil extended beyond two weeks, we would know, either way. Camilo would be in Miami, or in prison, or "lost at sea." We would not even have a body to arrange in its casket, an inert painted face to gaze at while mourning.

I made my exit gracefully, leaving poor Marisol to her protective maternal charade. She reminded me of those mother birds that feign a broken wing in order to lure predators away from their nests. I pitied her but not nearly as much as I admired her. She had pulled it off, showing up at work, chatting with her colleagues, creating the illusion of a normal home life, all this while waiting for another seven o'clock report of the names of survivors and the silence of death.

I PASSED EACH SOLITARY HOUR IN THOUGHT, WAITING FOR SEVEN o'clock, strolling through the Museum of the City, finding, on its archaic second floor, the very machete flourished in battle by the poet José Martí as he challenged the Spanish tyrants, striving (a noble yet futile effort) to make his poetic vision come to life, an island free and just. "I hide in my wild breast the sorrow that wounds it: the son of an enslaved people lives for it, is silent, and dies," shout-whispered the poet's ghost, following me through museum halls and cobblestone passageways, a transparent wraith reciting solid verse.

We strolled the sea wall together (the poet's ghost and I) as we searched for Camilo's phantom, for some message of his, a remnant of anything left behind, some word spoken quietly to the sky before death, praise or curse, call for help, or perhaps one last satirical jest, followed by one last dark ripple of medicinal laughter.

The ghost, *el espanto*, left me. I moved on to Hemingway's seaside ranch, and the rooms of his house, preserved as a museum, his books, furniture, and shoes (the shoes he never wore while writing, the chairs he left empty while writing, the first editions of books he wrote while standing uncomfortably to meet the challenge of a typewriter, Cuban rum in hand, Doña Inés always there, always waiting), rifles, stuffed heads of trophy beasts (an African water buffalo still raising its horns defiantly, mouth downturned in a perpetual grimace, eyes lifelike, fixed and threatening), and the lovely tropical Cuban beach where the expatriate author had launched his yacht to go out searching the Gulf Stream for Nazi submarines.

My mother, in her youth, had posed on this beach, and my father, a dashing sportsman, a rebel, intriguing Hemingway with idealistic tales of heroism not yet tackled, and valor not yet proven.

I hunted my parents' ghosts, but they escaped me, they lingered elsewhere, in the wake of Camilo's raft, perhaps, or perched on the crests of waves at his side, where he could see them and pursue their watery tracks all the way to Florida, to the Fountain of Youth, to safety, to a family reunion, to love.

*　　　　　　*

AT SEVEN O'CLOCK THERE WERE NAMES, FAMILIAR, YET STRANGE, NAMES we'd often heard before, Felipe, Carlos, Jorge, José. They were not the names we longed to hear, the six syllables we'd turned into a prayer, a chant, a plea, Camilo Peregrín.

We shared a spare meal of plain white rice and bitter Cuban espresso drowned in a sea of sugar. "We have more sugar than coffee this month," said Marisol. "I am thinking of trying a pudding of sugar flavored with coffee and wild fruit from one of the beaches, coconut or sea grape maybe, or of Black Bag cashew fruit from the mountains, or rose apple. What do you think?" She looked at me with a firm, steady, confident gaze. "For tomorrow night's celebration, seven o'clock sharp, no excuses." She held up my bottle of Havana Club rum, where the medieval bronze vigilant Doña Inés still stood poised and erect on her shiny paper label, watching for ships.

Marisol switched off the radio, folded its antennae down, like wings on a resting butterfly, and sighed, "Tomorrow."

We were exhausted. I knew we would need to sleep or pray or pace the seashore. We couldn't sit there in that kitchen staring at Doña Inés and a silent radio. We couldn't sit in any of the half-open rooms visible to upstairs neighbors, stared at by curious eyes hidden beneath the shadows of immense turbans (the turbans, Marisol had assured me, were symbols of Santería, of voodoo, signs that the upstairs neighbors were the willing horses ridden by evil spirits, calling for curses to fall upon the earth). By now the spying neighbors must be wondering why Camilo hadn't been seen for two days. Soon, Marisol shout-whispered as we rose from the kitchen table, neighbors would begin asking questions, taking mental notes for a report to the secret police.

They would be performing bizarre rituals, sacrificing small wild creatures if they couldn't find Black Bag goats and roosters. They would be asking the spirit of war to help them destroy Marisol, begging the spirit of the sea to be satisfied with Camilo's death. They would be piercing the cowrie shell eyes of carved figurines, and feeding voracious invisible mouths with precious Black Bag meat and with bowls of blood. They would be dancing and casting coconut shells for augury and arranging color-coded flowers on homemade altars.

For now, I had the solace of translucent wings, and gleaming fireflies, pale greenish luna moths, named for the moon. The angels (some big, with many faces and multiple wings, others small and simple, all reassuring, fiery, windy) were serene despite their constant glowing motion.

"¡The concert!" Marisol suddenly remembered, "I have to sing." Our glances met and tangled. How could she sing? How could a mother dress herself in finery, stand in front of an audience, stretch out her arms and force pleasing sounds from her horrified mouth, all while waiting to hear the fate of a son lost at sea?

She rushed through the house gathering clothes, shoes, sheets of music, decorations for her hair (pre-revolutionary river pearls and lace), the old blue silk fan with peacock-tail embroidery. She handed me the fan and advised me to use it in the concert hall, saying it would be hot, always hot, always stifling, never fresh. She said it would be hot in the concert hall even if the government had fuel for air conditioners. The hall, Marisol explained, was just a roof supported by pillars. "Open sides," she added, "letting in all the heat and rain, all the insects and wind and sounds from afar, to mix with the music and make it different than it's meant to be. You sing in that hall," she gasped, "and birds accompany you, cicadas, crickets, the whistling of bicyclists as they pass along the road.

"Because the building is so old. Today the new buildings in other countries, I'm told, are different, but similar, glass walls, skylights, mirrored walls, so, like us, the people can't really tell whether they're indoors or out."

Despite my dread of the stares of upstairs neighbors, I liked the sound of a concert hall without walls. I wanted everything out in the open. I felt exhausted by Cuba's ubiquitous secrecy. Secrets lead to slavery, I found myself thinking, to betrayal and more secrets, and pretty soon a cycle is released from hiding, feeding on itself, cannibalizing all the secrets, then giving birth to more.

I accepted the blue fan. "We need to sleep," I said, opening the fan to cool my face, waving it through the air like a signal, like a call for help.

"Maybe tonight," Marisol nodded. We were thinking of rafts and Rescue Brothers, sharks and airplanes, and waves and ghosts and storm clouds and angels and God. Our minds were far from the concert, far from sleep, far from song or dream.

It rained in the concert hall. water came pouring in horizontally between stone pillars. Swept in by wind, the rain made the ceiling appear to be weeping through the eyes of murals painted on its surface: angels, conquistadores, Indians, beaches, palm trees, parrots in an intricate green jungle.

Marisol posed in front of a crowd of the island's upper class, the Commander's loyalists. She clasped her hands, roused a pert smile, and sang like a mockingbird, the melodies flowing into each other and out through the space between pillars, absorbed by night.

The men wore embroidered shirts and sharks' teeth pendants, a symbol of some sort, a Santería talisman, Marisol later explained, to attract more power to the powerful, make the strong man even stronger. These men applauded enthusiastically, calling out, "¡Bravo!" and "¡Socialism or death!" and "¡Life to Cuba!" They occasionally peppered their between-song conversations with slogans and winks and knowing tilts of the head.

The women fanned themselves, smiling graciously, holding their poses with studied elegance. We could have been surrounded by eighteenth-century noblemen and their ladies instead of Communist Party members. I fell asleep.

I DREAMED I WAS IMMERSED IN A SOLIDIFIED SEA OF HARD, TANGIBLE reflections, garnet, steel, pyrite, topaz, amethyst, a sea of minerals and helmeted miners, dark tunnels, dynamite, blind creatures burrowing under layers of stone, finding veins of crystalline light.

I dreamed with Camilo, with drowning. My brother and I looked up from our sunken raft and saw the sky, its egg-shaped stars gleaming from their nest of galaxies, indigo-blue space with the soft sheen of silk, airborne sharks circling.

I felt the sting of salt on my eyes, the lick of a tide passing through my hair. Seaweed grew from my tongue.

I slept through most of Marisol's concert, dreaming with food riots, women standing out in the rain, beating spoons against the sides of empty pots and pans. . . .

The pots were numerous and varied: sky-blue porcelain speckled with tiny pebbled clouds of white, shiny aluminum, old black iron streaked with rust, copper beaten in smoky forges, enormous kettles, the Big Dipper, cauldrons, sieves, a floating pot spilling gold from the top of an inverted rainbow . . .

In the dream there was a clamor of angry housewives (in Spanish the archaic matriarchal term, *ama de casa*, means owner of the house, mistress of the house, landlady) as mothers demanded milk for their children . . .

In the dream, secret police were baffled, and soldiers watched, perplexed, as their own mothers and sisters swarmed the sea wall, demanding food, shrieking for beans and corn and bread, shouting "even the Black Bag is empty." In my dream no one whispered. Angels followed the women, stroking their heads, resting lightly on their shoulders, humming, breathing flame, shouting. Even the angels were shouting . . .

I was awakened abruptly by lightning, rain, applause, fireflies, thunder, a sweltering tropical heat. I looked down at the program in my hands, wet paper curled at the edges, paper the color of sand. According to the rain-streaked concert program, Marisol had just finished singing a piece called "Oath," *Juramento,* and then another called "If You Only Knew," *Si supieras.* Most of the songs boasted romantic lyrics written long ago by famous Cuban poets and composers. None had anything to do with economic theories or political intrigue or Ministries or sugar or curses or codes. This, I decided, was Marisol's reason for choosing to join a choir. Her small gesture at an escape from her daily reality. This choir belonged in the past. Only tonight it was not an escape, but a net, strands of lace twining around her hands and hair, holding her still, making her smile in a bronze, vigilant pose, like Doña Inés.

She ended her solo with one of José Martí's most famous verses, a refrain from his "Simple Lyrics," a poem set to music, with a background of a tiny, high-pitched peasant guitar, and a native Cuban Indian flute and paired African drums crafted from a polished wood striped dark and light:

> *Yo soy un hombre sincero*
> *De donde crece la palma*
> *Y antes de morirme quiero*
> *Echar mis versos del alma*

> I am a sincere man
> from where the palm tree grows
> and before I die I want to free
> the verses from my heart

Now I was truly awake. Here I felt at home. Here, inside this simple verse, with the poet's ghost and my fugitive wandering half brother and his courageously serenading mother, here I could belong, in a land where a soothing rain could erase words (my concert program was suddenly blank now, the ink washed away) a land where flaming wings could carry invisible words to anyone lost at sea.

Many other people performed in that official government choir along with Marisol, after her solo of three brief wistful songs. Both men and women sang, but I couldn't see them, I couldn't hear their voices. My eyes were heated, all I could see was Marisol, heroic, metallic, molten, mother of my half brother, this woman who could carol in public while she mourned in the place we keep hidden away, cradled, swathed, rocked for comfort by an unseen hand.

All I could see now was Marisol with her inflamed eyes and

lacy white dress, ornate, antiquated, dressed like a child at First Communion, white from head to toe, incandescent, white embroidered ribbons, ruffles, layers of lace petticoats, satin shoes, chains of river pearls, a mother-of-pearl clip holding the black cascades of angry hair, clutching at the fury of her internal rebellion.

No wonder the Commander (even after so many decades of failed sugar harvests and disgruntled cane-cutting brigades) continued to crave Marisol's savage grip of loyalty, the grip of a parent pulling her child out of quicksand or tar pits or a whirlpool in a rushing stream.

Marisol's old-fashioned choir sat down, and another, dressed in Young Pioneer uniform (red, white, and blue) took their place. These fervent young Communist Party hopefuls sang in Vietnamese, and waved paper fans embossed with the slogan "Socialism or Death." I was seated near the back of the concert hall, next to a pillar. My clothes were soaked by rain. The air felt like the hot mist inside a wet sauna. I shoved my knapsack a little farther under my chair (antique colonial mahogany carved by slaves seized from the Congo and carried in the holds of ships across an ocean so big and so treacherous that no one ever tried to cross back to native shores), wondering what Camilo's parcel concealed, what stunning secrets it might eventually reveal. Did it contain treasured photographs that could be ruined by water? I dreamed with my father in the jungle, my mother on Hemingway's placid beach. I was glad I had thought of wrapping the entire knapsack in a sheet of black plastic before leaving Marisol's house. I had done it because I thought a traveler's backpack might look inappropriate at a concert, but now I was glad, because I really had no idea what Camilo had put in my trust, and how soon he might want it back, expecting it returned intact and dry, free of Cuba's heated rain.

Marisol had repeatedly sworn that she herself had no knowledge of the parcel's contents. She'd insisted that whatever it was, Camilo must have some crucial plan for it, because he was a linguist by nature, meticulous and cautious, a perfectionist. He never did anything without considering all the consequences.

"He must have planned all this in great detail," she had assured me. "If he decided to trust you and only you, he knew why, knew what he could expect of you. It could be some favorite possession perhaps, or his university diploma from the Soviet Union, or his notes on the dialects of Spain. You know he was recently instructed, by the Commander himself, as a personal favor, to prepare a treatise on Galician colloquialisms."

I sat in the concert hall beneath a sheet of horizontal rain, listening to Vietnamese march songs, wondering about Camilo and the packet of mysteries he'd entrusted to my care, and about Marisol, about her vulnerability when the Commander finally noticed that a son of the inner circle was gone.

Marisol, while we paced the beach sands, had confided that someday she planned to start a small business in her home, in one of her houses. She said she preferred the strange chimney-shaped house in Old Havana even though its open central courtyard meant she could be spied on. Of all her houses, only that curious one had been a family one, a Peregrín house. It was the only one with history ingrained in its roof tiles and ancestral heel marks scuffing its marble stairs. "After *el triunfo*, 'the triumph' of capitalism," Marisol had shout-whispered, "I will have my little business, there in my own house where once so many of my husband's cousins used to come and go, in the only one of my houses which was never handed to me as a gift from the Commander." Marisol had looked behind her as she spoke, and from side to side. She had even checked the sky (for listening birds, she chuckled, since some of them know how to talk and might repeat what they hear) before saying, "We know, of course, all of us do, that *this* is ending now, and soon we'll lose our pensions, and we'll have to start over with nothing, just as we did when the Commander told us to accept his version of communism (nothing for anyone, everything for one). Marisol didn't tell me what type of business she had in mind. I knew she owned several homes in different parts of Havana, personal rewards given to loyalists after each challenge to the Commander's authority. A beach house after the Bay of Pigs invasion. A country estate after the CIA tried to poison the Commander's cigars. An Embassy Row apartment after an unpopular purging of poets from the Ministry of Culture, when the island's most famous poets were issued shovels and reassigned to gardening tasks in Lenin Park, and responded by producing verses even more independent than before, and by smuggling the verses overseas, where the first tiny sparks of doubt were ignited in the minds of admiring intellectuals who had, until that time, consistently referred to the Commander as "savior of the Third World."

The Commander himself kept at least thirty homes of his own, scattered across the island. He slept in a different one each night, as protection against assassins. Only his doctors and bodyguards knew where he was hidden at any given moment.

Now, beneath horizontal rain and a painted medieval conquest of the Indies, I wondered how Marisol would manage after the Commander's inevitable fall, how she would learn to run a business, what kind of enterprise she would launch from my father's tribal Peregrín home.

She had bemoaned her regrets, said she wished she'd spent less energy praising the revolution and more getting to know her only child. She wished she'd passed every moment holding Camilo's hand and none at all setting harvest quotas and production goals and export predictions.

She said she had measured her life in metric tons of sugar instead of hours or days or years. Now she wanted the years back. She said she had no use for sugar. She yearned to reclaim her son's infancy, his childhood, his adolescence. She wanted to go back to the holidays they spent at the beach together, and put her mind on his eyes and smile, seize it away from the petty anxieties she'd felt in those days, the worldwide glut of beet sugar, the plagues of cane-chewing insects.

She'd sworn, as we paced those beach sands, that someday she would learn to drink her coffee black. She'd confessed that sugar and slavery had walked together through history, accompanied by secrecy. She'd confessed that she was tired, disgusted, fed up. "Overflowing" was the word she used to describe her exasperation. *Inundación*, a flood. Now, seated beneath painted jungles and painted angels, listening to polite applause, I pictured Marisol's tenacious eyes overflowing with tears made of sugar instead of salt.

Of course, I didn't think Marisol should blame herself for Camilo's dilemma. I couldn't imagine a grown man fleeing on a raft just because his mother had fretted about the collapse of the East Bloc barter system (no more trading of sugar for wheat or petroleum) or the absence of hard currency, or even the intensifying food shortage, the lack of medicine. No, Camilo must have guarded much greater secrets than the ones Marisol and I had imagined as we paced those beach sands, greater or more personal, less abstract. He must have been outraged, terrified, desperate beyond belief, beyond all the ordinary everyday circles of possibilities.

DAWN, AFTER THAT NIGHT OF THE DREAMLIKE CONCERT, WAS CLEAR. NO more rivers of lightning floating in sky, no more tributaries of fire or cascades of electricity. Marisol had gone to the Ministry, and I was alone on the sea wall. The sky was such a vibrant blue, so close and dazzling and tangible that it looked like it had been painted by a mad genius, the wet pigments still visible in thick curling swaths, parallel sets of brushstrokes running in all directions, crossing each other, a maze of turquoise-blue layered upon royal-blue and peacock-blue and aquamarine.

I was afraid that if I stared at that generous sky too long, it might absorb me, submerge my hopes beneath its expanse of brilliance. Staring at those blue layers seemed as dangerous as staring directly into the sun.

Below, the sea lay flat and smooth, a robe of silk dropped onto a marble floor. I imagined Camilo pulling himself up to a dungeon window, peering out to watch solar flares disrupting the transmission of Radio Martí's treasured list of seven o'clock names.

The intensity of sunlight reminded me that at this moment the real Camilo might already be dead, draped across his raft, inert, glaring up at this same layered sky and flaming sun. Or he might be wondering whether we'd had sense enough to call the Rescue Brothers, whether planes from Miami were out searching for him. He could be speculating, wondering whether we'd already given him up for dead, decided he was lost at sea. Wondering whether we'd called off the search too soon.

That day crept along with nothing but wall and sky and sea, everything parallel and flat, interrupted only by the motions of seagulls and frigate birds and would-be *balseros* carrying their black inner tubes from rock to rock along the sea wall guarded by soldiers. I had grown used to the ubiquitous soldiers. They were as familiar as birds or lizards, a form of wildlife.

At seven o'clock there were no names at all. Not a single name. No one had been rescued.

Instead of ending, our vigil, it now seemed, was just about to begin. That was the year I learned how to wait. It was the year I learned how to love and to see how closely fastened people can grow by waiting together, like vines on a fence or roots in the cracks of sidewalks, lichens on stone. Even when separated by a deep, triangular, shark-infested sea.

I was astounded by the experience of waiting, by the alteration of time that occurs as one lingers. I actually waited in Havana, at Marisol's side, for only a few of the hundreds of days that followed Camilo's attempt to escape from the Commander's grasp.

I barely knew Marisol at all. I barely knew Camilo. Yet for the rest of our lives we would remain related, connected, a family. We had been forced to claim each other, belong to each other, to need, fear, dream with each other.

In two hours I had learned so much about Camilo, absorbing his surroundings, his house, city, sky. I had grown attached to my half brother, like the tendril of a creeper, or the cocoon of a caterpillar. We had spoken for two hours, scanned each other, appearance, gestures, posture, hair, smiles, skin. We'd found out, during that two-hour visit, that Camilo had an unquenchable sense of humor, and that I had two half brothers, one illusory and another authentic.

Yet in two hours I had learned so little! No secrets, childhood sorrows, lifelong ambitions, visions of a future. I didn't even learn Camilo's opinion of our father, or his feelings toward my renegade mother, or his memories of me as imaginary half sister on a continent distanced by tides and waves.

In two hours we had seen just enough to know that we'd both shifted from our fanciful forms to these new, solidified ones. We'd grown into each other's memories.

In two hours I'd moved from wondering about Camilo to caring. It had been a painless transfiguration, followed by the drama of his escape attempt. During the days of waiting with Marisol, I didn't even notice that I was being altered, adjusted, modified, while God, the sculptor, busily scraped bits of wet clay from my unfinished eyes.

Here was the fantasy of my childhood brought to life, the half brother I'd taken along on every expedition, called out to during every adventure, cried to after every small wound.

When I took him to the headwaters of the Amazon (my mother was searching for bark paintings depicting piranha and serpents), we sat in a dugout canoe, confronted by endless jungle on both shores of the Río Napo. I asked my imaginary sibling, "Is this how Cuba looks?" My mother, seated in front, on a bench of wood so perpetually wet that moss and seedlings sprouted from its cracks, was busy bailing rain out of the canoe, using a turtle's empty green shell to scoop the water. "What was that you said, Carmen?" my mother asked without looking at me, but I didn't answer, and my imaginary half brother, hiding in a cloud above my head, winked and smiled and teased my mother with an extra spurt of rain.

I'd longed, all my life, to dwell in a hot, green, tangled place, birdsongs, frog chants, nocturnal shrieks, monkeys dangling like flowers from trees. Yet each time we visited one of those places, I eventually returned to the windswept desert, to dust devils and scorching sands, and a sun so alive I thought the earth must have lost its orbit and gone racing inward, ready to crash in flames at any moment.

I collected winged horses and mentally embroidered birds and the hallucinations brought on by fevers from distant jungles. I had my assortment of invisible souvenirs, but always, on every trip, I searched for my father's island, asking my imaginary half brother, at predictable intervals, in the Congo or Bali or Ecuador, "So is *this* how Cuba looks?"

My mother would hear my question, and say, "Maybe someday you'll see." She meant maybe someday I would see Cuba (from the womb I had barely glimpsed its indigo sky) but when I was small I thought she meant maybe someday Cuba will look like this, so I came away from Thailand and Malaysia and Senegal, always thinking, "Cuba will soon be here, it's on its way."

MY MOTHER TOLD ME THAT WHEN HEMINGWAY SPOTTED HIS GARDENER trying to shear Cuban trees, he chased the poor man away with a rifle, refusing to allow the insolence of pruning in a place meant to flourish beyond all barriers, a place without borders.

She said the Commander, unlike Hemingway, loved to see things trimmed and clipped. During a sorcerer's ritual he'd sacrificed a rooster, but first he yanked out its tongue, saying that way it wouldn't be able to tell what it had seen. My mother said the Commander had worn a pendant of sharks' teeth to increase his appearance of ferocity. She said he would have been happy to wear a lion's mane if he could have found one on the island, or a rhino's pronged horn, or a gargoyle's claw.

My father's appearance was not ferocious at all. He looked just like Camilo. His water-stained photographs, resting in the piles of memory on Marisol's cluttered desks and bureaus, showed a bearded revolutionary smiling in the Cuban jungle, his eyes cheerful, like scintillating planets seen through my desert window on moonless nights.

Marisol said the jungle was an odd place to be cheerful, especially during a war of liberation (she still hated the Commander's tyrannical predecessor enough to remember the war against him as an act of courage and emancipation). She said her husband, my father, had a gift for cheer. Like Camilo, he loved to recount long anecdotes ending in humorous dilemmas with double meanings, misinterpretations, foggy views of clear images.

MY MOTHER HAD ADAMANTLY REFUSED TO DISCUSS MY FATHER. SHE HAD refused to describe his island home. Her only concession to my reality was an occasional grudging conversation about Camilo, how someday I would meet him, how I might not like him, because men, my mother scowled, were too vain, too bossy, too taken with regal visions of heroic knights fighting just and noble battles against fire-spitting dragons freshly emerged from long centuries dreaming in caves.

My mother, when questioned with enough persistence, would gradually concede that I might have liked my father. She would not say why. I imagined I would like him because he would buy me ice cream flavored with saffron and cashew, or give me a flying horse, or teach me magic tricks and show me how to hide when I was being chased through a jungle (chased by anything, ogres, devils, crocodiles, mad dogs, cannibals wearing bones in their ears) but no matter how hard I tried, I could never dream with my father in the Cuban jungle, in his noble war. I would plan these dreams, but once I was asleep, they would vanish, and I would be left alone, or dreaming with Camilo, a boy I knew only from a few snapshots of Young Pioneers and student work brigades and militiamen and linguists.

When I dreamed with Camilo, he was never in uniform. He was North American. He lived in the desert and ate hamburgers and spoke English. He found new uses for ancient artifacts, showing me how to make slingshots out of necklaces of Chinese coins, or a spear from the plank of an authentic Spanish galleon. He roamed the sand dunes at my side, finding strings of shell-bead money, and the ashes of cremated shamans, and slick concave chips of obsidian brought to the desert from distant volcanos by trade, each tribe exchanging one treasured object for another until everyone had a little bit of everything God had ever invented.

4

Buried Treasure

Quiero, a la sombra de un ala,
Contar este cuento en flor:

I want, in the shadow of a wing,
to tell this flowering tale:

JOSÉ MARTÍ

I RETURNED TO MY REAL LIFE IN THE DESERT SOUTH OF PALM SPRINGS, where I lived alone in an old adobe house built by some long-forgotten family of pioneers. It became my mother's house, perched on the sloping gravel surface of an alluvial fan, at the mouth of a canyon where bighorn sheep still moved silently down rugged granite slopes at dawn to drink from a hidden spring.

From the mud-and-straw patio I could see, now far below sea level, a long dry valley which was once a prehistoric lake. The ancient water level could still be distinguished as a stripe of dark minerals staining the sunbleached rock. Stone fish traps lay tumbled along this watermark. Above them, on granite boulders, petroglyphs outlined the angular chiseled forms of frogs and rattlesnakes and turtles.

After each windstorm I would wander across sand dunes, collecting seashell beads, bone awls, shattered grinding stones, soapstone pipes, even the brittle fragments of deergrass baskets once carried, centuries earlier, by nomadic desert women as they gathered mesquite pods and cactus fruit and fibrous, yam-flavored chunks of roasted agave.

Sometimes the money-beads shaped from seashells were charred and blackened. These came from cremation sites, where the dead had been torched along with their possessions, along with their brush and palm-frond houses, stone tools, rabbitskin blankets, obsidian-tipped arrows, winnowing baskets, ceramic water jars, sleeping mats, wild tobacco, pigments for face painting, eagle feathers for striving to fly during ceremonial dances.

All of this had seemed natural to me, a creature of the past, my life layered on top of the lives of the dead. I always left the cremation sites intact, bones, ash, skulls, broken finger bones.

WHEN I RETURNED TO THE DESERT FROM CUBA I FOUND A NEW GOLF course draped across the sand dunes. Stark white condominiums were springing up all around the slab of green. A shiny blue lake had drifted into my view of salt flats and mesquite thickets. I had known the golf course was coming, but I didn't realize that it could be thrown up overnight, changing the land from gray to green, the lake from ancient to modern.

My trip to Cuba had lasted less than two weeks, but during that time, a mirage had been transformed into substance, air into fluid. I felt like all the world's primeval mists were now being converted into dew.

After my mother died, I began planning to move away from

her desert and start over someplace mountainous and wild, the Yukon, Kilimanjaro, a cloud forest above the Orinoco basin, the highlands of New Guinea. My mother had left me exactly enough money to start and finish college, if I could manage to stay on a narrow four-year path and take no wrong turns.

My mother had found and lost many small fortunes, always selling her antiquities too soon, for less than their potential value, always anxious to get them off her hands, into a museum or private collection, always determined to control the past by moving it from place to place, by turning it into an accident of geography.

She had done her best to become a reclusive desert rat, a cactus gardener subsisting on steamed yucca flowers and stewed prickly pear pads.

She died half a year before my trip to Cuba. It was the half a year I'd spent in Miami, preparing finally to meet my Cuban half brother.

AFTER SEEING HOW RAPIDLY THE GOLF COURSE HAD EMERGED FROM gravel and sand, green and wet and hideous in its defiance of nature, I decided to stay. Camilo, if he was alive, would be needing help. If he was lost at sea, Marisol would be the one in need. She would find herself unable to keep up the travesty of sugar harvests. She would long to join her cousins in Miami. Either way, I would need cash to make sure no other Peregrín ever left Cuba on a raft, to make sure they always knew they could turn to me for exit visas and airplane tickets and bribes for the Commander's hidden treasure chests.

I raced into the new resort demanding work. They gave me a temporary job managing condominiums. With the dunes now obscured by green turf, whirlwinds no longer carried sand into my eyes. There were no more dust devils, no blinding curtains of windblown salt. I no longer felt like a camel in an old Hollywood safari movie.

A flood control project took form. No more flash floods, no walls of water crashing through the canyon during winter storms. The bighorn sheep now came to swimming pools for their morning drink. I told myself that I, like the wild creatures, would manage. It was my new job title, the first job title I'd ever had: management.

Humidity rose from the golf course sprinklers, intensifying the desert heat. One hundred and twenty degrees Fahrenheit now felt like one hundred and thirty. Most of the condos would be occupied only from November to May. Every summer the white bedrooms would be abandoned by golfers fleeing north. The pastel-hued kitchens (coral, mint, a pale version of nautical blue) would stand empty, strands of artificial chilis and glazed ceramic onions left hanging beneath skylights.

I promised myself a winter of management. I would work until the new dwellings were vacated, then send every penny to Camilo's mother. I would create a fountain of bribes to help her free her son. If he was alive.

I found it an odd way to think of freedom, and yet, it fit everything my eccentric mother had ever led me to imagine, an island of fanged cannibals and one-eyed titans.

AS A CHILD I HAD GROWN ACCUSTOMED TO MY MOTHER'S REBEL DIET OF homegrown seeds and the flesh of wild rabbits. Now, in my mother's desert garden, the remains of last year's blue corn and sunflowers still stood, shriveled and papery dry, mummified by sun and wind.

Throughout my childhood we had moved from one wilderness home to another, always desert, always naked rock and shifting sand, always a log cabin or a geodesic dome, or a canvas teepee erected on a flat landscape devoid of shadows.

When my mother died in her hang-gliding accident, blown by shifting winds into a rocky cliff, she left me with a desiccated garden, four authentic adobe walls, enough money for college, and the skills for treasure hunting and rabbit-skinning and the gathering of wild plants. She left me, however, without any knack for management in a world filled with humans.

The tenant in 124 shot his wife three days after moving into their new condo. The inhabitants of 273 stopped paying their mortgage almost immediately, and refused to move out. Number 112 set his garage on fire trying to burn a black widow spider. An overdose of barbiturates emptied number 208, her stomach pumped, her mind as smooth as glass.

Graffiti appeared as if by magic along the long walls separating golfers from desert. Black symbols formed on the surface of white paint, left behind by youthful taggers from struggling immigrant communities where gates had never been guarded and swamp coolers had not yet been replaced by air-conditioning.

THE HEAT BROUGHT HALLUCINATIONS. A BEARDED DEMON FLOATED across my kitchen, hovering near a bowl filled with miniature white pumpkins and gold-striped decorative gourds.

I ran outside. I kept running. I felt myself flying. After that, I was afraid to go home. I set up a tent and slept in it. I dreamed with attacking lions and drooling hyenas. In the morning an earthquake cracked the brand-new walls of several condos. I moved back into my lonely childhood home, leaving the tent up just in case.

*　　　　　*

A HUGE STRAY DOG MOVED INTO MY TENT THAT NIGHT. IN THE MORNING she licked my face and demanded a breakfast of ice cream and wild doves. I kept her and named her Rocky Path, thinking of our barren desert surroundings and the chocolate, marshmallow, and nut dessert she consumed in rationed spoonfuls, whining for more.

The Sheriff came by in his striped car, warning me that I could be arrested for stealing such a fine animal, so obviously a mix of Irish wolfhound and German Shepherd, with perhaps a trace of husky (the silvery mane) and labrador retriever (loose, floppy lips like the lips of a mischievous grinning chimpanzee).

I told the Sheriff that I had *not* stolen the dog. *She* had stolen my tent. I promised to call the Humane Society and search for the real owner.

They offered to take Rocky off my hands for three days. Then, they explained, she would be killed unless I paid a sixty dollar fee to reclaim her. Instead of saying what they meant (killed) they said euthanized.

I kept Rocky, and I kept my sixty dollars. I kept my distinction between killing and euthanasia. No one came to arrest me for stealing the enormous dog. She continued growing every day, until she was so lanky and clumsy and tall that every time she entered a room its contents would go flying off tables and walls.

Rocky was my only companion during the early days of my northern vigil. I was young. I longed to fall in love and leave the desert. But I was waiting for Camilo's freedom. His note had instructed me to wait awhile before opening the packet he referred to as "our chronicle."

I was afraid to open it, paralyzed. What if it contained voodoo dolls and *Santería* talismans, amulets of tooth and claw and hair, shrunken heads? The parcel taunted me. Venomous herbs, I imagined, the fangs of a serpent, vials of clotted blood.

It was still wrapped in black plastic, still immersed in the depths of my knapsack, still smelling like hurricane season.

I waited a full three months before opening the chronicle. I spoke to Rocky about Camilo and his foolish raft and about my imaginary castle dungeon with its angel hovering under a single high window.

Together we ate breakfast, lunch, and dinner. "Ice cream is bad for dogs," I warned, as I licked up my piles of thrice-daily ice cream, chocolate malted crunch, fudge brownie, tin roof. Rocky always managed to sneak a tiny lick from each of my bowlfuls. Maybe it was bad for me too, I found myself silently arguing, but ice cream was sugar, and sugar was Cuba, and I had forgotten how to survive without the island's taste. The big dog accompanied me on long walks in the canyon, where I carried a thermos filled with a homemade double fudge espresso flavor I'd invented. I let the ice cream melt in my thermos just long enough to provide a thick cold slush as we hiked uphill and a tepid milk shake for the return journey.

Sometimes Rocky would sniff too close to the four-inch spines of a jumping cholla cactus as she chased a jackrabbit or a desert iguana. Then I would have to spend entire evenings pulling the spines through her flesh to remove them from her quivering lips and nose. I wondered how I had ever managed to survive without a companion. Autumn in the desert seemed gentle, with companionship and a mountain breeze.

I dreamed with statues gazing at the sky, and rafts sailing across sand dunes. *Soñé con estatuas mirando al cielo, balsas navegando en la arena . . .*

Marisol began sending me letters. They arrived in two forms, some smuggled, others trusted to the Cuban mail, stamped with colorful images of tropical fish and Olympic athletes. These cautious letters, perused by official censors before being allowed off the island, were crafted in a mysterious, ornate script that reminded me of Arabic or Hebrew, as if Marisol had intentionally made her words impossible to decipher by anyone who hadn't yet cultivated the stoic and deliberate patience of a Cuban mother. These flowery lines were laced with metaphors and riddles, subtle wit, parables, and vague hints. Each of these brief censored letters required hours of reading, re-reading and constantly revised interpretation. What did she *really* mean when she wrote (the words hidden by loops and swirls of ink) "difficulties" or "complications" or "plans"? Did she expect me to understand only partially or to break her code and become fully enlightened? Should I be able to click my tongue at the end of a sentence, and say, "Aha, so that's how it is."

"For hard bread, sharp teeth," wrote Marisol in one of the deliberately scribbled censored letters, *"Para pan duro, colmillo fino."* The words were submerged beneath a sea of curlicues and connected eyelets ending in wavy flourishes.

Was Marisol hoping the Commander's censor would read for a few minutes, grow weary of the fancy script and double meanings, give up with a sigh, and let the letters flow from one wire basket to another until they were out of Cuba? Did she imagine that her forbidden thoughts could flee the island intact and free of condemnation?

I pictured Camilo in a sunlit dungeon, pictured him wondering, as he watched his translucent angel, whether we, the living of this human world, remembered him. I pictured him in the Viper, daydreaming and inventing jokes to entertain the angel.

Each of Marisol's censored letters ended with a quote from the poetry of José Martí, the infinitely revered poet of nine-teenth-century Cuban liberation, his verses still claimed a century later, both by exile and Commander.

AFTER A MONTH, THE SMUGGLED LETTERS CAME LESS FREQUENTLY, bearing stamps showing wood ducks and North American flags. These had been hand-carried to Miami by refugee Cubans or wandering exiles, I imagined, by sons sneaking across the sea to visit aging mothers one last time before they died, or brothers sneaking from exile to homeland to present their Cuban sisters with exit visas obtained through bribery and dedicated years (sometimes decades) of persistent Black Bag diplomacy, or simply with enough food and medicine to survive another month of plummeting toward Option Zero.

These smuggled letters, postmarked from Miami or Coral Gables or Key West, came infrequently, each one consisting of a few clear, concise pages, stating exactly what the simple words meant. In these Marisol would say, "this entire island is a prison," or "¡How we suffer!" or "You must pray very hard for Cuba . . . pray . . . pray . . . pray . . . for . . . us." *Ora por nosotros.* She gave warnings and spoke of illusions and delirium, and of weeks spent in a fog of indecision and alarm. She used the word illusion in its Spanish sense, *ilusión,* meaning, instead of apparitions or legerdemain, a dream, a wish, an attainable goal, the heart's desire.

She used delirium in its Spanish sense also, *delirio,* implying sincere passion and a clear but all-consuming obsession rather than a clouded and feverish lunacy.

*   *

IN THE FIRST OF THESE UNCENSORED LETTERS, MARISOL ABRUPTLY revealed Camilo's fate: "He was arrested," she printed in tidy block letters, "only six kilometers off the coast of Cuba, on that very first night, while you and I were so anxiously awaiting his safe arrival on the Key of Bones, while we listened to Radio Martí and planned our celebration."

Her unveiling of Camilo's imprisonment continued in a straightforward, matter-of-fact style, as if the current sugar harvest were being analyzed for an economic report. "They took him to Villa Marista, the headquarters of State Security. Once a Marist monastery, now this building houses all initial secret police investigations before prisoners are transferred to more permanent facilities. Villa Marista is in a quiet suburban Havana neighborhood called *La Víbora*, perhaps you remember it, tree-lined streets, wide avenues, parks with statues. Here, if I tell someone my son is in Villa Marista, they know just what that *means*, but you, perhaps you don't realize. Someday we will talk. For now, this is what you must do, understand that Camilo is still inside Villa Marista, that he has been inside for three months now, an unheard of eternity, and that soon he will be executed (secretly) or brought to trial or transferred to a prison, probably Combinado del Este or one of the forced labor camps (if he's lucky) in the sugar fields or God forbid, in the tunnels.

"I, in the meantime, find myself undergoing a crisis of the spirit, of love. *Una crisis del espíritu, del amor.* All these years I have felt myself being smothered beneath this loyalist mask, and now I must lift it, for Camilo's sake."

AS I READ THESE WORDS, A FEVER OVERCAME ME. I FELT LIKE DR. Livingstone's portrayal of a lion's attack. I was entering the dreamlike state he'd described, detached from pain, rescued from fear.

Villa Marista was not the medieval dungeon I had imagined. It was in placid suburban *La Víbora*, the Viper. It was once the residence of reclusive priests, converted by the Commander into a chain of linked cells for interrogation and the determination of futures. Human futures, just like the northern grain elevators where farmers and gamblers haggled over corn futures.

I closed my eyes and saw Camilo digested in the Viper's entrails, his angel at the window, whirring its hot wings.

Marisol described his raft as a makeshift one of inner tubes connected by frayed rope and machete-hewn slabs of palm log. As I read her smuggled words, I pictured Camilo's arrest as a sort of amputation, his raft cut away from his flesh, the two, dissolved by water, melted by sun, the two having become one. I pictured him in his dungeon, crouching, legs chained or chopped off, gazing up into the single eye of a colossus.

Yet it could have been so much worse, a solitary death at sea, insanity brought on by dehydration and isolation, a hurricane, the Bermuda Triangle, man-eating swamp-dwelling octopi. My imagination took me into the bellies of drifting ghost ships and giant carnivorous sea creatures.

Camilo could have been washed ashore in Florida, already eaten by gulls, his bones picked clean. Or he could have reached the Key of Bones still alive but too weak to wave his arms and call for help, dying in the promised land, within reach of the Fountain of Youth.

He might have been shot from a Cuban patrol boat. Instead, Camilo had simply been arrested for his raft. He was, I hoped, just one more *balsero* among so many thousands. Yet there was also the specter of a Commander's memory. The Viper guards, by now, might know about our father's work, about the contents of the package.

Marisol wrote, with the clarity of her smuggled script, that she would need money to get Camilo out. She asked for a loan. She reminded me that she had ideas for a business she would start when the Commander fell.

MY FEVER REACHED ONE HUNDRED AND SIX DEGREES. I SHOULD HAVE BEEN dead. Now the desert, in November, was cool by comparison, only one hundred degrees by day, and eighty-five at night.

Rocky curled her long gray body at my side as I trembled with chills. She peered into my face for reassurance. I left the door open so she could come and go as she pleased. She brought me lizards and kangaroo rats, offering them gently, like a folk healer offering herbs brewed into an aromatic paste.

I knew my life was changing, irrevocably.

I WAS USED TO DULL ROUTINES, A QUIET DAY-TO-DAY PROGRESSION FROM birth to death. True, I had been ushered through rain forests and Greek temples and Afghani rug markets, but it had always been simply a matter of watching (accompanied by my imagined half brother) my mother barter dollars for pitch-sealed baskets that smelled like the meat-and-blood diet of lion-maned Masai warriors, or for horses from the frieze of a marble column, or wool (crimson and azure) designs looped by children with veiled faces.

After leaving Cuba my mother had devoted all her love and energy to the antique trade, specializing in tribal artifacts, Peruvian mummies, Apache burden baskets, feather headdresses from Borneo.

She had whisked me through Burma and the highlands of

Kenya. Yet none of those adventurous forays into other people's lives had ever affected me with the intensity of Camilo's arrest off the shores of his lovely (so green, so lush, so many sinuous vines of orchid and hunter's robe and cup-of-gold), serpent-smothered, tropical island.

I no longer thought of Camilo as a half brother. He was a whole brother now. I was the one reduced to halves. I knew that a part of me would have to enter the Viper along with him and would not be free to leave until he was released.

IN ONE OF HER ORNATELY FLOWERED CENSORED NOTES, MARISOL mentioned that she had caught a fever, and that her temperature was hovering near an impossible one hundred and six degrees Fahrenheit. She said there was no aspirin to be found on the entire island, not even in the Black Bag, and she had to plaster wild herbs on her forehead to cool the skin.

I HOVERED IN THE HEIGHTS OF MY OWN PERSISTENT FEVER, ACCOMPANIED only by my big dog who didn't know how to find aspirin either. Instead, Rocky brought me a dead scorpion and half a dozen golf balls. She comforted me with her clumsy swaying tail, which sent plates and cups and magazines flying all over the house, and with her huge dreamy wolfhound's eyes.

I knew I might eventually have to contact my father's relatives in Miami, ask them for money to help Marisol bribe Camilo's way out of the Viper. In the meantime, I started with my mother's artifacts. Still weak and feverish, I drove to Los Angeles to sell her collection of beaded Sioux moccasins, porcupine-quill necklaces, and birch bark water jugs. I sold Mayan figurines, jade funeral beads, specimens of Roman glass from an excavation in Spain, and a handful of old first editions signed by Hemingway.

I sent the profits to Marisol by way of a smuggling ring based in a suburb of Los Angeles. Surprised, the ringleader said he usually filled requests for contraband VCRs and stereos, or computer software, or calculators, but bribes for getting people out of secret police holding cells were less common. I asked him to include a bottle of vitamins for Marisol, and another for Camilo, and some powdered milk, and cans of spiced beef, and several bottles of aspirin.

As soon as the money was gone, my fever broke. I slept for three days, dreaming with gargoyles and cobblestones and castles facing the sea, and pirate ships, and keys attached to dancing strings, and buried treasure, and a gallows constructed on the sand of a palm-lined beach . . .

WHILE I WAS IN LOS ANGELES SELLING MY MOTHER'S ARTIFACTS AND making the arrangements for sending cash to Marisol for my brother's ransom, I was stranded by the heat of my fever, stranded in a sea of smog and strangers. I had managed to locate a motel that allowed dogs. I called in sick, but my job as a manager was already lost by then. During my absence, several condos had been flooded by defective plumbing, and no one had been able to locate me. My replacement, I was informed, had already been hired.

From the hotel (after I finally awakened from my three days of post-fever sleep) I called cousins in Miami, just to hear the sound of rapid Cuban Spanish. Each of my father's exiled aunts and sisters repeated the same generous offer, "¡Come and live with us, little Carmen, no one should have to live alone!" Of course, I knew I was no longer little, and living alone, as they insisted, was no longer a nightmare, no longer the most lonely and dangerous path I could imagine.

I dreamed with all the frequent ecstatic *conga* lines of my six months in Miami, the months I'd spent studying for my reunion with Camilo (if only I had known that he would not be dancing when I arrived in Cuba, nor would I need any of the pre-revolutionary Cuban recipes I was taught, on an island where food was more common in memory than on tables).

I dreamed with the *paso doble* and the *rumba* and the *mambo*, and with a thousand tidbits of gossip served wrapped in sweet deep-fried pastries, dripping with dark viscous cane syrup.

I dreamed with mountains of rice and black beans, with pans of simmering onions and garlic, sweet peppers and spices in olive oil the color of liquid gold. I dreamed with *Miamense* cousins standing at banquet tables, announcing that spaceships were landing in sugarcane fields, and benevolent aliens were climbing out, promising a free Cuba. . . .

I dreamed with long circuitous paths leading nowhere, and with my father flying out of the jungle, vanishing into thin air.

I dreamed it was New Year's Eve, and I'd eaten twelve grapes at midnight, and my mailbox was stuffed full of seed catalogues and museum journals and letters from Marisol. . . .

WHEN I RETURNED TO MY ADOBE HUT, THE LETTERS WERE THERE, JUST AS I'd dreamed. Marisol had documented her outrage at the length of time her government had taken to inform her of Camilo's detention in the Viper. The month's worth of letters were out of sequence, mailed weeks apart, yet all arriving at the same time, as if they had been sitting idly on someone's desk, or hovering in Cuba's sky, before finally deciding to land in my eager hands.

"¡All that time," Marisol printed clearly, "as I listened every evening at seven o'clock, hearing that list of strangers' names and imagining the worst for my son, imagining the sharks and the salt and thirst and sun and waves, the storms, the loneliness, all that time, he was already inside the Viper, and no one took the trouble to let me know! For you to understand this will be impossible, but imagine it, they waited to let the mother know, not to punish *her*, but to punish her son.

"We have an official saying: '*En guerra y en paz, mantendremos comunicaciones.* In wartime and in peace we will maintain communications.' Yet in back alleys the young men jest, changing this to: '*En guerra y en paz, mal tendremos comunicaciones.* In wartime and in peace we will maintain poor communications.' ¿You see?"

IN ANOTHER LETTER MARISOL SAID THE ENTIRE PEREGRÍN FAMILY WAS NOW a tribe of pariahs, now known as dissidents, the island's untouchables, *los intocables*. Categorized, she lamented, by Camilo's raft, no longer the loyalist old guard, no longer courtiers of the king.

EVERY TIME SHE USED THE WORD *BALSERO,* RAFTER, I PICTURED CAMILO floating on a chunk of balsa wood, as porous and absorbent as a sponge. Vulnerable and desperate, valiant and determined. A sponge absorbing his future, saving it for later, to be squeezed out one drop at a time.

I DREAMED WITH A PIRATE'S TREASURE, BUTTONS RIPPED FROM THE clothes of ransomed victims, chains and crosses, rings, cascades of glittering gold and silver coins, a gilded toothpick for the mouth of a king, rivers of star-shaped jewels . . .

The chests bearing this imaginary treasure were so heavy that three men, straining together, could not lift them. A gold whistle in the shape of a dragon, ruby eyes, emerald fangs, a cloud of poisoned smoky breath . . .

Symbols on treasure maps, cryptic paths leading to petro-

glyphs instead of gold . . . the forms of birds and serpents
pecked into granite and limestone . . . the crests of kings burnt
into the wood of the treasure chests . . . yet my dream hand
crumbled the wood, leaving only a brass lock and the mass of
stars held together by time, fused . . .

"YOU MUST THINK OF YOUR FATHER'S WORK," MARISOL INSTRUCTED.
"Now I know it is in your hands. Consider it from the perspec-
tive of our daily lives."

A few weeks later a brief smuggled message arrived: "Received
vitamins, etc. Thanks! Here every day the same, feverish, smothered by mask. Camilo in Viper very skinny, pale, desolate."

I TRIED TO ASSIST WITH THE DELIVERY OF ADDITIONAL BRIBES. I WRANGLED
a job at the golf course. The men on the mowing crew grumbled.
No one had ever heard of a woman gardener. They accused me
of receiving the job as a reward for my mother's friendship with
the president of the Condominium Association. It was true, my
mother had known everyone involved with development of the
golf course, but she had fought them all tooth and nail, trying to
save her sand dunes from the spread of green. She had failed.
Some said that was why she let the wind hurl her winged form
against a cliff. They said she knew enough about hang gliding to
avoid treacherous breezes when she wanted to. I refused to let
the rumors bother me. My mother was already gone. I hardened
my heart. Only Camilo mattered now. And Marisol.

Citizens' committees were already patrolling their gated community's long white wall to combat groups of hit-and-run taggers who persisted in scribbling spidery black warnings along its
flat surface. Each mark enraged the condominium dwellers, who
insisted that the wall should remain blank, a separation of golfers

from desert, nothing more, nothing less. They said the wall was meant as an absence of communication, not as a vehicle for silent messages. They said if a tagger wanted to say something he should call a radio talk show or write a letter to the editor of a newspaper, or rent a billboard, or print leaflets and slip them under the windshield wipers of cars scattered across supermarket parking lots. Secretly, I disagreed, seeing that the young taggers had never learned to speak except in code.

WHEN I MOWED THE FAIRWAYS I WORE A HELMET TO PROTECT ME FROM flying golf balls. But protection against the imagination had not yet been invented. I could think of nothing but Marisol's letter, Camilo's dungeon (the image of an angel persisted, along with the high window and scent of the sea, the migrating flamingos, luna moths and fireflies, lightning and rain, *los relámpagos, la lluvia*) and my father's work, his careful mapping of the Commander's human cosmography.

FINALLY, KNOWING THAT IT COULD WAIT NO LONGER, THAT WITH Camilo in the Viper and Marisol depending on me, and my father's ghost (and Martí's verse, and Hemingway's old Cuban fisherman) urging me on, the time for feeling Cuban had arrived. I would overcome my paralysis. Let the package expose its horrors.

I told myself this package was *it*, my illusion, my delirium, my murdered father's veiled obsession, his buried treasure, our past dug up by Camilo and handed to me against my will.

5

Conga Line

Cuba es tu corazón, Cuba es mi cielo.

Cuba is your heart, Cuba is my sky.

JOSÉ MARTÍ

I COULD FEEL MY FATHER'S GHOST SHOUT-WHISPERING FROM THE DESERT air. The parcel brought Camilo's Viper too close. There was a scent of venom. I draped myself in the same dark garments I'd worn on the day Camilo vanished and tried to face his reality. For months, I had been afraid even to touch those memory-smeared clothes. They'd lain hidden in a closet while I rushed around the maze of condos, managing. They remained hidden while I sold my mother's antiquities, while I mowed the golf course, while I roamed the canyon with my giant dog, drinking the softness of cream and sugar. Those Cuba-stained clothes had remained hidden while I imagined Camilo's raft at sea, the wind and waves, the sharks, the desolation.

Now I put on the blue jeans and black T-shirt I'd worn when I met Camilo, when I grasped his dancing key out of the sky and opened his locked door, when I talked to him for two hours, one just before midnight, and one just after, when I forgot to ask him all the things I'd spent a lifetime wanting to know. The jeans were faded indigo. The soft dark cloth of my shirt boasted a surfer's image and, in bold white block letters, the words NO FEAR, followed by a tiny explanation scrawled in cursive: *for those who are scared to be afraid.*

I now had to face things I'd hidden from myself because they had reminded me of my only sibling's courage and my own vast sea of fear. Camilo's note still framed the parcel, although his words had been smudged by the horizontal rain of Marisol's concert.

"Come on Rocky," I sighed, "this is going to change my life, I can tell by the way it's been changed before." Each of my mother's excavations had altered me slightly, my heart, my mind. Each cremated seashell, each winnowing basket, each water jar exposed by a windstorm. Only this time it was my own ancestor hidden by time, about to be uncovered, revealed, imagined, remembered.

I was barefoot. The sand scalded my toes. Racing from shadow to shadow, I reached the shade of a blue-gray smoke tree that looked like it had been splashed onto the gravel by a careless artist's sloppy brush. Rocky followed me anxiously, sniffing at Camilo's mildewed note, sniffing at Cuban rain.

I sat cross-legged in the shade, our chronicle balanced on my knees. It was a large packet, yet I had smuggled it out of Cuba easily, and past U.S. Customs, and into this desert where it didn't belong. Tattered leather and linen straps bound it into its packet form. It was obviously very old. Centuries, I guessed as I folded back the straps, revealing an embossed leather cover.

Beneath it was a stack of weathered folios with frayed edges, the pages stained by rain, by sea water, by the dripping residue of a cave's underground stream. Some of the parchment sheets were torn, some accidentally ripped in half, missing corners. Grains of sand clung to the pages. There were remnants of a wax seal. The handwriting was a series of elaborate chains, linked loops, as if each page had been filled with nothing but the letter *e* and the letter *l*, creating an entire document of abbreviations and symbols, an artistic array of profuse but illegible flourishes, like a spider's web or a fisherman's net or a female ancestor's crocheted bedspread. I would have to be a magician to decipher these pages, an alchemist to make the transition from form to meaning, from seeing to understanding!

At first, I was certain that none of it could ever be interpreted by any human eye, not even by an expert at a museum. I held a Rosetta stone with no key to the hieroglyphics.

As I sifted through the stack of parchment, I found, hidden beneath the larger ancient ones, a tidy stapled pile of modern pages, painstakingly hand printed by a loving hand. The paper was obviously post-revolutionary Cuban, a rustic yellowish brown with crumpled edges and visible threads. Cheap paper, the kind you write on when you can't find anything else.

Most of the pages were covered by my father's writing. The rest were in Camilo's. My father had translated the old parchment chronicle into modern Spanish. A brief foreword preceded his transcription, followed by a detailed analysis of attempts to control thought, a track of censorship from the Inquisition to the Commander.

Perhaps I had expected an apology from my father, a message written directly from him to me in anticipation of my birth and my awareness, my passage from the womb into light. Secretly I'd hoped for some explanation of his marriage to one woman while he was still married to another.

Instead, I found, "Censorship is achieved by swallowing the language so thoroughly that wherever an intellectual or any other citizen looks, only the words of the tyrant can be seen. The prescribed words, phrases and slogans become an entirely natural aspect of one's surroundings, like rain, wind or heat. People dress to protect themselves from this mental weather, a permanent storm.

"And yet, we have the enduring lament of *el poeta* Martí: 'Every time a man is deprived of his right to think, I feel as if one of my children were being killed.'

"We are taught to think of these words as a warning against tyrants worse than our own, tyrants of unnatural proportions, monstrous, deadly, invincible once in power.

"So we plod along, making jokes and dancing, followed, at every step, by the Commander's face and words, trailing across the posters and billboards of wide boulevards, on our television screens, our State newspapers and State magazines, the only publications we are allowed to receive.

"Eventually the tyranny becomes so pervasive that even journalists are unaware of their gradual conversion from reporters of fact to creators of myth. They express opinions of the absolute ruler, nothing else, filling every space on every page emerging from every officially authorized printing press and typewriter (all other presses and typewriters, at this stage in the development of the tyranny, have been banned) always the same images, past, present and future, all illusory . . ."

MY FATHER'S WORK, I SAW INSTANTLY, WAS SIGNIFICANT TO CUBA, portentous. It had been written long before anyone else realized that the Commander would cling to his dictatorship for more than a few years, more than a few decades, for his entire lifetime. No wonder my father had vanished, no wonder my brother had awaited my arrival on his island so anxiously as he planned his own departure, an escape that required some outside hand to safeguard the chronicle and its modern sequel. Camilo had needed me as courier, the bearer of messages. I had inadvertently helped deliver a document of great value, my father's meticulous and extensive collection of documented outrages, atrocities, and absurdities, first encompassing five centuries of unspoken fears, secret languages, poetic metaphors, flowery enigmatic phrases, codes, gestures, facial expressions, sign languages, signals passed from drum to drum through tangled green jungles, parables, fables, myths-told-as-truth, folk sayings, street jokes, talking-animal stories, tattoos, carnival masks, double meanings.

The work was magnificent, worth dying for, floating away for, disappearing so that the words themselves would not vanish. His analysis of censorship was followed by actual case histories, poets imprisoned for bold similes, ordinary laborers tortured for remarks overheard by secret agents, even the details of solutions to mysterious crimes. Even the details of disappearances, the documentation of Camilo Cienfuegos's trip into thin air, and of Ché Guevara's elimination from Cuba's hierarchy to prevent his popularity from increasing, to keep him from usurping the Commander's role.

And there was the medieval chronicle itself, legible in its modern version, my father's work. *Our* father's work. Camilo was part of this document too. At the bottom of the massive pile of ancient folios and modern papers, my brother had hidden a tightly folded sequence of letters he'd written to me over a period of undetermined length, during months or years of anticipating my arrival. He'd thought of me as the only outside link to freedom, he said, the only potential smuggler of our inheritance.

Reading through Camilo's letters swiftly at first, then slowly, I learned that he had waited for me a long time, waited for me finally to decide that it was time to make my journey. Waited in silence, writing to me secretly, saving the letters, knowing that I wouldn't come until I was ready, and that once I did, I would have the chance he'd never had, the chance to carry our chronicle out of the Commander's island prison, all the Cuban people held there, like endemic creatures, along with the island's fragrant butterfly jasmine, wrapped around green riverbanks, and 8,000 other kinds of plants, 1,000 species of insects, 900 fish, 4,000 mollusks, 300 birds, *jutías* and *almiquí*, indigenous Cubensis frogs, manatees, hummingbirds, butterflies, flamingos, crocodiles, and parrots.

I PICTURED CUBA THE WAY CAMILO DESCRIBED IT, AN IMAGINED ISLAND, *LA isla imaginaria*, formed into its shape by the Commander's powerful dream, *el sueño poderoso del Comandante*. . . .

Then, reading my brother's greeting: *"Querida Hermana Carmita,* Dear sister Carmen," I chuckled, because Camilo's formality made me sound like a nun.

Rocky panted and drooled. Her eyes roamed, following the jerky movements of a lizard, but she was too hot and lazy to chase it.

I read in Spanish, out loud, pretending that Rocky would listen. She curled her loose dog lips up over her teeth, apparently smiling. I grinned back at her, resuming the path of Camilo's discovery:

"Ahora ya sabes que salí de balsero. By now you will be aware that I have attempted to flee Cuba on a raft. Astonishing numbers of

young Cuban men (and some women, and some old people, some whole families) have all done the same, or so we estimate (we, the human rights movement operating secretly on this island) and by now you will know whether I survived or merely succeeded in feeding a few more sharks.

"If my action strikes you as extreme, consider the Chronicle of Antilia which you now hold in your hands. You will realize that we, you and I, descend, through our father's pilgrim name, from two races, the Extreme Ones, *los extremeños* of Extremadura in Spain, and the timid Hidden Ones, *los escondidos*, native to the caves of this island, so lonely within its pearly chain, *las Antillas*, the Antilles (you see the origin of the word, ¿no? Named for the refuge which never existed, Antilia from the Greek for bilgewater or a pump or the hold of a ship. An unlikely name for a refuge).

"Perhaps you will protest, 'No, there is no such thing as a human right, man is born with nothing but his memory of the womb,' but I remind you that when we say rights—we really mean gifts—the gifts we all received from God in that primeval garden, which, even though access to the verdure is now denied us, remains our ideal and our dream, the place to which we always strive to return. That itself, the yearning, the effort, that is our gift, and we will not renounce it, we will call it a right and say that it can best be described as hope.

"Yes, my answer is yes, of course I know how few *balseros* survive, of course I know the odds. Every true gambler studies his game. Remember that I am not the only one depending on this throw of the dice, and that I am not the only one planning this shocking venture. You have many cousins here on this island, stranded, all planning to do the same, secretly, all pacing the beaches, stashing fragments of rope, purchasing Black Bag rubber hoops, these inner tubes I've hidden under my bed (no, my mother never looks there, afraid of what she'll find) and the dreams I've hidden inside my skull. If I am lost at sea or consumed by fish or oxidized by sun, the rest will be up to you.

"Of course, you will be asking yourself (if you have any empathy at all), '¿Why doesn't the Commander simply let the young men leave?' and perhaps, if you have learned any of our Cuban folk refrains (from the cousins in Miami, I suppose, or from my mother) you will now be thinking, as you read this: 'A enemigo que huye, puente de plata. To the enemy who flees, a silver bridge.' But this Commander does not follow the tradition of his predecessors, burn the enemy or expel him into exile, force him across the sea, no, this Commander, unlike the others, has tried to keep us all concealed here, enclosed. Three possible explanations, one: sheer demonic cruelty; two: slaves for his fields (yes, my own mother's beloved sugarcane, the carnivorous fields which should have been ripped up long ago and replaced with nourishing native crops, manioc, corn, vegetables); or three: fear of the secrets we will reveal when we have crossed the sea with open, gaping mouths, ready to shout into the sky that cry which is nothing less than a reflex of the human spirit. . . ."

I DEVOURED MY BROTHER'S LETTERS EAGERLY, IN FRAGMENTS, SKIMMING them, first tasting the ones that caught my eye, saving the rest for later.

None was dated, none signed. Camilo had been careful. Nowhere on any document did his name or address appear.

IN ONE NOTE HE OFFERED CONDOLENCES FOR MY MOTHER'S HANG-gliding accident:

"¡But how glorious," he added, "to fly into one's death instead of crawling!"

He went on to say that his dream, his *ilusión*, his *delirio*, was flying. He longed to soar, float, glide, propel himself into blue space, perform acrobatic stunts in midair, trace the smoky loops and dips of skywriting.

He said he was raised by his mother to believe that my mother was a sort of feral saint, the one who gave way and fled into a forest of time and distance rather than bare her claws and fight the other woman: by fleeing she had become a peacemaker. Peacemaking was the most difficult role, my brother asserted, more complex than the warrior's strategy or the hunter's silent crouch.

This letter, like all of Camilo's, and all of Marisol's, and all of my father's documents and notes, ended with a boldly printed line from the verse of José Martí:

> *Con letras de astro el horror que he visto*
> *En el espacio azul grabar querría.*

With astral letters I would carve
In blue space the horror I have seen.

I HELD ONTO THOSE WORDS OF THE POET, JUST AS I HELD ONTO MY brother's desire to fly, and my father's flight from injustice, and my mother's futile attempt to defy gravity, and Marisol's sugar-stained ferocity.

I read of Camilo's vigil for a raft-borne escape attempt. When he was in Moscow, he'd had a Cuban lover whom he'd intended to marry. She was a student at the Linguistics Institute, as skilled with language as he, the two of them experts by birth, born with a gift, masters of simultaneous thought and speech. They could repeat a Russian phrase in French before the speaker had finished pronouncing it. They rarely failed to guess the next inflection or nuance. They spoke to each other in the same way, guessing at tricks of the mind, finishing each other's thoughts.

Camilo had longed to defect while in Russia, or on the way home after graduation. He and his true love had stood together quietly at the entrance to an airport cafeteria in Norway. Her name was Alina. It was the same name as the Commander's grown daughter, the famous Alina who became, against her powerful father's will, a dissident held captive in Cuba for criticizing the Commander to foreign journalists whenever they interviewed her, for saying she wanted to leave Cuba, her father's paradise; everyone who heard about the Commander's trapped daughter automatically thought of her as a fairy tale princess held captive in the castle tower by her father, the stubborn king.

Camilo's Alina, however, had made her escape, stepped away from her true love's side, and shout-whispered a plea for asylum into the ear of a Norwegian airport official. Without looking back to see if he would follow, Camilo's love had ventured away, ending up in a refugee camp somewhere in the frozen North, where she patiently waited for permission to be resettled in Spain, the land of Cuba's voyaging ancestors, the land of the Extreme.

"OF COURSE I YEARNED TO DEFECT ALONG WITH ALINA," CAMILO WROTE, "but I couldn't, I wouldn't, partly for my mother's sake, because I thought she might be punished for my rejection of the Commander's myth of generosity (now I have already accepted her punishment as inevitable), and even more, because I couldn't leave without our Chronicle. I'd left it in Cuba, along with all its implications, our father's work, my notes for continuation of his investigations. I couldn't leave that all unclaimed, unfinished. When I was sent away from Cuba to study in the Soviet Union, circumstances were such that the Chronicle could not go with me (I knew my luggage would be searched). But later, while I was in the Soviet Union, that monolithic nation crumbled before my eyes, simply vanished, as if erased by the back end of a giant's pencil.

"All of a sudden I saw what it was to be free, knew that now if I went back to Cuba and claimed the Chronicle, and whisked it away from the island, searched and found a way to take it with me (the way, of course, appeared like a miracle when you sent us your note announcing that your mother had died and in a few months you would be visiting us on our lonely isle) all of a sudden I saw what the Chronicle could accomplish outside of Cuba, how its words could be spread and understood and could have an effect on minds, true, but especially on hearts, that more than anything, was what motivated me, the effect of the Chronicle on the heart of its caretakers.

"Yes, I blame my parents' generation (and your mother, for she did as much damage as any native Cuban, meddling in a war where she didn't belong) for our suffering and sorrows here on their island. Yes, they created this, our inherited nightmare. They dreamed it so beautifully, but in transition from their minds to our hearts, the dream changed spontaneously, mutated. They dreamed utopia, and created prison, dystopia.

"They were youthful, idealistic, revolutionaries in action as well as thought. But their chosen leader became a mirror image of the preceding tyrant (one right-wing, the other left-wing) and this was accomplished with their help, their cheers, their worship. When their struggle was over and the old king was gone, the knight in shining armor was crowned, and so it proceeds, link by link, a lengthening chain . . ."

Camilo wrote, "We used to call the Commander 'Lord' or we called him by first name, affectionately, but now we say 'the lunatic' or we simply say 'you know who.'"

CAMILO HAD CONTINUED OUR FATHER'S WORK, BUT STILL HELD IN HIS memory all the essential details, and had not yet spelled them out on paper. He'd extended and updated our father's investigations, not for our father's sake, but for the sake of his own unborn children (and mine) and for the memory of the Chronicle of Antilia, for our distant ancestors' love, the merging of Extreme and Hidden. And for the dream of José Martí.

He said that if he survived at sea, his life would be no more than another chapter in the Chronicle, his work would become, instead of the translation of diplomatic exchanges from one easily understood language to another, the translation of yearnings of the heart, cravings of the spirit, of hungers and thirsts, for justice, for freedom. "For the hungers," he concluded, "of this island refuge, Antilia, our worldly destination, the place which never existed, u-topia, no place."

If he survived, he would be designated traitor, and his mother would remain behind in Cuba as suspect, as outcast, as hostage. For her suffering (which had not yet begun), he would now have to take responsibility. Their roles would soon be reversed, he the dreamer, she the recipient of a nightmare.

Camilo ended this prophetic role with a postscript:

"P.S.

"If Dante were still alive, he would come to Cuba to research a new chapter of the *Inferno*."

IN ANOTHER NOTE, WRITTEN HASTILY ON SOME OTHER DAY, CAMILO SAID that after he left Cuba on a raft, his mother would have to stay behind. "The Commander," my brother explained, "divides our families in this way, by keeping the *balseros'* abandoned relatives as resentful hostages. If I'd defected along with Alina, Marisol's fate might have been even worse, because then the Chronicle was still hidden in her house (without her knowledge, because the Chronicle no longer belonged to anyone but you and me, our generation, to us, our father's accidental heirs). If I had defected, sooner or later, the secret police would have found it, and held my mother responsible for its twentieth-century appendix.

"But she knows nothing of my plans. I will soon leave her without saying good-bye. Ignorance is safety in this system my mother helped create. I blame her, and I blame our father. They put the Commander where he is. True, he was small then, and they didn't stop to think how much he might grow, but if my mother suffers now, she has no cause for complaint. The serpent that strangles her was her pet. As they say, 'He who sows wind reaps cyclones. *El que siembra viento cosecha ciclón.*' "

CAMILO WROTE OF ISLAND DWELLERS OF THE PAST, OF TAHITIANS following a shark to Hawaii, of cannibals rowing their canoes to Cuba for a ceremonial meal of human flesh. Camilo wrote about lizards clinging to the debris of shipwrecks, and coconut seeds floating from one shore to another, already sprouting and ready to swell from seed to tree.

He wrote, "Our father's work will be continued. It will tell of the many forced labor camps and of the mothers who gather twice each month (and also on the birthday of José Martí) in front of a church in Havana to shout-whisper '¡Life to a free

Cuba!' I will tell of the Association of Mothers for Dignity, and of the organization called Sons for Love of the Homeland and for Liberty, and of the Movement for Harmony, and the Association for Free Art, and the Committee for Peace, Progress and Liberty, all secret, all banned, as if their goals were dangerous.

"You will be asking yourself, '¿Why don't they just rebel?' ¿Why not put the Commander on a raft, and float *him* away, instead of choosing that danger for ourselves? And I will have to answer, 'Because at sea we face the less terrifying of two dangers, ¿no?' "

THESE NOTES FROM MY VANISHED BROTHER MADE ME THINK OF DOÑA Inés on her pedestal, facing the sea, and of Marisol's turbaned neighbor singing and staring and twisting the neck of a Black Bag canary, then pouring liquid sugar-syrup onto its tiny golden carcass, still singing (but no, it was no longer the yellow bird singing, now it was a flock of translucent angels humming above the sound of flames in the courtyard) and Camilo's prediction that Marisol would be a hostage made me think of our father flying, propelled into thin air, leaving behind only his germinating seed and his modern appendix to our medieval Chronicle.

I stroked Rocky's woolly gray head, then got up and fetched her a single tiny lick of extra rich blueberry cheesecake ice cream pie, Camilo's notes still haunting me. Even his punctuation disturbed me, the question marks before his questions, the emphatic upside-down symbols before any statements he was sure of, and the uncertain "¿no?" after any reality that could still be altered by time or by God. Did his apparent uncertainty confirm or deny the statement it followed, was it really indecision, or simply finality, simply a new, imagined end negating reality as it had existed up until that moment of the appearance

of that first upside-down question mark before the single word
¿no?

"P.S.

"You will by now be saying to yourself, '¡But my
brother was born into the privileged *nomenklatura,* the
Communist ruling class!' You will say that I, of all
people, had so much less reason to flee than the others,
laborers starving in the cane fields, young men assigned
to demolition duty in the madman's tunnels, dissidents
harassed and beaten by Rapid Action Brigades. You
might assume that I fled because I wanted three meals a
day (everyone in Cuba knows that you in the North eat
at least that much, perhaps with tidbits in between, and
midnight snacks, and feasts on holidays) or blue jeans
and T-shirts, or a stereo, a fast shiny car, street lights
that don't go out at dusk. But no, those are not my
dreams.

"My dream is an open mouth, an open mind. For this I
leave my home and my past. For this I entrust to you our
Chronicle. Read it, and think of our ancestor Vicente
Peregrín, who left his native Extremadura for the very
same reason. Think how much longer was his journey,
how much less certain of success. When he set sail from
Spain, fleeing the claws of the Inquisition, he didn't
know whether his ship would reach the imagined refuge
of Antilia (a place that never existed) or the teeth of
some terrible sea monster. He sailed onto a map that
showed more dragons than islands. And think of his
choices when he arrived in Cuba: conquest or love,
destruction or creation. Escape, or the perpetuation of

secrecy. Unfortunately, as everyone knows, but no one cares, history repeats itself. I will try not to do the same, even though as a translator, until now, I have been limited to the altered repetition of others' passions, never my own."

CAMILO'S HAPHAZARD NOTES HELD MANY JESTS, JUST AS THE TWO HOURS I'd spent with him had been a repository for his suffering island's medicinal Black Bag laughter. "The Man of the Future," Camilo quoted some anonymous verbal cartoonist, "will have huge ears for listening to interminable speeches, four feet for laboring like a beast, and no mouth so he won't have to eat."

Camilo must have roamed his own mind searching for these messages. "I wonder about so many odd insignificant little facts, perhaps because, like you (I can tell by your choice of Northern postcards) I am constantly seeking order in this maelstrom, sanity in lunacy, humor in tragedy. Here for instance, is a typical Cuban street joke:

> A woman went into exile. Her sister stayed behind, yelling at her as she climbed aboard her raft, '¡Traidora!' Traitor, the sister hears sadly as she floats away. Twenty years later she returns to ask why her sister called her a traitor at that painful moment of departure.
> 'No, sister, *hermana*, you misunderstood,' comes the answer as the two women embrace, 'I did not shout *traidora*, but *trae dólar*, bring dollars.' "

HE ALSO WROTE OF THE CHATTERING OF WHALES AS THEY LOAFED IN groups beneath the world's oceans, talking and singing. "When they're hungry, whales shout," he said, "they click, roar, rumble, squeak and whine, even though they're underwater. The sound is very wistful, like the calling of a mother to her lost child. Some of these submerged songs are mournful, like weeping, but a whale can sing loud enough to shake a passing boat, it can serenade for twenty hours, never resting. They memorize their songs, learn new melodies from other whales, repeat them, pass them on, teach their young. We (Alina and I) learned this at a Linguistics seminar a few years ago. We learned that no one knows why dolphins spin as they leap into the air. We learned that the fastest-moving stars in our galaxy leave behind them a guitar-shaped cloud of glowing gases, and that water in a Northern Hemisphere sink swirls counter-clockwise as it drains, while in the Southern Hemisphere water swirls clockwise, and if you build a sink located precisely on the Equator, water will move straight down without circling at all. All of these patterns can be taught as language, even though they are also biology and astronomy and physics. The speaker tries to say, I believe, that we do not yet know all the codes, that these forms of sign language are not accidental but are attempts at a communication we cannot yet interpret. In some cases, we do not even know how to *hear* these hidden languages, so we are not even aware of their presence in our daily lives. This explains why we can't see God, who created the world from the invisible, from words."

I was beginning to see that my brother had given me more than a packet of old documents and new letters. He'd asked me to smuggle his reveries, his skywritings, his preoccupations, his expressions of hope wrapped up neatly and tied with straps of leather and linen.

It was evening, the time for Radio Martí's list of survivors, but I was not in Cuba, and my only task was the reading of Camilo's notes. Waiting was now a job for Marisol. Although, more than ever, after reading Camilo's letters (the words seemed passionate enough to become winged and fly from my hands) I longed to help him, and to help his mother, to extract him from the Viper and her from an ever-lengthening vigil.

I set the Chronicle down on hard gravel and closed my eyes, thinking of migratory birds and butterflies fluttering back and forth across highways and rivers, flocking in all directions, and of my mother gliding into a cliff, and of the way she'd lingered briefly in a coma, waiting to die, her thoughts a mystery.

DURING THE DAY, ROCKY AND I RETURNED TO OUR ROUTINES. I ALLOWED myself to wait to read the Chronicle. In my leisure hours, be-tween reading and re-reading Camilo's letters, I took up the embroidery of fanciful birds. Rocky watched me with one ear up and one ear down. Eventually, I assumed, she would become civilized, obedient. She would stop pilfering food from the pan-try, stop seizing half-cooked steaks from the barbeque grills of perplexed condominium dwellers.

Instead, she kept growing. Throughout the pleasant aridity of autumn, Rocky consumed more dog food, lizards and kangaroo rats than all the other neighborhood pets put together. She followed me to work, breaking her chains if I tied her, and gnawing through doors if I tried to lock her up, and I was warned that if I couldn't keep my "beast" off the golf course I would be fired from the mowing crew. But Rocky followed be-hind me as I worked. She chased golf balls and frightened old ladies. She splashed through water traps and dug craters in the carefully raked surfaces of sand traps.

Finally, the golf course superintendent let me go. I wished I could go home and sit with Camilo above the expansive view of desert vanishing into man-made rolling green hills and pristine artificial blue lakes. I wished for a chance to laugh with my brother about the euphemism for getting fired. Being "let go" sounded more like a gift than a punishment.

I searched the desert for the sibilant angel that, I felt certain, still confronted my brother in his dungeon. If I found it, I would think of important things to say, and the angel would carry my words to God, and everything would be resolved.

BUT I HAD NO IMPORTANT THINGS TO SAY, AND NO LETTERS CAME FROM Marisol, and Camilo seemed to have sailed off the edge of the earth, which no longer felt round and continuous. I could not forget the way my brother described our ancestor Vicente Peregrín and his efforts to master the art of navigating by fantasy. *"Navegar por fantasía,"* Camilo had explained, was the medieval mariner's way of finding his path at sea, by dead reckoning, by imagining his ship's position in relation to the stars and to landmarks already far from view. "So it is with us," Camilo had added, "as we leap from one position to another, never sure how close we are to some finite edge, but moving blindly, migrating."

I bombarded Marisol with a futile series of telegrams, censored letters, and smuggled pleas, but she did not respond, or if she did, her answers were intercepted, destroyed, or diverted into some official file. The Cuban postal censor, I imagined, must be steeped in sorcery, an evil being, brutish, deformed, a gargoyle's permanent grin engraved on his lips, his fingers coiled into beastly claws.

I embroidered birds on silk cloth with silk thread. Wings poised for flight, beaks open for song.

I dreamed with women watching as their children fell from the limbs of trees and, transformed in midair, became birds lost in flight.

Awake at dawn, I thought of Marisol trying to help her son escape first from the Viper and then from the island, knowing (¡certainly she knew!) all along, that if she succeeded, she might never see him again.

I walked, once again, through the mind's landscape, remembering our moments of waiting together in Old Havana and on the Blue Circuit beaches, wandering along the medieval sea wall and white-hot sands, through quiet palm-lined plazas and turbulent Black Bag alleys, mazes of marble sculptures and concerts offered beneath verdant painted jungles. . . . I wondered whether now, isolated in her vigil, Marisol would see the island through my eyes, as I was struggling to see it through hers.

I dreamed with my imaginary brother in his dungeon cell with its small, high window. He had run out of paper, out of ink, cloth, and blood. There was nothing left to write on, no more cartoons to be sketched on toilet paper, no more jokes dotting the sleeves of shirts or the cloth of shrouds stolen from the dead . . .

He wrote in the air with his fingertip and eye. The angel carried these sketches into thin air, out the window, up to blue space, where they floated above Old Havana, viewed from the sea wall, from Black Bag alleys, from weathervanes and from second-story windows left open for the suspension of dancing keys . . . the floating words were viewed by Marisol as she waited, wrapped in bedspreads woven of pudding and sugar. The words were viewed by Doña Inés through her bronze eyes. . . .

I dreamed with buckets of brilliantly painted ice creams flavored by Cuban fruit, *mango, guanábana, mamey, marañón*. I dreamed with Camilo, asleep himself, in his dungeon, and dreaming of northern plums, apples, peaches, pears . . .

I remembered that in Spanish I could say "return to crazy" instead of "go crazy." *"Me vuelvo loca,"* I could say to Camilo if I could reach him. "I return to crazy." And he would understand, knowing that in the language of our ancestors we can recognize insanity as a primitive ancestral state, a place to seek out as refuge whenever we feel overwhelmed.

I walked the desert with Rocky, my imaginary Camilo and the blazing angel. We were wanderers, pilgrims, penitents. We watched as walls and turf grew, while our desert appeared to shrink (of course it was always there, underneath, the aridity, the sand and wind).

Bats swooped down from caves in the canyon to drink from swimming pools and startle evening golfers. New neighbors stopped by to ask if I needed anything, to invite me to bridge games and square dance lessons and cake-decorating workshops. Feeling like a hermit (like an old white-bearded man hiding and waiting for visions), I declined.

I embroidered tropical silk-feathered hummingbirds, nightingales, toucans, bee-eaters, macaws, birds-of-paradise, using storybook colors my mother once found in a Hong Kong street market, vermilion, emerald, saffron, magenta, ocean blue.

My silk birds, I convinced myself, might soon come to life. Hadn't I already spent enough sleepless nights daydreaming with lush indoor gardens and dancing keys, with skydivers and rescue crews and giants stumbling into fiery swamps? A miracle seemed overdue.

                        *   *

PHONE CALLS CAME FROM MIAMI. DISTANT COUSINS HAD HEARD ABOUT Camilo's arrest. Some had heard it from strangers (proving the impossibility of repressing secrets for more than a few hours or a few days or a few years or at most, a few centuries). Others had received, as I had, letters from Marisol, letters begging for help.

The Miami cousins warned me how herculean our task was going to be. They said getting a relative out of the Viper was like getting him out of purgatory; it could only be done by suffering. We would need a plan, connections, bribes, a miracle.

Long chains of linked dancers swayed through my embroidered aviaries, clinging to each other, feather and fist . . .

Some of the Miami cousins said soon it would all be over anyway, maybe Camilo should wait for the Commander's fall. But I was afraid (and I knew, through our shared memory, that Marisol would be terrified) that waiting was a game the Commander could appear to win, if his one-eyed giants pounded Camilo hard enough. I was afraid the angel might take pity on my brother, and carry him mercifully up out of that dungeon and into the sky. . . .

I thought of Marisol so far away. My own mother had always been close by, like a cactus in her desert garden, thorny and colorful, a picturesque nuisance, best avoided unless gloves were worn. I hadn't loved her the way daughters in movies loved their mothers. She never embraced me and rarely said anything warm or even friendly. She treated me like a remnant of my father, like an emerging fragment of something she'd tried to bury. She had protected me from love, kept me isolated, in hiding, on the move. We had been like pirates sailing through our adventures, making an escape with our booty.

I'd grown up planning never to love, never to marry. Men, my mother had said, were tricksters and magicians. They could fly, they knew how to disappear. Until I was eight years old, I had firmly believed that if I wished (and I did) I could choose to grow into a bird or a flying horse instead of a woman. Once when my mother took me to the ruins of a Greek island, I had listened as an old guide repeated the tale of a winged creature born from terror, Pegasus springing from the blood of Medusa. Bellerophon fell asleep, and upon awakening he found a golden bridle at his side, and when he went out into the fields he found Pegasus drinking from a spring, and with his golden bridle the hero claimed his winged horse, and together the two performed marvelous stunts, killing the fire-breathing Chimaera, a monster half lion and half goat, with the tail of a serpent. The monster's flaming tongue melted the tip of Bellerophon's spear, and when the molten metal ran down into the beast's belly, the monster died, and the man, with his winged horse, tossed boulders out of the sky. But an insect stung the horse and as it bucked, the hero fell out of the sky, lame and cursed, lonely, isolated from men and consumed by agony, a fugitive, wandering alone, as above him Pegasus, still flying, carried thunderbolts and hurled them down. . . .

MY IMAGINED WINGS WERE EVENTUALLY REPLACED BY REAL ONES. MY mother taught me how to leap from cliffs and from airplanes, carried by man-made wings or by a parachute, landing safely on the desert floor, landing alone on our desolate mirage-covered salt flats. My life now seemed like one flying dancer in a giant celestial *conga* line, moving from generation to generation, dancing from island through sky and sea to continent and back, each of us clinging to the ghost of the one in front, trailed by the unborn memory of the one behind, hands on waists, three short rhythmic joyful steps, then a kick to free ourselves of the chains dragging at our ankles. I constantly returned to the Chronicle, my father's notes, Camilo's letters, to our history and Cuba.

"P.S.

"When our father found the Chronicle in a cave, held between two embraced skeletons, he fell to dreaming about our past and our future. Suddenly nothing else seemed to matter, only the love that kept those two skeletons entwined, only the connection between dead and living and not yet born. He found the past in that cave beneath our ancestral home, that home built and later rebuilt, on so many separate occasions, by various descendants of the Peregrín line, once after a fire, then several hurricanes, and of course the pirate attacks, and many wars.

"Someday, when the Commander has fallen (no, he is not Atlas, yes, he will see that the world does not rest on his shoulders, that he too will fall) then you and I, Carmen, with our loves (I with Alina and you with one God will soon choose for you) we will journey together to that home and those caves, and I will show you the two skeletons (and many others as well) which still recline near a wooden chest that was once filled with Inca gold. You must know by now that it was not I who stole their golden treasure, nor was it my father, but someone long before us, someone Vicente knew nearly five centuries ago, his own brother.

"Promise that if you hear I have been arrested, and if there is no other recourse, you will contact the descendants of that thief, and ask them to share with us their gold (Vicente's gold) so that you can use it to get me freed. Because, despite the noble ideals of our parents' rebellious generation, we ended up with a renegade society that still kidnaps ordinary people (yes, I am very ordinary, my complaints are not unique) and demands, in exchange for our freedom, a pirate's ransom.

"You will be reading this there in your safe, pleasant North, saying to yourself, no, surely he has not been arrested, by now he must be in Miami, but I tell you that *just in case* I end up in the Viper instead of on the Key of Bones . . . well, given the circumstances (our father's work) you can imagine the size of the bribes that would be needed. . . .

"Prison is my heart's dread, but as they say, 'He who covers himself with honey will be stung by bees. *El que anda con miel anda con abejas.'*

"So if this turns out badly, if you hear that I am in prison in Cuba (surely my mother will find a way to keep you informed) then you must trace our genealogy, find the thief, and ask his descendants for help. By now, after five centuries, surely they will realize that the gold truly belongs neither to them nor to us, nor to those pirates from whom Vicente seized it, nor to the previous claimants or the ones before them. So if you and the Miami cousins are not wealthy enough to meet the Commander's ransom demand, then ask those who . . ."

CAMILO'S PLAN SEEMED SO COMPLEX AND SO IMPROBABLE THAT I COULD barely stand to read the words. Just as he'd feared, he was in prison, in Cuba, and now I was supposed to dig up someone who'd taken gold from a wooden chest in a distant cave nearly five centuries earlier, and I was supposed to find a way to make sure that the descendants of that person helped Camilo, "for old times' sake" as he (deadly serious, not, as usual, jesting or tongue-in-cheek) so naïvely instructed.

It was that very naïveté that made me love Camilo so much, while knowing him so little. That innocence that had allowed him to float away from home beneath the barrels of machine guns pointed at the sea. Yes, God and Camilo and our ancestor Vicente Peregrín were conspiring to teach me about myself, to show me how little innocence I had retained, how skeptical I'd become. They were being used, by that unseen hand, to prepare me for an outlandish claim, an extreme claim. I was supposed to travel back through five hundred years of time and betrayal asking for justice and a chance at my brother's freedom.

I began to make my way through the Chronicle of Antilia, a tale of love that left me thinking of nothing but love day and night, daydream and true dream, falling into love headfirst, drifting into love like a leaf, like a feather. . . .

It was the story of our ancestors, Camilo's and mine, of the lovers who lived in a place that never existed, in the mythical refuge of Antilia. The Chronicle forced me to wonder about love, to wonder whether I would recognize love if I fell into it (was it like a marsh or like a canyon, or would it bounce back, a trampoline) to wonder whether I had ever really loved anyone at all.

Loving Camilo without knowing him taught me that I could eventually learn to love other strangers as well.

6

Antilia

En aquel país de pájaros y de frutas los hombres eran
bellos y amables: pero no eran fuertes. Tenían el
pensamiento azul como el cielo, y claro como el arroyo;
pero no sabían matar . . . Caían, como las plumas y
las hojas. Morían de pena, de furia, de fatiga, de hambre,
de mordidas de perros. ¡Lo mejor era irse al monte. . . !

In that land of birds and fruit the people were
comely and amiable, but they were not
powerful. Their thoughts were blue like the sky,
and clear like a stream; but they did not know
how to kill . . . they fell like the feathers and
the leaves. They died of sorrow, of fury, of
fatigue, of hunger, of the bites of dogs. It was
best to flee to the mountains. . . .

José Martí

THE CHRONICLE OF ANTILIA BEGAN WITH A LOT OF UNFAMILIAR MEDI-
eval formality and introductions:

"I, Don Vicente Peregrín del Castillo, Old Christian, Extremeño, Hijo de Algo, Noble Descendant of Faithful Vassals to
the Catholic Kings, Humble Son of the Honorable Cosmographer Don Vicente Peregrín Torres, Native of Extremadura,
and of his beloved wife Doña María del Castillo y Aguilar, I son
of Valor and Dignity, do hereby set my humble plume to the
daunting task of justifying my status as weary renegade and

beleaguered fugitive in this green wilderness of caves and forests we commonly refer to as Cuba even though its Christian name be given as Juana.

"There are those who will say that I am mad, and they would, if they could find it, destroy this my history, or discredit it, because they would say that the words emerge from a madman's hollow plume.

"Yet surrounded as I am entirely by blue sea and green forest, this land I call my home has given me more than madness. Since the moment of my arrival in Cuba as a youth of fifteen years, I have been blessed and plagued with the most mysterious dreams and waking visions, both terrible and wonderful, and with the sounds of enchanted songs, and the sight of fiery celestial wings, and with a fountain of love so deep that even Satan in his fury has not been able to destroy this gentle passion.

"My native wife is much the same as I. She says that before we, the Extreme Ones, came to Cuba, the timid people of this generous land dreamed with us, dreaming peacefully with our hollow ships and our giant horse dogs, and with our shining armor and thundering spears of fire.

"She says they knew we would arrive in the bellies of great stinking calabashes filled with filth and biting vermin, and that knowing this, they were not surprised when we stayed, having no place better to go. She says she never believed we came from heaven, because her father hid behind a bush and observed our natural functions, and thereby knew that we were human and needed to relieve ourselves just like these flame tinted cave-dwelling hidden natives, of which my wife is the last.

"And in the same way that my beloved wife's people had dreamed our arrival, so I have dreamed the arrival of he who would steal my gold, and so I leave this message for my half-breed descendants, that if ever they are in need, they should go to my native village in the cork forest of Extremadura, and demand recompense from the offspring of my brother, he being the cause of all my agonies, and yet, also the fountain of my blessings, because through the trials he set upon me, these being the dreaded wrath of the Holy Brotherhood of the Inquisition, I was forced to flee my pleasant homeland and seek out refuge in this, Antilia, my new and perpetual home, which neither exists, truly, as refuge, nor does it lack existence either, but simply floats in time, allowing me to stretch upon its verdant back, dreaming.

"At my side is the faithful Sirena, this woman whom I loved from the first moment of our encountering. She was, as a child, properly baptized after some brief trials of the flesh imposed on her by the Holy Inquisitors, but she will not tell her names, neither her baptized name nor her native one, and so I have simply gone through this entire lifetime of calling her Siren of the Sea, a blasphemy, no doubt, yet the least of my sins.

"When first I did hear the sweet singing voice of Sirena on a beach of this marvelous island, I did think her an enchantress, and named her without a thought to her possession of other names both Christian and pagan, and without thoughts for the heresy I perpetrated by choosing for her not the appellation of a Holy Saint but merely that of the legendary mistress of the serenade.

"I, proud son of Extremadura, born on the Day of the Three Kings in the Year of Our Lord fourteen hundred and ninety-one, on the eve of Castile's arrival in this New World at the end of our earth, and on the eve of the expulsion of all heretics from a free and united Spain, do now find myself nearly dead, and nearly mad, and my beloved wife Sirena is even closer to death, and much closer to madness.

"Yet I take it upon myself to dream with a safe and joyous new world for my sons who live aboveground and wear garments of finely woven cloth, and ride on saddles of tooled leather, and tend their cattle without thoughts of death or madness. The same I dream with my daughters who now wear silks and no longer remember their mother's way of decorating her skin with red seeds and with lace from the delicate bark of a forest tree.

"And even more so for this the only one of our many sons who still remains with us in these caves. For him, my son Vicente, bearer of my name, I recount these terrible adventures of our lives, that he may not consider the possibility of repeating our errors, nor hold himself above us and invincible, but that he may take pity on us and comfort us in our last days, and that being, at this time, a young man and bold, half Extremeño, skilled with both sword and plume, and with his tattooed tongue that has inherited my natural facility for dialects, that this my youngest and most rebellious yet most beloved son may know the joys and sorrows of his parents' time on earth."

My ancestor went on to tell, in great geographic detail, how his own father had mapped the Lands of Spice and the Forest of Cinnamon, and the legendary refuge of Antilia, all without ever leaving his own quiet home in the cork forest of Spain.

"To Antilia," Don Vicente testified, "my father swore that enough fugitive monks had fled during the very first onslaughts of the Moors nearly eight centuries ago, so that even if all the Catholic Kingdoms were to be overcome and every Knight put to the sword, a few Holy documents would be safely guarded on that distant island, and a source of repopulation would survive.

To this end the refugees did abandon their vows and take the gentle women of Antilia as wives, and did learn to paint their skin with cinnamon, and to bring red children into the light as heirs."

Don Vicente said that he knew by now that Antilia had never existed at all, and that the fugitive monks had probably perished at sea after fleeing the Moors. He said that when he arrived in Cuba the name he gave to the patch of jungle he claimed for himself was a false name, yet he swore by God that he would never change it, because Antilia was still a real place in his dreams. He said that even if he were to fade into a stupor from which he could never be roused, he would continue to dream with Antilia and to believe that somewhere a refuge from fearful attacks did exist.

Vicente was named after his father, who in turn had been named for Vicente Ferrer, rabble-rouser and scourge of heretics (canonized by the deluded Church as a saint) the man who, long before the proclamation of expulsion, single-handedly traveled across the kingdoms of Spain convincing mobs that all Jews and Moors should convert or be burned alive, and that those who did convert should never be trusted.

"Never did my grandmother imagine," lamented my ancestor, "that the name she gave my father, and which he passed to me, would be the name of a man who set the sails of a ship of thought which would eventually put me to flight."

DON VICENTE THE YOUNGER LEFT HIS CORK FOREST IN 1506, DURING "A fever of denunciations" so fervent that his very own brother was inspired to denounce him to the Inquisition, accusing him of practicing black magic and Moorish necromancy, of conjuring genii, and of hiding stolen Church treasures through devious and secretive means.

So even though he, Vicente, was the oldest, and should have inherited all of his father's lands and goods, the treacherous younger brother ended up as heir, and Vicente, so frightened by the threat of torture and flames, took leave of his homeland and fled. The act of fleeing, he later realized, incriminated him further, so that even though he had always claimed full allegiance to his father's faith, and even though he truly knew nothing of magic or Moorish rites, and even though in the Parish church where he had been baptized, full documentation of his ancestry and *hidalguía* was chronicled, thereby proving truly that his father and all his forefathers had fought against the Moors, even so, Vicente's status as Old Christian was challenged by his brother, who bribed a priest to alter the records, eliminating Vicente from the chain of verified descent, transforming him into an adopted rather than a natural son.

Vicente, being of dark skin and Moorish features, dreamy, volatile-tempered, and poetic to a degree unknown except within the Alhambra's garden walls, found himself alone in the world, falsely accused, listed as a criminal, and fleeing the dungeons of darkly hooded men who would take him to the fires.

Fortunately, he could speak numerous tongues, all learned easily from his father, who had never traveled, but had always listened carefully to those who did. Vicente knew all the dialects of the Kingdoms of Spain, as well as French, Latin, Greek, Aramaic, Arabic and Hebrew, these last two incriminating him even further.

He stole one of his father's mules, and rode to Granada, where, it was said, so many abandoned Moorish treasures now lay hidden beneath alabaster citadels and vermilion towers that the carved lions of Moorish fountains now shed tears instead of spring water. Vicente rode boldly through Granada as if he had every right to be anywhere he pleased. He was not questioned. His theater of respectability gave credence to the illusion he created of confidence and ease. "I wore a mask," wrote Vicente Peregrín sadly. "I had no other choice."

He passed through Granada dreaming of the legends he'd grown up with, talismans, enchanted caves, divinations, and buried treasures. Terrified by his forbidden daydreams, he raced out of the last stronghold of defeated Moors, reduced now from conquerors to fugitives like himself. He raced to the river port of Sevilla, where by proving his skill with tongues, he was signed on for an arduous and dangerous journey to the edge of the earth, where, as sworn by the ship's navigator who took him on as novice apprentice, he would find himself either eaten by cannibals or heir to a fortune of nutmeg, cloves, mace, musk, and myrrh. "Sandalwood," Don Vicente quoted his mentor's recitations, "camphor, amber, extract of mummy, indigo, aloe, forests of cinnamon. Pearls and gold, silver, emeralds, rubies."

The people, he was told, would run backward on feet attached the wrong way at the ankles. Their heads would be square and their faces blue, their ears so monstrous that they could be used as wings. Some had snouts like dogs, and fed themselves voraciously on human flesh. There were tribes of dwarves, and of warrior women, and perennially weeping clans whose tears, once shed, solidified and became precious nuggets of gold.

Vicente, having no reason to doubt and little experience with truth, believed every word. He left Spain through a maze of shifting sandbars, expecting to tread beaches covered with a sand of gold dust, where kings sailed in gilded ships, and where neither the Inquisition nor his own vicious brother could hope to find him.

Until his first encounter with treachery, Vicente had assumed that the worst that could happen to him would be capture by the Moors, followed by castration and enslavement as a harem eunuch. Yet the Moors were on the run, so his fear was not great.

Now, as he sailed away from his homeland, Vicente gazed out to sea, over waves of the unknown, beneath a sky of towering volcanic flares and careening meteors, and he thought how strange it was that after torturing Moors and Jews to force their conversion, the Inquisition then doubted their sincerity of belief. Belief, he decided, must always come from within, from the invisible, from tenderness, from God who comes to us in the form of a tiny sweet baby, and does not choose to torment our flesh. Otherwise the conversion could not be called belief, but remained nothing more than a carnival mask. Vicente's only consolation was the certainty that like Torquemada and all Inquisitors, like all informers, along with the tormented ghost of the deluded saint Vicente Ferrer, like all of them, his own treasonous brother would ultimately face a Celestial Judge and be cast into the slow eternal fires reserved for perpetrators of the greatest evil. Betrayal of trust, Vicente decided, surely must be the most odious of all evils. A special fire, much hotter than the rest, he thought, must wait for those who provoked the distrust of loved ones for each other. He knew his thoughts were heretical and blasphemous, and that he himself would burn if any wizard read his mind and betrayed him to the Holy Brotherhood as a challenger of the institutions of power.

¿What if he were really a Moor, Vicente mused, wouldn't he still be just as infuriated as now? ¿Or if he were descended from a

Hebrew, Turk, gypsy, or one of the black African pagans carried up to Spain from far beyond the Canary Islands? ¿Would the flames of the Inquisition then bring him to the Holy Cross? No, not in spirit, not inside himself, only in the outward masquerade that should not be called faith, but fear.

He found it curious that the Inquisition, designed to protect him from untruths, had instead turned him into a masked liar. He loved God, but he hated the Inquisition, with its patrols of the Holy Brotherhood, much more than he had ever hated the Moors or the Hebrews. He thought of all the quiet mornings at home, all the hot, pleasant afternoons, all the familiar connected days he would never know, the parents he would slowly forget, the brother he would long to forget. Instead, his days would be separate, distant, remote, unknown. They would be wide open, like the gaping mouths of dragons.

Accompanied by horses, hounds, and pigs, by ships' rats and penned chickens, geese, and sheep, Vicente found himself a corner of the deck suitable for sleeping. He studied the stars and found that no matter how hard he tried, they always looked different to him. Everything in the sky was constantly changing, and he couldn't find a way to make it stay still.

"IF WE SHIPWRECK AND RUN OUT OF FRESH WATER, WE HAVE TO DRINK our own blood," the older sailors would tease him, whispering and cackling, urging him to drink until he could barely stand. "More wine now means less blood later," they would say, and he, imagining that liquid could be stored in the flesh for later need, believed them. They told him he must practice drinking his urine, in case he ever found himself drained of blood, and was left with no other choice. He tried it once, but soon caught the glint of hysteria in their laughter, and then began to tease them back, saying he was prepared to eat insects and serpents rather than let himself starve on the mysterious frontiers of the unknown Indies.

They hissed about worms that could eat the ship's wood from front to back, leaving only a flimsy shell you could easily put your fist through without even trying. Again, Vicente thought they were joking, but later, in the Caribbean, the cannibal sea, he saw that it was true, and that the other tales were true as well, and that men and women were capable of enduring horrors much worse than the guzzling of blood and urine.

"If they catch you," he was told, "they'll tie you up and cut off your arms one by one, eating them raw before your very eyes, and then start in on your legs."

Vicente was convinced of every Carib peril, although he tried to hide his terror. He cursed, at first secretly, and later openly, while drunk, the crimes of the hooded Inquisitors and their informers. "No better than cannibals themselves," he accused, spitting into the sea and vowing that no matter how many hardships he found in the lands of spice, he would never go back to Spain, not even if he, like the men of biblical times, were to live five hundred years.

The sailors instructed young Vicente in the survival skills of exploration. "If you get lost on some deserted shore," they warned him, "you must raise a wooden cross, carve a sign on the trunk of the nearest tree, and bury a jar or a wooden chest with the mouth or the lid sealed by tar. Inside this receptacle, leave a narrative of all that has happened, and of your intentions for the future, with a map if possible, so that you can eventually be found, even if only after your death, for burial of your remains, and that others might learn from your journal how to avoid the dangers and horrors to which you have succumbed."

*   *

"Now that I am old and nearly dead," Vicente explained as he continued our Peregrín family Chronicle, "I remember those wise instructions, and considering myself still a mariner lost, I do follow those words of my mentors at sea, leaving behind me this narrative of all that I have suffered and enjoyed."

Vicente quickly learned the sailors' codes for distress, the beating of a drum in fog, the calculated raising and lowering of a flag by day, the flashing of a lantern at night.

He struggled with both Old and New World constellations, the Bear, the Indian, the Sisters, the Eagle, Swan, Hunter, Harp, Toucan, Peacock, glowing Dorado fish, golden Bird of Paradise, Southern Cross.

He sailed in a caravel of oak and iron spikes. So many dangers were feared beneath the depths, that one sailor, when it was his turn as lookout, drove himself blind by staring too fiercely into the labyrinth of sun reflected by waves.

In the Canary Islands they took on a store of fresh water, along with wood for the stoves, and onions, garlic, goats, sheep and hens. Vicente, of course, could afford none of those officers' luxuries. He ate the crew's staple of salted fish with wine, cheese and the hard, dry ship's biscuits, which, after a time, were so riddled by white worms that nearly every sailor chose to wait until after dark for his rations. "That way," one old man explained, "you can't see the maggots while you eat them. Trust your memory, but lose it when you must. It always helps to forget."

Vicente refused to sleep below decks. Despite the danger of waves and storms, he stayed above, where the stench of bilge and rats and roaches could be carried away by wind.

While the others talked of fortunes to be made, Vicente silently imagined that he could learn to dream of nothing more than freedom and safety.

He learned to use a sandglass for measuring time. He watched as the navigator counted knots on a moving line passed over the rail, to guess at their speed. The other, more complex tools of navigation escaped his understanding. For depth, a sounding lead; for latitude, the bronze astrolabe, tables of the sun's declination, celestial fantasy.

"You have no heavenly skills," the pilot concluded with distaste, obviously disappointed. "For the son of a cosmographer you seem more suited to farming." Vicente's employer advised him to claim a village of natives in Cuba. "Take everything, land, jungle, beaches, natives. Teach them how to run cattle, that will be your best chance at making a fortune for yourself and your heirs. Our ships will need hides for saddles and boots, tallow, salted meat, horn for our weapons. Soldiers of the King will come to you for provisions before setting out for other lands, for the forests of spice and rivers of gold.

"But whatever you do," warned the navigator with a stern shake of his head, "give up the task of sailing. If you can't follow the stars, you can't find your way. It takes more than a sandglass to tell time at sea. And space, well, for distance you have no sense at all."

Vicente knew it was true. He looked out over the sea and enjoyed its terrifying wild beauty, but he couldn't guess how far they'd traveled or how soon they might land. He gave himself up to a life with no further measurements, closed his eyes, and simply drank in the sounds of night and of waves, the music of stars and of wind pushing against taut sails.

Yet he did begin, quietly, to measure the gold he might someday collect, the pearl beds he might encounter, the tracts of good ranchland, already equipped with men to work them. He arrived in the Indies surprised by their welcome appearance, surprised by the cool steady breeze that drove the sails and the cinnamon-hued girl who stood singing on a white shore, guiding the ship with her voice, "a voice," Vicente wrote four decades later, "of liquid gold, a voice like sunlight.

"I loved her immediately," he testified repeatedly throughout the Chronicle of Antilia. "I defy the man who says we should not marry women of the spicelands. To any who say we should merely bed them, and marry others of our own breed, I say that I am happy, and that any sorrow I have received has come from my devious brother and from my own moments of madness, that lunacy driving me away from this my beloved wife, in search of other more respected treasures.

"¿Have the others not sired half-native children? ¿Have they not married the beautiful daughters of the native *caciques* chieftains of this land, producing handsome red-hued children who are now cultured Hidalgos and do they not speak perfect Castilian and treat their families with respect? These high-born half-breeds have gone on to the conquest of Florida, flourishing gold-handled swords and galloping fine Andalusian steeds, masters of many houses, slaves, and herds of cattle, and all the characteristics we admire: valor, piety, generosity, perseverance. Did Cortés himself not sire the Cuban Indian Catalina, daughter of the Indian Leonor Pizarro?

"Yes, I loved my dear Sirena immediately, but I did not stay at her side. I moved on, to other islands, to unknown shores. I sought the pearl beds and gold fields of my daydreams. My night dreams were reserved for love and fear.

"Sirena, when I first saw her, stood naked upon the sands, singing. She laughed easily, smiled enchantingly, and spoke readily, in sign language, of the most intimate matters and of all the most secret bodily functions."

VICENTE TOLD OF HIS EXPLORATIONS. HE DESCRIBED JUNGLES, BATTLES against warriors with fierce magic and poisonous arrows, fevers, storms at sea, starvation. There were times, he said, when he had to chew ox hides and swallow sawdust. He said that once he finally returned from all these perils, still poor and much scarred, he found Sirena and told her of his adventures, and she laughed, saying, "Until your people came here, no one had ever starved in Cuba." She showed him how to gather enough shellfish and wild fruit to last a thousand lifetimes.

Yet by then her own tribe had been reduced to a few lean stragglers hiding in caves. The troops of Diego de Velázquez had nearly finished them off, burning many at the stake, feeding others to their trained mastiffs. The survivors were now suspicious of Vicente, all except Sirena. She presented him with his first son, whose name she would not tell him. He took the boy into town and had him baptized Vicente, forgetting, momentarily, that it was a name he'd once longed to renounce.

He had tried, but failed to explain his fear of the Inquisition to Sirena. Now he taught her to read and explained that most of the books his father had read as a young man had since been banned, and that there was very little of the written word left on earth that Spaniards were allowed to possess. "On pain of death," he said sadly, "of the rack, the noose, and the flame."

Then he told her of his journeys and showed her how he would write them down if he were lost, placing them in a sealed chest. "On our ship from Spain three men died spitting black blood," he mourned, "and another perished behind a barrel of brined fish, his feet gnawed off by rats. If they had known how graciously this island of Cuba would welcome them, they would not, perhaps, have died so soon but would have struggled to live long enough to hear your song."

Sirena's songs could not save their son from the pox. When the tiny body was buried, Don Vicente Peregrín wrote of his sorrow and swore that he would never, unless his memory failed him, name another son of his Vicente.

He promised himself a lifetime of permanence, everything the same, his love for Sirena, and hers for him, their happy days together in the forest, their nights in the cave, with occasional feast days in town. He offered to build her a house, but his wife refused, saying she was much more used to hiding than he could imagine, and would have no other home beyond the walls of her cave. So Don Vicente realized that now he was exactly what the Holy Brotherhood had falsely accused, a man enchanted. He laughed and hung his hammock in the cave, which was always cool, and by the glow of a firefly lamp, he read anything he wanted and taught Sirena to do the same.

He kept his regrets secret. He himself had burned innocent people alive during his travels, demanding the locations of the vast cinnamon forests everyone promised, but no one could produce. His shipmates took gold and pearls back to Spain to be shared with the Crown. Cinnamon, however, remained the next most coveted prize.

"We sailed through the land of a one-eyed Knight," Vicente wrote on a folio of sheepskin, "and a land of spotted tigers, where insects the length of a finger could kill a man with one bite. There were man-eating fish, and serpents so huge that they could eat a goat in one swallow, and spiders that consumed whole birds."

Vicente had picked up many languages along the way. He taught Sirena all the forms of sign language he'd invented to ask natives about cinnamon trees. They were continually showing him various red woods, mahogany and many others, but none with the taste of spice. Sirena could soon sing in any of two dozen languages. She had taught her husband her own people's tongue within days of his first arrival in Cuba. He seemed to understand it without trying.

Her tribe was a small band of old men and timid women hiding in caves who were called the Hidden Ones. They were given the name by the conquerors who could never find the last of them to burn. Most of the men had already been killed.

Sirena mourned from time to time, but she was young and was easily distracted, easily cheered. She said she found Vicente's language as fluid as water, a tongue dreamed for song. He, in turn, learned her names for forest creatures and sea beings. Vicente found that Sirena firmly believed there were tribes of devils to the south. He, in turn, told her, with great assurance, that he'd heard of lands where everyone dreamed the same dreams, of stars drowning in rivers and birds wearing helmets and skies turning to fire. He told her of the giant sea horses that can consume entire ships, and of bulls with golden horns, and women half fish who comb their hair all day, and of nocturnal creatures that glow like fireflies but are protected beneath hard shells like turtles and can only be killed by fire. He told of winged heads without bodies, and the men who awakened to find their wives' heads flying away, and of birds filled with eggs of gold, flying only at night and emitting such a brilliant light that men follow them to the edges of cliffs and then suddenly, the light vanishes, and the goldseekers plummet to their deaths.

Vicente spoke of tiny birds with songs so sweet and soothing that all listeners instantly fall, doomed, into a perpetual sleep. He said there were cities built entirely of gold, but they were invisible, and would remain so until the end of the world, when angels and men became one.

He described trumpet-blowing apes and griffins, and fire-breathing dragons, and feathered monkeys, and flying unicorns. He said he had perched on top of a green mountain hidden by cloud and had spoken to people who pointed toward Cuba and said that it was home to demons.

"Of course many of these wonders," wrote Don Vicente my ancestor, "were told to me by those who saw them, and others I viewed for myself, by day or in dreams, and now I find that all have merged and blended, so that for me there is no longer any distinction between legend and truth, vision and dream."

Vicente described, with outrage, the hanging of Sirena's cousins in groups of thirteen. "To honor Our Redeemer and the Twelve Apostles, the Inquisition testifies, yet when these hooded devils light fires beneath thirteen sets of feet, I cannot help but wonder, may God forgive me if I blaspheme, ¿Does Our Savior truly feel honored by these flames?"

Vicente said he settled at the heart of the island, with his beloved Sirena, even though she would never tell him her name. "In her youth she decorated her black hair, shining like silk, with the living bodies of fireflies. Her garments of lace came by slicing bark from the guana tree and pulling these delicate strands out until they opened into a fabric of fine threads that could be worked with embroidery in the shapes of birds and flowers."

Vicente became a cattleman. He gathered honey from wild bees and sold it in town along with hides and tallow and horn. "We drink milk and honey," he wrote, "like the slaves escaping with Moses, or the monks of Antilia.

"On Saints' Days and other feast days we join with several mixed-breed families in town, to play games of chance, and celebrate goose fights, and dances of the Andalusian style.

"Sirena tells me that when she was a child her people ate nothing but corn, manioc and fish, iguana and jutía, all foods hidden in sea and jungle. She says they lived in palm-thatched huts, but during hurricanes they had to flee to caves, as they did when attacked at regular intervals by cannibals from beyond the sea, and so, she explains, this hiding has been for her a very natural existence, and one foreseen in many prophetic dreams.

"She has taught me to enjoy the fume of a large roll of tobacco, a plant native to this island, which, when placed in the mouth and lit by fire, does send smoke emerging from the nose and ears, and induces a pleasant stupor. Sirena's people perform this smoking trick from the time when they are very little. They also learn to plot the course of sun and moon, and the winding paths of stars, and though they have no weapons except those invented for hunting, and they do not attempt to defend themselves against cannibals or Soldiers of the King, they are very wise in celestial fantasy, and can find their way on any shore, and they reproduce the paths of heavenly orbs by carving them as designs on the walls of their caves, to be studied and memorized.

"Even their dogs have been bred for hiding, being silent creatures, incapable of barking or howling. These represent, according to my beloved Sirena, a magical dog that she says will escort us all to the other world when we move on.

"Sirena, while we were still young, gave me a stone ax head carved in the form of a shark, and with rasps of coral and shark-skin she fashioned for me a tray of wood to be used for serving my food, which, she said, would be buried with my body in the cave when that enchanted dog leads my spirit away.

"I learned to fish with a spear, and with hooks made of conch shell, and nets woven from a jungle vine.

"Sirena has tied a doghead amulet onto my forehead, and around her own neck she wears a talisman of green stone carved in the shape of a frog, although she will not tell me its meaning.

"We often play a native game by trying to hit a rubber ball through a stone ring, and Sirena, saying the ball is a person in a small canoe, and the players represent hurricane winds at sea, does seem to enjoy this diversion greatly.

"She secretly continues to believe in many of her people's old falsehoods, saying that if she takes all her wounds to a pain tree she can live forever. She pierces the trunk of this tree and leaves her pain there in the wood, but she ages just as I do, and now is close to death, even though all her life, as instructed, she has greeted the sun each morning, coming up from the caves, and has painted her body crimson with a mixture of achiote seeds and wax, so that she looks and smells like a fragrant red torch, her hair the flame, her smile the glow.

"Even now, as she dies, she combs her hair with an ornament of mahogany and bone, decorates it with parrot feathers by day and fireflies by night, and wears no clothes on her body except when we go to town, where the priests would tell her to dress or burn. When she has to wear garments of wool or linen, she complains of the heat.

"When she was with child, my beloved suffered headaches, and to cure them she would pierce her temples with the spine of a stingray, but once, when we had twins, she said it was a good omen, and I was told to rest in a hammock for one month after the birth, holding the infants, a custom Sirena said was reserved for fathers. She said in this way I would become accustomed to their touch and sounds.

"She nursed each child until it was old enough to smoke a cigar, generally three or four years.

"Through all our years together, I continued asking my wife her name, but always she refuses to answer, saying Hidden Ones never pronounce their own names. Now that she is the last of her tribe, I know I will never be able to call my wife anything other than Sirena, because not a soul remains alive on this earth who knows her name.

"It was with some horror that Sirena first realized she would die first and I would be the only one left to speak her tongue, unless our youngest son learned it too, he being the only one of our offspring who enjoys the gift of words and in fact, the only one who visits us or appears to remember where we hide, or why, this last being a mystery of much duration now, since hardly anyone in the countryside or in town can say who it is that lives in the caves and why we choose to keep ourselves hidden.

"I have recorded here as many of the intricacies of Sirena's tongue as I can, along with her legends, so that when she is gone our youngest son can choose to remember us or not.

"When her last cousin died, Sirena mourned for one month, speaking lovingly of the dead girl, then weeping for several minutes, and abruptly stopping to laugh.

"Her people knew only three seasons, the time of rain, the time of sun and the time of winds. She was always terrified by any eclipse of the moon or sun, and when she was with child her greatest fear was that she might give birth to a serpent like the one she claimed to see in the stars. The Pleiades to her were a turtle's nest in the sky, and she also saw in the heavens a white bird, and a river of the dead, where a man struggled to swim away from the stream of stars, helped by two friends who tried to pull him out from shore.

"When I told her of my failure at navigation by fantasy, she laughed and said that if I could not travel by the positions of moving stars, then I had better stay in one place, as she did, and eat the fruit of the Tree of Life, which always yields a delightful and bountiful harvest. She told me that a long time ago people asked God to stop giving them food because they were getting bored, and they already knew where to find it themselves. God agreed, but He was angry, so He chopped down the Tree of Life, and then the people had nothing but the few scraps they had gleaned from salvaged seeds and twigs. Now, suddenly, they had to work for their food, and they were no longer bored. We often sit by the stump of the Tree of Life, Sirena and I, and our youngest son Vicente, whom Sirena named in a fit of memory loss, cursing him, I fear, with repetition of the past. We contemplate, by that marvelous tree stump, our fate. We play music on the instruments we gather from its wood and fallen fruit. These instruments spring spontaneously from the soil near the magical tree, guitars, flutes, drums, and rattles.

"After the tree was cut, a flood rose, and the people had to make tiny canoes from the beaks of ducks, and in this way they floated to the top of the highest mountain peak, and were saved. From that dry refuge they tossed rocks down to test the depth of the waters, and these mounds of stone can still be seen scattered around the base of the mountains at the heart of the island.

"From a talking bird the people learned how to make fire. This was in the time when God still lived among men in His visible form. The fire came as a glowing toadstool that could be stored in caves to hide it from the rains.

"Sirena has always been terribly afraid of evil spirits, who, she says, appear in the shapes of men but are very wild. Certain rocks can be pointed out as the bones of evil spirits, and certain forest vines as nooses set to trap people who are traveling along the pathways of hunters.

"Other spirits are harmless and gentle, much like Our Lord's angels, but not lit by fire. These live in pools of fresh water, and hurt no one.

"This island of Cuba is inhabited by a giant serpent of such enormous proportions that it swallows people and grinds them up with rocks hidden inside its body, and it can turn itself into a man, and although it lives near a clear lake that no one ever visits, it can also move through these caves, and it has a breath like strong wind, and a red human tongue, not forked like that of an ordinary snake.

"Sirena says that when people fall into water they go on living there, just as a frog would. Perhaps that is the significance of her green stone amulet. She also believes that orphaned children turn into frogs, and that parrots have their own kingdoms with their own rulers, and that because of this they fly away to visit them and pay tribute. She says that animals used to speak like men, and that in that time everyone was able to understand each other. The walls of these caves are covered with many mysterious and frightening drawings and carvings, but no one has ever known their meanings.

"The first men and animals were, of course, fashioned by God from clay, and they had dreams that became real, so that when they slept well, their souls were able to rest, and when their sleep was restless, their souls had flown away and gone walking in the forest. The same is true now of the dreams of men and the sleep of their souls. For this reason, we share our dreams with each other every morning at dawn, and until the dreams are told, Sirena does not feel safe or complete.

"Her language is very strange to me, even after all these many years of faithful marriage and lengthy conversations, and yes, alas, occasionally even arguments and disagreements, these lasting seldom more than a day, and ending always with songs of lament and embraces of pure and enduring passion.

"When the chieftains of her people were still alive, they spoke to commoners through intermediaries, even though all spoke the same tongue and there was not one in these caves who could not understand the others. All the natives, in fact, these Hidden Ones here at the heart of the island, and the Taíno tribes to the east, and the Siboney, and many other small groups without name or memory, all could understand each other until we Extremeños arrived and sent them fleeing into the deepest recesses of their wilderness.

"When I think of a ruler of such a humble group as my Sirena's people, speaking through an interpreter even though everyone understands his words, I find the image ludicrous and most unusual, yet common and comical at the same time, rulers always being the ones, may God forgive me if I blaspheme, to distance themselves from subjects through the creation of one device of sorcery or another, through illusion or conjury, again, may God forgive me this blasphemy, which, no matter how hard I try, cannot help but escape my maddened plume.

"We, the subjects, do always strive to believe these monarchic illusions, knowing that the flame or the sword is fate to those who fail.

"No matter, it befalls me now to recount the intricacies of Sirena's tongue, that my son may not forget his mother's voice of sunlight and blue sea. Colors are described by naming birds of that certain hue, and size is described by age, so that a large bead is known as an old man bead. The plural is expressed by repetition, two beads being known as bead bead.

"The morning greeting is '¿Are you awake?' and the greeting on forest trails is '¿Are you there?'

"Animals are always known in relation to dogs, so that Sirena may speak of a turtle dog or a cow dog or a horse dog. This is true with all except insects and birds, these being named by imitating their sounds of clicking, grating or whistling, so that a conversation between two women may soon take on the drumming and shrieking of an entire forest of strange wild creatures."

VICENTE WENT ON TO DESCRIBE THE FOREST IN GREAT DETAIL, BEGINNING with the Tree of Life, its leaves like the fingers of a hand, with white flowers and black seeds attached to a soft fluff used for pillowing the heads of travelers. He told of a thunder tree with sap so poisonous that anyone seated beneath its leaves during a rain would be instantly blinded, and of a tree of fire with scarlet blossoms, and a wood of life so heavy it would sink in water, and a rain tree that showers the "juice of cicadas" all night, a juice taken as drink in the morning. There was another tree with thick dark green leaves shaped like teardrops, found growing on every beach and useful for writing messages or making playing cards by scraping designs into the leaf with a sharp stick or thumbnail.

Paradise, said Vicente, was known to Sirena's people as a mountainous place in the sky. Demons, on the other hand, were often seen dancing on waves of the sea in the form of calabashes, leading people out so far that they were drawn into the depths.

Creatures such as snakes and insects, which shed their skins and then grow new ones, were thought to live forever. There were long, elaborate legends recounting adventures of the sun, of lizards and crocodiles, and men who suddenly turned into birds of the morning, and entire villages that sometimes came out of the caves, newborn.

Vicente said stealing food was considered the most terrible of crimes among Sirena's people, and that, if captured, a food thief would be impaled on a wooden stake and be left to die slowly, in agony.

He told how his tongue was pierced by Sirena with the sharpened beak of a mockingbird, to help him learn her dialect quickly, and how, before the deaths of all the people by fire and hanging and smallpox and fever, they used to tell two distinct kinds of legends, the first a set of ceremonial stories passed from generation to generation, and considered entirely truthful. From knowledge of these, all women, children, and outsiders were jealously excluded, so that once the last of the Hidden men had passed on, history vanished. The second set of tales had been invented specifically to delight and confuse the Extreme Ones. These told of nations of warrior women, and of golden sands bordering great rivers, and golden lakes, and women with hair of gold and teeth of pearls and eyes of sapphire.

These devious tales, Vicente speculated, had been designed intentionally as a ruse to lead the explorers away from Cuba. With arms waving to indicate great distances to be traveled between islands, the Hidden Ones had managed to give the Spaniards a sense of urgency, convincing them that the journey was long and someone else might get there first unless all haste was taken.

"They protect themselves with fantasy," wrote Vicente, "just as we do, just like our navigators and our Kings, may God forgive me, and our Inquisitors, may God forgive them, because I do not."

VICENTE CONFESSED TO INQUISITIONS OF HIS OWN, TO THE TORTURING of islanders during his searches for pearl beds and lands of spice. He concluded, in the Chronicle of Antilia, that after many horrible incidents, he, unlike so many of his countrymen, eventually realized that any tale might be invented to escape pain. "That," he testified, "is why I gave up the search, that and even more than that, the memory of my dear Sirena's melodious song."

THE CHRONICLE RECOUNTED ALL THE FAMILIAR OUTRAGES AND absurdities of the conquest of the Indies. Vicente told of the appearance of Hernán Cortés at the heart of the island, promising fame and riches to any man who would join his expedition to the mainland of Mexico. Cortés, according to my ancestor Vicente, was particularly interested in recruiting him, because of his noted facility for languages, as verified by the cave-dwellers having tattooed his tongue, an honor granted only to those most gifted in the realm of speech and understanding. While the Armada of Cortés grew daily in numbers of ships, men, horses, and cannon, Vicente continued laughing off invitations to conquer the mainland. He said he was not good at traveling, grew seasick easily, and had no luck with celestial navigation.

Yet he was known as a native of Extremadura, the fountain of Spain's most ferocious warriors, where men were "born on horseback and nursed in armor."

To Sirena's secret displeasure, Cortés took with him as many Cuban Indian bearers and servants as he could find still alive in the mountains, jungles and new Spanish towns, so many natives, in fact, that one thousand were said to have died of the Mexican cold as soon as they arrived on the mainland, and not a single one survived to see the fall of Tenochtitlán.

To Sirena, this news seemed more than strange, because she had always found great cause for delight from the touch of anything cold: fresh mountain water, a cool breeze from the season of northern winds, the feel of stone in a cave, the cool metal of Vicente's armor when he stored it away from the sun.

"She has the greatest illusions about cold," wrote Vicente, "and thinks it would calm her if she could truly find it, and she does not believe me when I tell her that cold can hurt the flesh and shrivel the soul, and that here in Cuba she possesses the world's most wonderful climate, a perennial heat that induces such delicious stupor and such soothing dreams, that no one of the island's natives has ever shivered except from fear.

"She loves to take fresh cream from a cow, and place it in a ceramic jar, and put this in a mountain stream until the cream is cold, and then drink it with pleasure as if it were a delicacy concocted by the masters of a King's kitchen."

Vicente wrote about Hernando de Soto, governor of Cuba, who, abandoning his wife Doña Inés, and ignoring the hardships chronicled by those who had already perished in the North, set sail for the unknown wilds of La Florida in hopes of finding vast fortunes. Today, Cubans believe that de Soto, not Ponce de Leon, went in search of the legendary Fountain of Youth. Vicente told de Soto's story in the fashion of the time, with much fervent belief in the existence of limitless wealth, and with flowery words, and fanciful descriptions of marvels beheld, and with a veiled regret for the failures of his own attempts, up to that time, to seek and locate an unimaginable fortune.

He said that he often came up from the caves with tears

flowing from his eyes, to watch his cinnamon-limbed sons riding naked on Andalusian mounts, and he would say to himself and to God how glad he was that the boys so loved their horses and their cattle, and how sorry he was that they, like their native cousins, might be swept away at any moment by the pox that took these Hidden Ones so easily, or by the hurricanes that often seemed to aim themselves directly at the land above the caves.

"Much jungle had cleared by then," he recalled, "and many changes had come to our surroundings, with only a handful of respected Spanish families living in the Villa of Trinidad, the men having gone off with Cortés to conquer Mexico, and the women to inland towns for safety from pirates, leaving here only the ones like my children, who are half-breeds, along with some full blood Taíno Indians from the eastern provinces of Cuba, and the first of a few black Africans, promised to the landowners here as slaves for the fields of sugar now being planted to sweeten the cacao brought from Mexico, this being a delicacy so wonderful that the seeds are used there as money, and have been brought now to Cuba for trade, along with some Mexican Indians from the mainland, who are being worked as slaves in the western provinces of Cuba, in those places where the Cuban natives have all succumbed to pox and to the fiery stake, or where they have hung themselves to avoid being hanged by others, or have swallowed poison and fed it to their children to escape the drudgery of enslavement, a condition, Sirena says, that these gentle ones can never tolerate, having grown accustomed over many centuries of lassitude, to their long afternoons of dreaming in hammocks, their only labor being the gathering of sea creatures and fruit, the cultivation of small patches of corn and manioc, and the celebration of joyful songs on sunny beaches, all of this now having come to an end for them, just as for me the days of pleasantries in my homeland were robbed by the betrayals that forced me to flee in search of Antilia, landing me not in that refuge, but in this other one called Cuba, a Taíno word meaning nothing more than "land" or "place," this designation seeming to me fitting for a series of hills and valleys surrounded on all sides by storms and waves.

"The worst and most heated of these storms are named for the native wind known as Huracán. The Hidden Ones have always faced these whirling storms by escaping into caves, but other villages that stay aboveground are sometimes swept away in their entirety, houses, forests, fields, and all inhabitants.

"It was to one of these winds that I yielded my dreams when I was but a small child, and heard of it from my father who always spoke at great length and with wonderful excitement and curiosity, with each of the returning Extremeño explorers. It was a wind in the Year of Our Lord 1502, so hot and so violent that it sank twenty-six galleons and all the gold contained within them, a quantity so vast that its weight and the brilliance of its glow can barely be imagined.

"That treasure," wrote Vicente sadly, "seized my mind with such a fierce yearning that I could never, even during my most pleasurable years with my beloved Sirena, forget that sunken glow completely. Each firefly in a cave would remind me, each yellow blossom in shaded forest, each song from Sirena's sweet throat. I thought of all that gold resting beneath the sea, and of the vast lands and the abundance of slaves it could purchase, and it made me sometimes long to run away from my beloved and return to the quest for cinnamon. And although that great treasure fleet was hurled by God's winds into the depths when I was only five years old, and had never yet heard of Antilia or Moors or the Inquisition, the storm captured my mind and held it, and I have, since then, been slave to its vision of riches unknown. My youngest son says he does not understand my longings. He says he fails to comprehend my continuing fear of the Inquisition. He says the dream I have of escaping pursuit by hiding is all illusion, and even more, he insists, is the dream of escaping by the accumulation of gold and lands. He shouts at me and says that Antilia does not exist, and that all I have is Cuba, all I will ever have is already here. He is disrespectful to a shocking degree, to such an extent that any other less forgiving father would, by now, have put such a son to the sword. Yet I find that I am old and tired of swords, and that when I lift my armor to place it on my back, it burdens me not only with its weight of metal, but also with its memories of Hidden Ones chewed by these snarling wickedly trained dogs that have now almost entirely replaced the timid barkless ones of Sirena's youth, native dogs that were used more as companions than as warriors, and that, instead of feeding their masters with captured prizes from successful hunts, had to be fed like children on scraps from the dinner tray.

"We dine now daily on roasted doves and the fried udders of our cows, and on a love for each other that cannot be destroyed even though my son says he hates me as he hates the other Extreme Ones, and even though Sirena is near that sweet death that will take her to the journey of a magical dog leading her across a river of stars to God, and even though I myself am named mad and am pursued by a brother I can barely remember, even so, I repeat again, that nothing destroys love.

"My fears have never left me, and this I confess only to my youngest son and to my God, because no one else can hope to see these words. My son Vicente, may the Lord forgive Sirena for cursing him with my own unfortunate Inquisitor's name, my son protects me from the attacks of that malevolent brother, only long enough for this the Chronicle of Antilia to be completed. Soon I will die either of madness or at the blade of my brother's sword. My son cannot protect our gold forever. It will be taken, and the boy will have to flee or die. I have told him to hide in the mountains. I have told him that in the wilderness of this island he can hide forever, so wild is it, and so intricately carved by trails of connected caverns. My son says he despises me for hiding, but at night I dream with him, and see that he will soon do the same. He says I was at first a renegade without a crime, and I am now a renegade of many crimes. He says I should not whisper, but should speak out loud, here where the Inquisition cannot follow and where no one cares any longer what I say.

"But I have not been able to forget my years of speaking in parables and rhymes to every stranger I encountered. I do not believe that God, being Good, wishes us His children to fear each other, brother against brother or father against son. My fear has often been with me in dreams, and if I had not spoken it every morning to my dear wife Sirena, perhaps it would have become something else less evil and less humbling, but no, it has stayed, and kept its own name, and now its most terrible form is the vision I have seen of my son inheriting its power. This, if it is true that I am mad, is the source of my lunacy.

"My wife and I have often moved out of the caves and into the house I built so that we might live as do others. Yet during every hurricane wind, and every appearance of any member of the Holy Brotherhood roaming about asking questions of the local priests (who are now so used to life in Cuba that like natives they carry palm leaves perched over their heads to protect their robes from rain) and during every attack by pirates, I dream always of Antilia, and may God forgive me, I did finally leave my beloved wife and all my family, and I did go out away from my home in Cuba to seek once again, golden treasure and the safe and blessed shores of my spiced vision.

"I came back without cinnamon but with a wealth of much more gold and jewels than I had ever imagined possible, much more than enough to cure the disease Cortés spoke of when he first came to the Villa of Trinidad in Cuba, saying all Spaniards should follow him to the mainland, saying we suffer a disease that can only be cured by gold.

"Fugitive and hermit, I left Cuba abruptly, promising to return, but my dear Sirena did not believe that promise, nor does she now forgive my forsaking her for a place she says does not exist and a wealth she insists can cure no one of any ill, no more than the pain tree has proved itself capable of healing pox and fever.

"I left my home and my sweet beloved during the conquest of El Perú, after the Villa of Trinidad had been so thoroughly destroyed by hurricane winds that not a single house, cow, tree, or ship remained standing. So ravaged by flooding and terror was the island that many families became scattered, and all my grown children took my grandchildren inland to Sancti Spiritus and other villas, leaving us desolate and lonely, thereby making my abandonment of Sirena even more dolorous for her than it might otherwise have been, may God forgive me the confusion of my tangled heart.

"Now it is said in Cuba by the few surviving natives and their many half-breed offspring, that bad luck will pursue any man who speaks the name of the discoverer of these lands, because he became a powerful man and had the chance to rule the islands well, but instead, he fell to the lunacy of greed, and is now referred to only as the Admiral, and never as Cristóbal Colón, unless the name is pronounced secretly and as a curse, evoking the evil that caused the man to lose his sense and be carried back to Spain in chains. This, at least, is the way my son Vicente tells the tale of the great and noble discovery of these spice lands, and he laughs, because he says now everyone in Spain already knows that neither is this India, nor does it hide forests of cinnamon, but only of achiote, which he says should be enough to satisfy us since its crimson seed can flavor our food just as well as any other spice, and color it at the same time, and decorate our skin, and ward off the bites of flying insects as well.

"My son, may God forgive him, swears he will refer to me only as father when I am gone, and never by name, since he holds against me still that betrayal of his mother that took me away from her and out to sea in search of my dreamed Antilia and my sunken galleons of gold.

"Sirena still speaks from time to time, although she is very ill and suffers much from attacks of demons and fever. Yet when she talks it is mostly of her childhood, in a longhouse above the ground, in the open, where sun came in to light her mother's hammock, and tame birds sang in the rafters, and silent dogs lounged near the cooking fires, and musical instruments came dancing all by themselves out of the red soil at the foot of the stump of the Tree of Life. My wife moans now and asks how can seven men capture seven thousand. She complains that when we came with our extreme demands for golden tribute, we cut off the hands of her father who could find none of the shining ore in his caves, and I answer that still I love her even though I was not the one who chopped her father's hands, and I know little of what she means when she speaks of the spread of sorrow across this earth.

"While I was gone from Sirena, a foreign pirate ship came to the harbor near this pleasant Villa of Trinidad and did spread its crew of scoundrels across the town and ranches, and the thieves, exploring these caves, did find and steal my wife, so that while I myself was away at sea seizing gold from the foreign pirates who rob our Royal Treasure Fleets (keeping always for myself an assigned portion, and often, I confess, much more than the amount to which I was entitled) during all this my poor wife was suffering terribly, and alas, she was already pregnant with our youngest son at the time of her capture and enslavement.

"So she has had her own adventures, although they are not of the sort she would have me leave for our son (in this chest with its seal of pitch and its noble image of our honorable Peregrín family crest, honorable, that is, until my brother shamed it by accusing me falsely and until I, driven by fear of him and his hooded demons, did dishonor it myself by becoming a gentle coward who would hide in caves, discard my armor, and become confused about the very nature of our conquest here in this hot dragon's mouth at the edge of the earth's abyss).

"And so, in place of my own adventures, I recount here, for my son's sake, those of my dear and beloved wife Sirena, who still, even in madness, and even in the jaws of death, does continue to serenade me sweetly, using first the words of her tongue, and then the words of mine.

"I, Vicente Peregrín del Castillo, having failed to learn the intricacies of navigation by fantasy at sea, have not, however mad or sane, failed in my King's quest for gold, nor have I failed to learn the art of protective deception on the solid land of this earth, a skill that I fear bears much similarity to that of celestial navigation."

Vicente then told, with great passion and much heartfelt regret, how Sirena had been carried away on the ship of pirates, and how she had suffered even more, he believed, than her ancestors the Hidden Ones, who had so often been forced into caves to escape hurricanes and, according to legend, the attacks of cannibals, and who were so timid that they even feared the peaceful chieftains of the Taíno of eastern Cuba, who moved every year a little farther to the west, and might have eventually taken over the entire island if they had not been stopped by pox and fever and the troops and flames and mastiffs of Velázquez.

Vicente knew nothing of his wife's agony until it was all over. By then he was a wealthy man. He returned to the heart of the island with his treasure of Inca gold, confiscated from pirates who'd stolen it from the ships of the Royal Treasure Fleet as they attempted the arduous passage from the mainland to Sevilla's Tower of Gold, stopping first at Havana Harbor to gather strength and provisions. The treasure ships traveled in large groups for safety, with pirates secretly following close behind, and privateers like the ship of Vicente Peregrín pursuing, in turn, the foreign corsairs, so that the sea became so filled with sails that it had the appearance of an immense blue silk-covered book with many white pages opened and fluttering in the hot Cuban breeze.

Returning to the Villa of Trinidad with his store of golden tribute extracted by the Incas from the many tribes they'd conquered, Vicente laughed to himself, thinking how strange it was that he, a man who could not map his path at sea, had become the captain of a corsair, simply by demonstrating his daring and by speaking well enough to convince other men that his was a ship gaining wealth, and that those who followed him would soon have lands of their own and cattle and sugar and slaves.

The gentle ancestors of Sirena, Vicente noted with sorrow, had, according to legend, been seized by cannibals and taken to the southeast in big canoes, to an island where all the men, being natives of that land, spoke one language, and all the women, being captives from Cuba, spoke another. Hardly anyone ever escaped. The Cuban men, said Sirena, were castrated and stored in wooden cages like penned livestock, until the day they were butchered and served as a ceremonial feast, their captors dancing on the surface of a wooden drum so large it could only be played with the feet.

The captive women (Sirena recalled hearing this from old grandmothers who escaped these dreaded raids by hiding in the caves) detested their masters so much that in the absence of weapons they fought with poisonous snakes found secretly in the captors' fields and hidden in baskets until just the right moment for rebellion. During these fits of serpent-tossing, the female insurgents would die along with their enemies, gaining neither freedom nor safety, and exhilarating only for a few seconds before going down in defeat against a force of warriors more numerous than any den of fer-de-lance.

The result of such a female rebellion would eventually be another raid against Cuba, with more men captured from the shore while fishing and more women dragged from the caves while hiding.

Before each war the cannibal chieftains, according to my imaginative ancestor Vicente, would fast for a year, drinking nothing but a brew of dream-inducing roots and herbs. They surrendered themselves to tests of courage, to the stings of wasps and biting ants so ferocious and so venomous that no Spaniard would have been able to survive the fevers and visions produced by their attacks. The cannibals, said Vicente, tortured themselves willingly, with fire and whips, and when they were satisfied with their own courage, they set sail in search of even greater reserves of boldness.

Yet none of that legendary suffering, my Hidden ancestor Sirena accused her Extreme husband, matched the horrors of the voyage she'd endured on that ship of pirates. No one on that ship had understood her tongue or her mixture of it with Spanish. In panic, she forgot all the other words her husband had drilled into her mind, remembering neither the Arabic poems nor the French ballads. She gave her last child to the light, Sirena revealed, with so much incomprehensible wailing and moaning that the buccaneers tossed her overboard to be rid of the noise. A merciful current washed her onto an unknown shore, where her infant emerged from its hiding place with ease as she crouched on the sand and watched it fall. She was silent now. The pirate ship sailed away into storm winds, which, Sirena quietly hoped, would crash its wood onto some hidden reef, destroying every memory of her bondage.

Vicente, when faced with these accusations, swore to his angry wife that when he left her he had no idea she was with child, believing she was long past the age for giving light.

The Chronicle of Antilia went on to tell how Sirena, after giving birth, had wandered through a violent hurricane wind, confused, clinging to their child, hungry and feverish, on the shores of a wilderness, until she encountered the wreck of that very same evil ship from which drunken pirates had, only a few days earlier, tossed her into the shark-infested waves. She found, among the scattered corpses, chests filled with mounds of gold, and with huge silver crosses stolen from newly constructed churches on the mainland, and sacks of emeralds, and silver baptismal fonts, and so many Inca pendants and masks that she thought, so this is what the old ones meant when they used to tell the Extreme Ones of a land where men wore skins of gold and had faces shaped like strange creatures from a distant forest.

Sirena called the infant Vicente after her husband and in an effort to replace her dead firstborn son and the happiness of their days together as youths both wild and hopeful. She followed, in this, the Spanish tradition, and when Vicente returned to Cuba and learned that once again he had a son baptized with his own misfortune, he was both furious and grateful, and he refused to change the name to a nickname for daily use. When he asked his wife the true name of his newest son, she said no, there were no longer any true names. She said the time of secrets had ended.

Vicente learned that on that unknown shore his wife had built a hut of palm leaves and gold. Her fragile walls, she told him, were decorated with all sorts of jewels and chains and with stacks of gleaming masks. She used silver basins for cleaning the fish she caught with hooks fashioned from the clasps of golden earrings and bracelets.

Then suddenly, as if possessed by a demon, the gentle Sirena went out singing to the beach, her infant slung across her back in a makeshift hammock of golden chains padded with gold-embroidered garments taken from the shipwrecked treasure chests.

On that uncharted shore, while her son watched, she butchered the corpses of the pirates, using their own scimitars to slice the flesh from their bones. She chased away the seagulls, and kept the meat of her tormentors as food for herself and her child.

It was a custom abhorred by the Hidden Ones, and never, to

Sirena's knowledge, had it been tried by any of her tribe or any other on Cuba. Yet now she felt drawn to this absorption of the strength of others. She cooked and ate the men one at a time. She soaked the strips of flesh in salt water, then hung them from a rack of palm fronds to be dried by the sun.

It was a sustenance she didn't need. She had fish, turtle eggs, and coconuts, crabs, birds, the iguanas that sunned themselves on hot stone. She knew how to dive for conch shells, with their rare pink pearls treasured by the Spaniards, who still, after so much sailing, knew nothing of the floor of the sea.

Sirena told Vicente she could have survived for a hundred years on that mysterious shore without ever touching the corpses of her captors. Yet she took from the act some strange satisfaction that she did not try to understand at the time and did not want to understand now.

She stayed on that beach in her hut of palm fronds and gold for nearly four years, so that when the child Vicente finally came home to Cuba and met his father, the boy was already a smoker of cigars and a wild, unruly and insolent creature, much like the playful barkless puppies Sirena remembered from her youth.

The child had learned only his mother's native tongue. Now, after hearing his wife's tale of sorrow and rage, Vicente struggled to teach the boy Castilian and many other dialects. He forced him to sit still and learn to read and write. The boy would often close his eyes and say he just wanted to sing or sleep. "You're like your mother," Vicente would accuse, growing calm only after he remembered how much he'd grown to love the ways of the child's mother.

The three of them moved back and forth between the caves and the forest and a fine new house Vicente had constructed directly above the caves. Occasionally they would receive visitors from Sancti Spiritus, people who said they were Peregrín grandchildren, or the distant relatives of Sirena's dead cousins.

At these times Vicente would invite neighbors from the growing Villa of Trinidad, and everyone would dance and consume banquets and tie golden spurs to the feet of fighting roosters.

When guitars and flutes were played, Sirena would sing, and when tall tales were told, Vicente, instead of telling his own adventures, would tell how his kidnapped wife and son, stranded on an unknown shore, had finally been found by a passing ship on its way back from the salt mines of the south, and how Sirena had purchased their passage to Cuba by turning over all the waves of gold she'd found next to the bodies of shipwrecked pirates.

Vicente would laugh and tell how that gold was enough to buy a thousand ships instead of merely a passage for one woman and one boy. He said the sailors would have delivered her to Cuba for free, but his wife had hoped all along to rid herself of the shining gold, and when she got home to Cuba, ¿what did she find? A remorseful errant husband returned from the high seas and a fine house full of golden jewelry saved for her, food served in silver platters, and plump cattle roaming pastures that had once been forest.

Vicente did not tell how his wife had eaten the shipwrecked men, nor how the meat had slowly poisoned her mind so that now she believed only her dreams and never the events of her daily life. He did not tell how his youngest son would often shriek at his father, saying he would never forgive him for leaving Sirena alone in the caves while he went off in search of treasure. Vicente did not tell his celebrating relatives that the boy, now nearly grown, was a child of bitterness and rage.

*   *

I<small>T WAS AT ONE OF THESE JOYFUL GATHERINGS OF COUSINS THAT THE</small>
Spanish brother of Vicente Peregrín suddenly reappeared, old,
withered, gray, and bearded, demanding a share of the now
famous Peregrín hoard of Inca gold. Vicente's madness struck
him like a sword at that moment of encountering the Extreme
man he'd struggled to forget. Fear of the Inquisitors returned.
Vicente fled the celebration and moved back into Sirena's ancestral cave, entering through a secret passageway and refusing to
leave. He took his chests of Inca gold down into the cave with
him. It was enough gold to fill a thousand lifetimes with banquets and dances, enough to put golden spurs on the feet of
uncounted generations of fighting cocks. His wife may have
sacrificed an entire fortune in exchange for safe passage across
the sea, but he, Extremeño and warrior, was not about to forfeit
this last revenge.

An angel moved into the cave. Sirena joined her husband in
the depths, and their son moved back and forth between their
dark refuge and the pleasant house above. When Vicente's
brother finally attacked, claiming the gold for himself, he found
only two sets of blank stares awaiting him, two bodies embraced,
and protecting them, the boy Vicente with a gold-handled
sword.

The uncle put his nephew to flight. He seized the gold and let
the boy flee deeper into the caves. It was a battle that ended
swiftly and secretly. "No one will ever know," the brother
shouted, hearing his voice echo gruffly through bat-infested
caverns.

The angel, fluttering nearby, drew Vicente the Younger back
to his parents' side once the gold was gone and the caves had
returned to silence. The angel, humming and whistling, placed a
translucent feather in the boy's hand. Young Vicente wrote, "No,

I don't forgive him." He wrote this in perfect Andalusian *en-cadenada* script, all loops and coiled chains like the Chronicle of his father's imagined Antilia.

"I don't forgive any of them, not my treacherous uncle from Spain, not the pirates who stole my mother's mind along with her body, not my brothers and sisters who have abandoned us except at these times of feasts, and certainly not my own father who dreamed he could protect us with this armor of gold.

"I know my mother's real name," the boy wrote, "because she told me when I was very little, when she thought I could not yet understand. But it doesn't belong to her anymore, none of it does. None of it ever belonged to anyone, not the secrets, and not the Inca gold, which did not even belong to the Incas, but to the mines and rivers dug by their slaves. My parents have died together," wrote young Vicente, "still embraced and still in love, as if their lives had gone well instead of badly. At the end they couldn't even understand each other's words, just as they couldn't on the day of their first meeting. My mother returned to the language of her youth, and my father to the language of his, so that neither, during these last days, knew what the other was saying. He continually called our home Antilia, and said it was a safe refuge and could never be taken by any conqueror or Inquisitor. She, in her own tongue, would answer that she had been dreaming, and was now going out to greet the sun and eat from the stump of the Tree of Life. She told of dogs crossing rivers of stars. He spoke of angels with flaming wings. Their conversations were like waves at sea, tossing me back and forth. I told my father repeatedly that Antilia is a place that does not exist and has never existed, and I told my mother that the brief dreams of one night can no longer carry her through an entire day, and I told her that the stump is like any other tree, and the food she used to find there was left by her parents to trick her, and the musical instruments that seemed to come out of the soil were first carved and then placed there for her delight.

"And yet, even during these last few days when these two people who still loved each other could understand nothing of each other's speech, still they understood each other better than I could ever comprehend either of them. I feel that I am alone on the edge of the earth, with no one alive who understands me, even though I speak a dozen tongues.

"A winged angel has now moved into this cave to comfort me," the boy wrote. Nearly five centuries later, as I read these words penned by my forlorn young ancestor, I could see that even though he'd sworn never to forgive anyone, that even at that moment of setting a plume to the task of lamenting, the boy's rage had been released, and he'd traveled from childhood to manhood in one sentence. I saw him laughing at himself once the vow of resentment was written, knowing that even before it came out of his feather, the final word of hatred was cold and dead, all betrayals pardoned.

"I leave the bodies of my parents to this cavern," the young man wrote, "and the sheep of their souls to the Good Shepherd's care, and this the Chronicle of Antilia I leave guarded by the Lord's glowing angel. May all who pass this way remember that we dreamed the haven Antilia, where no one who is being chased by attackers can be found, and no one falsely accused of treason can fail to encounter solace and peace."

Young Vicente said that his parents both spoke the same last words, although in different tongues. "Nothing defeats love," they both said, he with the loud and rapid accent of the Extreme warriors and she with the shy and quiet murmur of the Hidden women.

The Chronicle of Antilia ended abruptly, without titles or flowery claims of loyalty to the Spanish Crown. It was signed Vicente Peregrín the Younger, son of Vicente Peregrín del Castillo and his beloved wife Sirena, native of the Hidden Tribe of Cuba. This long curling signature was followed by the location and date, Ranch of Antilia, Villa of Trinidad, Island of Cuba, Year of Our Lord 1550, Season of Winds.

7

Navigation by Fantasy

Ando en el buque de la vida: sufro
De náusea y mal de mar: un ansia odiosa

I travel on the ship of life: I suffer
From nausea and seasickness: an odious anxiety

JOSÉ MARTÍ

I IMAGINED LOVE. I IMAGINED SOMETHING BOLD, FEARLESS, VALIANT, foolhardy, superhuman, supernatural. Instead, an ordinary young man called Alec Larue came hiking out of the canyon searching for his dog. He saw me sitting in the shade of the smoke tree with Rocky, drinking melted ice cream and poring over the folios of my ancestral chronicle. He caught me daydreaming about the freedom of Camilo, imagining my brother in his dungeon longing to touch the crescent antlers of a new deer moon. I was wondering whether Camilo realized that some of the sharks in Cuban waters are so ferocious that they begin to devour each other before birth, cannibals in the womb. The angel would be singing now, I imagined. It would be the same angel young Vicente Peregrín befriended in the caves beneath his father's house.

"THAT'S *MY* DOG," ALEC SAID. ROCKY WHINED AND ROSE TO NUDGE his hand. "I lost her up there in one of these canyons." He pointed up toward the sheer cliffs of the Santa Rosa Mountains, which rose abruptly, like walls, from the flat desert floor. "Been looking for her ever since," he added. "Thanks for taking care of her."

He told Rocky to sit and she did. He told her to shake hands. He said, "Smile!" and the companion I'd grown so attached to smiled, lifting her lips up over long white teeth.

Amazed, I scanned this strange hiker's amused blue eyes. His hair was brown and disheveled. He wore faded blue jeans worn thin at the knees, army surplus hiking boots, and a denim work shirt with the sleeves rolled up. His clothes were much too hot for the desert, but they were sensible, protection from sunburn and snakebite and the grasping curved thorns of cat's claw acacia. He had obviously planned his journey.

"She looks like a mischievous ape when she grins," I offered. "How did you teach her to smile?"

"She looks guilty," Alec said. "That's the smile of a dog trying to promise that she'll try not to follow her instincts. No trash dumping, no cat chasing, no food stealing, you know. Not every dog can learn to smile on command, but this one can."

The hiker observed my sun-toasted hermit's face, the patio of my adobe house, strands of dangling red peppers and elephant garlic (my dead mother's spices) still hanging from the beams as if waiting for me to suddenly be transformed into an enthusiastic cook.

I offered Rocky's owner a plate of melted ice cream. "That's okay," he answered, "see, I have my own. It's freeze-dried ice cream, the kind invented for astronauts." He handed me a strip of hard chewy strawberry ice cream. It was the texture of taffy, and tasted like dried fruit.

"Camping food," I said. "Better than nothing."

My unexpected guest sat cross-legged on the gravel beneath the smoke tree, asking about the folios, telling me about his job (tree-ring research) and describing bright yellow inflatable rafts racing along rushing streams through the grandeur of wilderness canyons. He said he liked the mountains best, but the desert would do when it was too cold for white-water rafting or mountain climbing or hang gliding down from mountain to desert. I groaned, said, "Not another daredevil!" and then told this stranger about my mother's accident, her magical contraption flipped over by wind, her body tumbled against a cliff.

"She went over the falls," Alec commented with a sympathetic frown. "It's the worst that can happen, that or a dust devil, whirls you right back to earth."

We shared a chewy strip of freeze-dried S'mores ice cream, while Rocky licked Alec's hand, whining so loud and so long that she seemed to be singing.

"You can't have my dog," Alec said firmly. I nodded, although I'd been telling myself all along that if the rightful owner showed up, I would fight tooth and nail to keep my only companion.

"I need her," Alec said.

I needed her too, but I was too surprised to say anything.

"She's mine. I've been searching for her every single weekend since she got lost. I'll buy you a puppy," Alec offered, "to make up for the heartache, and all the money you've probably spent on her by now. Food, vet bills, all that."

I liked Alec. His name reminded me of the kid in the Black

Stallion books. Breathtaking scenes of a stranded child galloping along deserted beaches.

"I'm Carmen," I said, holding out my hand in greeting, "like the opera." Flamenco dancers, I was thinking, long ruffled skirts, doomed love.

CAMILO'S LETTERS WERE ARRANGED ALL AROUND ME IN PILES HELD BY rocks. The Chronicle of Antilia was open, exposed, its folios spread around me in cautious disorder. I explained it all to Alec from beginning to end, just as if he weren't simply a stranger who'd emerged from the wilderness without warning, claiming my dog. I carried the tale from long-lost brother to vanished father, filling in every detail, grieving mothers (both mine and Camilo's), plane flying into thin air, raft sailing in the dead of night, Antilia, caves, the Viper.

Rocky grew restless as the heat of day cooled to a glittering twilight. She ran off in search of moving prey, quail and road-runners.

I put all my Cuban papers away, wrapping the Chronicle carefully in its leather and linen packet, folding each of Camilo's notes, putting my father's documents in their proper order. I carried it all to the house, shut it away, and went hiking with Alec. Rocky found us eventually. The wing feather of a cactus wren dangled from her bloodied mouth.

"Why do you have to eat wings?" I sighed, scolding her. She hung her head and promptly swallowed the feather. Alec laughed.

"She's a dog, Carmen, not a child. You'd be happy to see her guzzling ice cream, wouldn't you? And she'd end up sick, diabetic, miserable. You'd be sorry then. We're always sorry when we turn someone away from his own realities."

That night we slept outside, under a full buck moon the color of saffron. It was not the pointed set of golden crescents I had imagined for Camilo.

ALEC, AFTER HEARING THE ENTIRE STORY, CONCLUDED, "YOU SHOULD DO what your ancestor said. Find those relatives in Spain and ask them politely to help you wrangle Camilo out of prison."

Later, when we knew each other a little better, when we were lovers, family, friends, when my adobe house was home, Alec took the Chronicle of Antilia to a genealogist in Los Angeles.

Alec worked at a tree-ring laboratory in Tucson. By counting the rings and comparing their widths, he could tell what had happened during a particular season a thousand years earlier. He could tell if the snowfall had been light or heavy, the runoff abundant or sporadic, groundwater basins full or dry. Anthropologists relied on Alec to help them figure out why a particular tribe had left its land and moved to another valley, or attacked a neighboring tribe, or fled into the refuge of a dense forest.

"You see these scraggly little desert creosote bushes?" Alec would say. "Well, underneath, the roots are all connected, they form a huge network. These aren't really separate plants, they're a community, like we are, everything attached. This branch might be old, but underground there's a root connected to wood that was alive thousands of years ago."

My tolerance for meticulous thought was limited. I had a mind carried by wings. I knew that work like Alec's would drive me insane. Yet watching him at his labor of detailed analysis made me think seriously about planning a career. "I'm wondering about studying folklore," I said one day. I told him that the Chronicle had made me aware of the power of belief.

"I think about those letters I get, the complicated ones from

Marisol, and I wonder about the censors in Cuba who read the ones that aren't smuggled, and decided whether to let them through. The censor, I think, must be someone with his own literary aspirations, biding his time with that tedious job, waiting to be selected for the writers' union. Not just an ordinary bureaucrat, you know? Someone chosen for his dedication to the interpretation of metaphors. A young person with creative urges."

I thought of all the questions Marisol said she had to answer when Camilo was little. Whether a star went out in the sky every time someone died, or did angels light a new one. What God would look like walking around up there without any skin. They were questions Marisol couldn't answer, but she tried, and trying made her feel younger, smaller, a child all over again. When Camilo asked her why God came to earth as a baby instead of a giant, she said she thought maybe we would have been afraid of a giant, so He sent Himself in a form we could tickle and laugh with.

I remembered those days of waiting with Marisol as if they had been a jovial time. Helping Camilo get out of prison and out of Cuba was the only thing I could think of, yet nostalgia was beginning to creep across my desperation. I was afraid that if I let it grow, Camilo's months in the Viper would stretch to years, and soon we would both be old, and looking back, he would wonder why I hadn't made the effort.

"While Marisol and I were waiting for news of Camilo," I told Alec quietly one night as we camped beneath a meteor shower, "she told me that when he was little Camilo found a sea turtle stranded on the beach. It was wounded. He put it in a tide pool. It was very big, very heavy, but he got some old fishermen to help him move it. They took care of the turtle, nursed it, and brought it food. Then one day a hurricane struck, and the waves carried it back out to sea. But by then it was well, and Camilo was happy that it had been taken back to its home. He'd been wondering how to put it back in the sea, only the wind did his work for him.

"The wind," I added, "had better do something for Camilo soon, or I'll have to stir it up myself, and you know what Camilo would say about that, 'He who sows wind reaps cyclones.' "

Then the genealogist sent my newly completed family tree. It was accompanied by a letter explaining that a parish priest in Spain had at first refused to cooperate, saying he suspected that I must have some other motive besides curiosity, that perhaps I was going to challenge a disputed inheritance, for instance. The genealogist argued that if I were to do so, it should not be up to them, the scholar and the priest, to hide the documentation of my lineage.

The priest finally complied, under pressure. He sent a record of the Peregrín family's births, baptisms and deaths in Extremadura, along with notes on the family's history. The brother of Vicente Peregrín the Elder had returned to Spain after "visiting" Cuba. He'd come back an extremely rich man, claiming to have made his fortune by capturing pirates in the Caribbean. His descendants, now wealthy, had clung to their village in the cork forest, going away only long enough to be educated in Paris or Naples, then returning to establish cattle ranches, wineries, and a profitable import-export trade handling everything from Chinese silks to Cuban cigars. Their business grew to include branches in Madrid, Barcelona, Rome, New York, and Tokyo.

Of all the Peregrín family, the parish priest verified, only Vicente had ever left his native town for any length of time. Only his loyalty to the Spanish Crown had ever been questioned. The accusations of his practicing Moorish necromancy had at first merely cheated Vicente out of a title and a small inheritance, then put him to flight to escape the Inquisition, and later, had kept anyone quiet who might have protested when his brother seized from his home in Cuba a fortune so vast that its possession was enough to buy any alteration of history, temporarily at least.

During all these centuries, the priest verified, the name of Vicente Peregrín had been abhorred in his native cork forest. Tales were still told of the evil spells he'd cast from enchanted castle towers. He was said to have a been humpbacked man of monstrous appearance, with three eyes and long curved fingernails as sharp as claws.

Yet the alteration of documents purchased by his brother could be easily discerned. Church records still showed that Vicente was as much a Peregrín as his greedy brother.

The family tree was accompanied by proof of inherited *hidalguía* (the medieval Spanish version of nobility, obtained by blood or by valor) and a surname derivation explaining the various meanings of peregrination at the time of my medieval ancestor's flight from Spain. Peregrín, in the Middle Ages, could mean that someone had made a pilgrimage for repentance, or it could mean that he had wandered away on a rare, wonderful, or strange journey, or it could simply mean the family was migratory, a family of foreigners.

They hadn't always been in the cork forest of Extremadura. Someone had been a migrant at some forgotten time. We were all the descendants of travelers. We were still traveling, still fleeing toward Antilia. No matter that it didn't exist. We would end up in the sky sooner or later anyway, transformed. We would end like the dreams of Martí, spinning from flame to wing.

The Peregrín family tree was accompanied by copies of all pertinent documents, taken from Church records in Spain, Cuba, and the United States. Camilo was verified as the legal heir, my birth being considered illegitimate because my father was already married to Marisol before his marriage to my mother.

Yet I was the one expected to handle a renewal of ties to these ridiculously distant cousins in Spain. They weren't likely to welcome my correspondence.

I called Camilo's girlfriend. Alina had settled in Barcelona, and the Miami cousins had sent me her address and phone number. When Alina heard the whole tangled story of betrayal and theft, she laughed hysterically, then gathered her reserves of solemnity and volunteered to serve as messenger to the descendants of Vicente Peregrín's brother. "We can go back in time," she said, her voice coming to me across the Atlantic, "and send the greedy brother to trial. ¡We can be his Inquisitors! ¡After all these centuries of confusion, the poor tormented ghost doesn't stand a chance! We'll create a scandal in one of Spain's wealthiest families. We'll drag their family crest through the mud. ¡They'll beg us to share the Inca gold!"

We laughed because we knew the gold wasn't really Camilo's, because it had been taken by Vicente from pirates who'd stolen it from the Spanish fleet that had seized it from Inca monarchs who'd extorted it from their conquered subjects, but by the unwritten laws of medieval honor, Camilo might still retain his right to all (¡or at least a portion!) of that sorrowful and scandalous gold; the Spanish cousins might be happy to settle for half of it, just to avoid an embarrassing contest of accusations.

I felt like I was holding a rooster wearing a golden spur,

prepared to launch a fierce battle with weapons attached to some other creature's leg.

MUCH LATER, WHEN I FINALLY MET ALINA AND HEARD HER VERSION OF the labyrinth of diplomacy she'd tackled in Extremadura, we laughed so hard that we became instant friends. Tied together by the absurdity of our efforts, we grew as close as sisters. When we reminisced about the Chronicle of Antilia and its effect upon our lives, we agreed that Vicente and Sirena had been right when they'd sighed, with their last shared breath, in their separate languages, that nothing could defeat love. Alina swore that without her love for Camilo she never could have convinced the Spanish branch of the Peregrín family to take up his freedom as a cause, their own cause. She said her love made her able to show them how they and Camilo were still connected after nearly five centuries. She said she showed them how none of the intervening migrations, conquests, revolutions, or revisions of history had ever really separated them at all. The suffering of Camilo, she convinced them, was their responsibility as well as hers and mine. His cell in the Viper, she insisted, was a direct outgrowth of their poisonous Inquisition. The venom had seeped across oceans and centuries. It had survived the Dark Ages and the Renaissance. It had been carried by tides into the waters of Cuba. It was the most insidious plan ever devised by any government, Alina accused, the plan to make neighbors inform against neighbors, brothers against brothers. There was no difference, Alina shouted in all of her many languages, between the Holy Brotherhood and State Security, between informers who whispered into ears hidden beneath hoods, and those who whispered to the Neighborhood Committees for Defense of the Revolution. Alina shamed my wealthy Spanish cousins in front of dozens of reporters and curious onlookers. Their town, after all, was still a small town. They yielded swiftly. To Alina's surprise, they seemed delighted to yield. Helping Camilo became, for them, a new adventure. They reminded her of knights taking up lances and armor. They galloped toward Camilo's rescue. Hearing Alina's voice streaming across the Atlantic as she praised the reckless courage of my Spanish cousins, I felt connected to her and to them, these cousins five centuries removed. I felt like someone waving a red cape, while others tossed harmless darts at an enraged bull. I hoped a gleaming sword would soon appear from the crimson folds of the cape.

I dreamed with scimitar moons and petroglyphs carved in the elliptical shapes of orbits. I dreamed with people baked on hot stones and serpents the color of flame.

With Alec, I could talk about time and space. We spoke of star clusters traveling toward the earth, the light from the year 1403 just now becoming visible.

He said that his grandmother counted her years as trips around the sun. "When she was eighty"—he grinned at the floating memory—"she would introduce herself to strangers as someone who had journeyed around the sun eighty times."

I dreamed with statues lit from within the stone and stars poured from pitchers in the sky, and of angels and flames, and rope ladders carrying people up and down, dancing into heaven and back . . .

I dreamed with Camilo's raft . . . strong, swift, invisible, impenetrable . . . indestructible, a magic-carpet raft . . .

ALEC AND I CAMPED IN THE CANYON ALMOST EVERY NIGHT, WHILE ROCKY chased bats and night-flying moths. We splashed love onto our arms and legs and hair, a soothing balm, a perfumed veil. We hid beneath the love, a plume of warm mist rising into the sky.

Then, by day, we crashed back down the mountain, streaming a trail of love behind us.

I RECEIVED A CLEAR AND SIMPLE LETTER FROM MARISOL. SHE EXPLAINED that a number of cousins had been accused of collaborating with her son in the planning and execution of his escape attempt, providing him with rope and rubber tubes, driving him to the beach in a Communist Party Lada, standing on the shore and waving good-bye.

She warned me that the timing of my visit to her home might mean that if I returned to Cuba I, too, would be accused. She advised me to stay away from the island until after the Commander's fall. "It is natural and inevitable," she said, referring to his fall, "a phase of the moon, a change of tides, the return of rains after a drought."

She said she had managed to visit Camilo in his cell inside the Viper. "Connections," she explained, "and the money you sent." Camilo, his mother wrote, was *"desesperado,"* a state of mind literally meaning merely desperate and hopeless, but implying furious and raving mad as well.

She said Alina had contacted her secretly, and she was aware of the plan. She said that if we pulled it off we would feel comical but triumphant. "All true rebels," she wrote, "are preposterous. *Son ridículos los rebeldes.*"

Marisol sent me three tiny notes Camilo had scribbled for me on scraps of shiny brown toilet paper:

> "Nothing defeats love. This is what scares them, the tyrants, *los tiranos.*"

" 'Stir it, the sugar's at the bottom. *Menéalo, que tiene el azúcar abajo.'* This is what Cuban women say when they cook a pudding, and the same can be said of life."

From the third note, I gathered that my imagination was not entirely out of touch with Camilo's reality. He described a guardian angel floating at his side, in the air above his shoulder, speaking to him in songs and sighs.

A TUMBLE OF EMOTIONS FOLLOWED THE RECEIPT OF THESE NOTES. I WAS angry with Camilo. How had he managed to get himself arrested before telling me of his need for help? Why did I continually return to anger instead of pity? I leafed through an imaginary album of possible explanations, trying to explain my fountain of rage. I wanted a less complicated brother. He was in anguish, while I was in love. He was desperate, while I was serene and hopeful. Every time I thought of him, he upset my vision of our world, his and mine, shared across the borders of our child-hoods, across a sea of flamingos and sharks. Our secret language, it seemed, was more than a myth. He had some way of slapping me awake every time I longed to fall into my delicious stupor of orchid and moon.

How many lives had been affected by Camilo's flight into the sea! His mother's, Alina's, mine, the accused cousins in Cuba, the Miami cousins, the Rescue Brothers, and in the distant cork forest of Extremadura, while bottling wine and bartering for Burmese rubies, another set of cousins so remote that we could barely remember why we shared the same last name.

Alec understood Camilo's position instantly. He said he wouldn't be surprised if my brother was never charged and tried as a *balsero*, but simply disappeared into the Viper and never emerged. The one-eyed giants, Alec speculated, must already know about my father's defiant work and the continuation of it so vehemently pursued by Camilo. They would not easily forgive my family's investigations of torment (accompanied, as always, by secrecy and a parade of hoods and masks).

We were warned by the Miami cousins that any money we sent to Cuba would fall into a bottomless pit of greed and deception. The guards would take our money and keep my brother. These were not ordinary bribes. These were a pirate's ransom. It would take more money than any of us had ever imagined, a king's fortune.

I returned to Camilo's portion of the Chronicle. Prohibiting the emigration of an unhappy citizen, he testified, violated international law. Camilo repeatedly quoted the United Nations Universal Declaration of Human Rights:

"Article 13: everyone has the right to leave any country, including his own, and to return to his country."

"Article 14: everyone has the right to seek and to enjoy in other countries asylum from persecution."

Into the chronicle my brother also inserted scriptures: "Are you a slave?" he quoted from a modern translation of First Corinthians. "Don't let that worry you—but of course, if you get a chance to be free, take it."

THAT NIGHT I DREAMED WITH EERIE ONE-EYED SHARKS GUARDING THE gates of an undersea castle. . . .

Alec told me the manuscript of our Chronicle must be extremely valuable, because the genealogist was begging for a chance to meet me and discuss its sale to a library in Sevilla. The charts, symbols, the elusive script, the descriptions of the customs of cave-dwelling Cuban Indians from the heart of the island, all were unique and should be studied by historians.

Remembering all the artifacts my mother had obtained through her trade, I now realized how different antiquities were when they actually belonged to you, when they came from the hand of an ancestor and were left intentionally, as a mark upon the walls of the earth, to be read and understood after one generation had passed, and again after another five or ten or fifteen lifetimes.

I refused to sell. I needed an image of the turbulent, imperfect love of Vicente and Sirena even more than I needed wealth.

I studied our family tree. It was intricate, like a real tree, the Peregrín surname fluttering back and forth across time, never in a straight, migratory line, but zooming in and out of tangled branches from father to son, the lines separating, joining, merging again as cousins married cousins on ranches near that small provincial Villa of Trinidad at the heart of the island.

Like my forests of embroidered birds, separate designs repeated themselves periodically across the whole, forming a solid mat of color, but made up of individual threads. Every generation or two, the names of Sirena and Vicente would pop up again, as someone tried to honor their memory by calling their names out to some new infant as it emerged into the light.

I dreamed with birds, maps, and flashing lights . . .

ALEC TOLD ME THAT HIS GRANDMOTHER HAD ALWAYS SAID GOD collects our prayers and keeps them in a bowl in heaven. He sniffs them, like perfume or incense. He enjoys their fragrance.

I dreamed with flowering vines and curling tendrils, smoke

signals in the shapes of butterflies and doves. . . . I dreamed
that God sent an angel to collect our human dances. . . . He
bound the dances together into a long chain, and draped them
all over heaven, like popcorn on a Christmas tree. . . . I
dreamed I was dancing with my ancestors, and their faces were
on fire, and their feet left footprints in the sky. . . .

MY LIFE ENTERED A PERIOD OF SLOW MOTION. FORCED TO BECOME STOIC,
I faced an emotional state of seige. Passion exploded in midair,
immobilized, frozen. I felt cold, like metal or stone. I struggled
to find purpose in Camilo's dilemma, in Marisol's anxiety, in my
helplessness. God was trying to teach me something, and I
wasn't listening. My attention span was too short.

Suddenly the fevers resumed. Whirlpools of conversation
reached me vaguely through the heat of a tropical fever. In the
desert it was midwinter. Christmas had come and gone. On New
Year's Eve, at midnight, Alec and I shared twelve grapes, one for
each of the coming months. We were ready to face 1993.

I pressed moist, aromatic leaves against my forehead, forming
a crown of herbs for my blistered mind and steaming emotions. I
felt my memory melting, fusing with the memories of others
long dead.

I dreamed with soaring Rescue Brothers and drifting rafts.
Cuba appeared to me as a sliver of flaming land embedded in a
sea of blue silk. . . . People were diving off the edges of the
flames. . . .

Camilo, in my dream, was free, his heart was free.

I HAD MALARIA AND A DOZEN OTHER COMPLICATIONS, THE RESULT OF A
childhood spent rushing from one jungle to another in search of

Cuba. My skin turned the pale orange of rice cooked with saffron.

Alec brought me ice cream. Rocky offered pack rats and side-winders. Alec tended my mother's garden. He said her ghost was still floating there. He sliced cross-sections through the trunks of creosote bushes and mesquite trees, tracking time, counting the years as a series of circles.

Marisol wrote, in her intricately crafted censored script, that now she was suffering unexplained fevers and a hunger so great it scraped against the insides of her eyelids. She said songs and memories were pressing against her lips and teeth, providing her only nourishment. She was too weak to stand in line for her rations. Food riots had repeatedly struck Havana. Women were going out banging empty spoons against hollow pans.

"At the Ministry," she wrote, "we are distributing recipes for sugar and corncob soup (cobs *without* the kernels, which were all eaten long ago). We are seeing new diseases, a blindness that strikes the center of the eye (peripheral vision is not affected). There is a new joke on the streets now: One man says to another, '*Compañero*, Comrade, I think I have that new eye disease, *la enfermedad del ojo*; suddenly I can't see anything in the kitchen, not meat, nor eggs, nor milk, nor butter.' "

Through my fever I marveled at Marisol's boldness in choosing to send jokes about hunger through the mail. Why had the censor let the humor pass? Other letters came, more bad news. Beriberi, unheard of in Cuba until recently, was suddenly spreading like wildfire. Marisol described it with simplicity in a letter smuggled through Miami. "A man will just be sitting around," Marisol wrote, "and without warning, his leg will break off at the knee. *¡Se cae!* ¡It falls off!

"Not even a dream of a horse or cow can be spotted in the

countryside. Everything that walks has been eaten. The penalty for killing livestock is five years in prison, so the joke on the streets is, 'In Cuba we eat meat every five years' (remember, every single animal in Cuba is owned by the government, even the fish, so if you go into the sea and catch a fish, you have to turn it in to the authorities).

"The factories have been closed due to lack of fuels, and the workers are still digging tunnels. They say the tunnels have been wired with dynamite. Everyone says the tunnels are being fitted with gas to kill us if we rebel. They believe the tunnels will be used to hide mass graves. I no longer know what to believe, so I believe nothing. Every day we pass a new law. Every day I am sent out with new recipes consisting of nothing but sugar. To lure crowds to his speeches and rallies, the Commander offers a bribe of fresh oranges. ¡As you can imagine, the speeches are well attended!

"Big waves have been splashing across Old Havana. Some of these waves tower high above the castle walls, even though hurricane season is over. People have been washed away, dragged out to sea. The sea wall is no more than a pebble to these waves. Phosphorescent jellyfish float down the street, and when the water recedes, it leaves a trail of stranded sharks and rays, and spiny sea urchins the color of wine. Lumps of pink coral are crusted onto our clothes, and today I saw one of those lacy lavender sea fans waving from the mouth of a gargoyle across the street. There are butterflies in the water, and bicycles. This is our winter, our 'dry season' in the tropics."

I ANSWERED MARISOL'S LETTERS WITH MY OWN FEVERISH HALLUCINATIONS. I cultivated a flowery enigmatic script, copying loops and flourishes from the Chronicle of my ancestors. I told Marisol I had dreamed that the Viper burst into flames and Camilo escaped. In the morning, tears were streaming across my pillow, and the taste of salt dried my tongue.

My constant fear was that something I wrote to Marisol would make things worse for her and for Camilo. As my fever passed, I hoped that the dream I'd described would not be interpreted by a censor as parables for some future escape attempt from the Viper. They might think I was planning arson or a bomb.

Eventually I was able to get out of bed and go outdoors. The hue of my skin returned to ginger mixed with cinnamon.

Fat Tuesday arrived. In Cuba, Tuesdays were considered bad luck. "On Tuesday don't get married, don't embark on a journey, and don't get separated from your loved ones," the Miami cousins called to warn me. *"En martes, ni te cases ni te embarques ni de los tuyos te apartes."* Of course, I had planned no wedding or journey, and Alec (on leave from his tree-ring counting job in Tucson) had promised to stay at my side, so I laughed and said surely Tuesdays couldn't be as bad as their reputation.

That was the day of the Commander's election. Marisol later wrote, describing it to me. "The first supposedly direct national election in over thirty years," she said, "and on the day before Fat Tuesday, secret police were sent to every single house on the island, to give advice and urge everyone to vote. The Commander ran unopposed. ¡He received ninety-nine percent of the vote! And now he tells me that he feels like a slave to his reign. He says he will step down only when the people let him. He says we still need him. I think he actually believes this, the illusion he himself created."

After that election, so many people left Cuba on rafts that the Rescue Brothers started finding fugitives by the dozen instead of in tiny groups. Three of the Commander's own cousins rafted to the Key of Bones. Marisol wrote to tell me that rain was coming in her open window. She said that she often walked to the sea wall to stare across the waves. She quoted biblical proverbs and Cuban folk sayings, "When one door opens another closes," and "The shrimp that falls asleep gets carried away by the current. *¡Camarón que se duerme se lo lleva la corriente!*"

Marisol wrote, "There's no such thing as a small enemy. *No hay enemigo pequeño.*" Her Cuban folk sayings always seemed to make sense. They always said something about her state of mind, or Camilo's. "*El que anda con lobos aprende a aullar.* He who roams with wolves learns to howl."

I answered that the detached head of a bearded demon sometimes drifted through the air of my desert, weaving its way between the baskets of onions and bowls of fruit on my kitchen counter. I said that Cuba felt like a lace shawl draped across my shoulders, warm and comforting, but moving, shifting, growing tighter around my neck. I said I couldn't decide whether to love or hate the island.

Marisol answered that she had been wearing a mask and was now removing it from her face. "Otherwise," she wrote, "I won't be able to breathe."

She complained that between visits to the Viper she couldn't remember her son's features. She said that at those times she couldn't have trusted herself to locate Camilo in a crowd.

ALEC HAD TO BEGIN LEAVING FOR TUCSON EVERY WEEK, RETURNING ONLY on weekends. Whenever he and Rocky were near me, the floating demon would vanish. "A by-product of love," Alec explained, "a beneficial side effect."

Alec always showed up with microscopes and pieces of trees

sent from regions struck by drought. It was his job to analyze weather patterns and estimate the duration and frequency of recurring cycles. He would spend hours seated in front of a computer screen, calculating statistical error and sketching graphs.

He took a lot of elaborate equipment along on his brief expeditions to Mexico and the Sudan. Rocky stayed with me. Alec said he'd named her Jo because he thought dogs needed short names, so they could respond quickly to instructions. He also thought they should be named after people, never locations, objects or ice cream flavors. He said he thought people would treat their dogs better if they thought of them as a kind of funny-shaped pseudo-human with floppy ears and lolling tongues. When I asked him what longer name Jo might be short for, Alec answered, "Almost anything you want—Jonas, Josephine, Joan of Arc, Josiah, Job . . ." But whenever I thought of the name Jo, I heard it in Spanish, so that the J sound became H, changing the name to Ho as in "Land, Ho!" on an explorers' ship, or "Westward, Ho!" on a wagon train, or "Hoe a hard row," or the rhythmic nonsensical "Ho, Ho, Ho" in department stores at Christmas. I decided to stick with my instinctive choice of names for our big, sloppy, loving companion: Rocky Path, like the desert, like the ice cream flavor, like a movie-screen boxer battling danger with his fists.

ALEC LARUE SPENT LONG HOURS IN OUR ADOBE KITCHEN, CONCOCTING stews of wild meat and feral herbs. How strange, I thought, that instead of someone cheerfully rebellious, like my father, God had sent me a love as passionately eccentric as my mother. We spoke of marriage, but I was so consumed by Camilo's dungeon that I couldn't imagine setting aside his anguish long enough to celebrate and change myself into Carmen Larue. I wanted to reach back in time and alter the dreams of Vicente Peregrín and Sirena. I wanted to change the ancient cosmographer's maps, move Antilia, make it real.

It was easy to imagine that the rest of the world was as obsessed by Camilo as I was. I considered a thousand possible approaches to his release from the Viper. I could return to Cuba and get myself arrested, smuggle in tools for his escape, then call on the United Nations to set me free. I could move into Marisol's strange chimney-shaped house, live under the scrutiny of her upstairs neighbors, and accompany my half brother's mother in her suffering. Or write to the President of the United States, pleading for help through diplomatic channels.

But over the years, *balseros* by the tens of thousands had fled Cuba, men and women exactly like Camilo, desperate for freedom; complicating the havoc, boats from Haiti and China were lining up along the North American coast, each filled with hundreds of refugees fleeing tyrants.

Anyway, the Commander had never listened to diplomatic pleas. He hadn't listened to protests, or threats, or logic, hysteria, reason, or lunacy. Camilo might as well be invisible. The world didn't want another runaway. Only the Rescue Brothers could see people like him, and they saw only because a few months or years earlier, they had been refugees themselves, at sea on the same flimsy rafts.

DRIFTING INTO LOVE WAS MUCH EASIER THAN I HAD IMAGINED. IT WAS neither cruel nor grueling and exhausting as my mother had

warned. I found this clarity of love intensely pleasing and surprising, a relief, an unexpected gift, like flowers tossed into a
wishing well instead of coins.

I wanted to concentrate fully on the love that had drifted my
way. I wanted to think of no one but Alec. How simple my life
would have been, I thought resentfully, if only I had never gone
to Cuba and met Camilo, if only I had never waited with
Marisol, never imagined a dungeon or read the Chronicle, or
come back feeling chained and frantic.

I argued with Alec about tidiness and food. I was messy, he
was neat. I liked to eat whatever I found whenever I felt hungry.
Alec enjoyed planning long slow meals served at deliberate moments, from platters placed on tablecloths, scented by tapered
candles and crimson roses arranged in sapphire-blue glass vases.
Whenever he cooked game hens stuffed with wild rice and almonds, or lamb ribs with mint leaves, only to find that I'd already filled up on leftover pizza or cookies and ice cream, he
would fall into a silent gloom, and I would argue my defense, as
if I were in court and he had accused me. Yet we always seemed
to patch our shredded emotions before too many starlit nights
passed, the desert a flash of shooting stars and ivory moon.

Rocky had never seemed more content. She would sidle up to
me, gazing with black doe eyes and pressing her head against
my ribs. She had grown so tall that I could now pet her without
bending over at all, just by resting my hand on her lanky back's
rough mat of gray fur.

Momentarily, I would forget about Cuba and Camilo and
Marisol. During those welcome tides of emotional amnesia, I felt
serene and joyful. Cuba couldn't harm me.

Then a smuggled note would arrive, ornate and cryptic, from
deep within the entrails of the Viper:

"¿If they kill me will you agree to continue our father's work and deliver his documents, and mine, to the United Nations?"

Aghast at the thought of meddling in international affairs, I would instantly deny Camilo's request in my mind. No, it would be too complicated, too dangerous, and anyway, people had been protesting the Commander's outrages for decades and one more voice would not make the shouts less hopeless. No. In one of her smuggled notes, Marisol had warned me against reporting Camilo's arrest to Amnesty International or any other human-rights investigators. She said that in Cuba a prisoner would be persecuted *more* if it was known that the outside world was watching. That, she explained, was the Commander's way of proving that he didn't care how anyone else viewed his actions. It was the Commander's own personal declaration of independence from all communities and institutions.

Now Marisol wrote that the Commander had called her into one of his many mysterious offices and scolded her for giving birth to a *balsero*.

"He complains," she wrote, "that no one will remember him. He says he is, to history, a mere speck of dust. At times like these I believe he is lucid."

ONE DAY ALEC QUIETLY SUGGESTED THAT WE GET MARRIED *SOON*. I WAS alarmed. "What if you're already married?" I demanded. He looked at me strangely. I no longer knew how to tell the difference between truth and lies, theater and secrets. Distrust had made me think that all men were probably like my father, idealistic and generous in some ways, greedy and treacherous in others.

But I said yes. Then I said we had to wait. First we had to free Camilo. We had to *be* free of Camilo. We could have a big family someday. We could be happy, share chains of cousins stretching across oceans and across centuries. Alec said he claimed Camilo as his own. He had no living human ties on earth. That was why Rocky (he still called her Jo) had been so important to him. Now he had a brother, and even better, a brother who needed help. He offered to take over the communications with Alina and our Spanish cousins. Negotiating had turned into a full-time job. Alina called almost every day from a village in Extremadura, with details of her progress, which bribes had been paid in Cuba, which were still being debated by various prison guards and Ministry officials, even, perhaps, by the Commander himself.

Alec spoke Spanish well enough to listen to these narratives while he cooked duck in orange sauce, or frogs' legs fried in a batter of creole-spiced cornmeal. He and Alina would laugh and banter, taking the whole thing lightly, optimistically, while I brooded with Camilo in his dungeon, scolding the angel and shrugging my shoulders away from the caress of a wide translucent wing.

I envied Alec and Alina. They were convinced that actions would produce results. They didn't let the absurdity of our situation prevent them from "plowing the sea." Alina spoke of the "dance of the millions," a term she used for referring to the lost wealth of Cuba, still legendary in Spain, a wealth of sugar, slaves, and secrets. She spoke of an emotional Bermuda Triangle in the Caribbean. She said that when a small snake tries to swallow a large bird, it will die before it will let its victim go free.

"Both," Alina told Alec, "suffocate together, predator and prey."

8

Home

*Dos patrias tengo yo: Cuba y la noche.
¿O son una las dos?*

Two homelands have I: Cuba and the night.
Or are the two one?

JOSÉ MARTÍ

MY TROPICAL FEVER RETURNED. IT WAS SPRING IN THE DESERT, March, season of the flower moon, season of moths and wild verbena.

So many caterpillars chewed through ephemeral blossoms on so many sand dunes that from my home of clay and straw I could hear the sound of their mandibles chomping.

Rocky chased jackrabbits and golf balls. She tried to show us happiness, seeing every moment of her life as an action rather than a past remembered or a future dreamed. Alec took her to a grooming parlor to have her shaved for the summer. She came back looking ridiculous, an enormous wide-eyed creature whose monolithic stature and affectionate character didn't seem to match. She looked like a caricature, some composite sketched by a cartoonist, the gentle expression of one dog stamped onto the fearsome body of another.

It was the season of winds and whirlwinds. Golfers spun in circles, struggling to control the direction of their movements. A roof blew away. A car was carried three blocks by a gust of wind, then abandoned standing on end. Rocky's tent disappeared into the sky, fluttering away like a large blue moth.

Sand stung our eyes and our tongues. We stayed indoors. We talked about time and space. Alec talked about love. We "made" love, or rather, simply discovered it. Love had been there all along, like a "rare" species of orchid in some tropical rain forest, waiting to be found.

ONE NIGHT A TREMOR OF SMALL EARTHQUAKES RATTLED THE DESERT. AT dawn a partial eclipse sliced one dainty morsel off the edge of the sun.

On that day of tremors and wounded sun, I met the genealogist. Alec invited him to dinner along with a curator from the Sevillan library dedicated to preserving documents from the Conquest, a time the curator referred to as Spain's Age of Gold, La Edad de Oro. He said that within the white Moorish walls of his library in Sevilla, visiting scholars could sift through journals like the one written by my ancestor. He said, "The Chronicle of Antilia will be treasured as a relic of our marvelous, brutal, and outlandish era of discovery."

He offered a considerable sum for the Chronicle. I refused to sell. Then he offered a small fortune. Stubbornly I refused. The curator said he could have the Chronicle confiscated as a national treasure. I answered, "No you can't, it doesn't belong to your Spain, it belongs to my Cuba." As I spoke, I was imagining Camilo in his dungeon, writing on air, continuing the Chronicle with puffs of breath, waiting to be reunited not with me, a half sister he barely knew, but with the documents he'd entrusted to my protection. I delineated the whole raft story, as much of it as I felt safe sharing with strangers.

Thoughtfully, the genealogist said he assumed my half brother must have known what he was doing, gambling, taking a risk, losing. "He determined his own fate," the curator agreed, "just as Hernán Cortés did when he burned his own ships behind him as he landed on the shores of Mexico ready to begin his conquest of the Aztecs. No turning back."

I continued refusing to sell. I had my own ships to burn. I had a commitment, an obligation to wait for Camilo, to wait for help from his mysterious girlfriend Alina, to wait for Marisol, to wait for some prison guard who might accept a bribe, to wait for the prison censor who might allow some note to pass that would explain everything, make it all logical and normal, turn us into a real family of adults who didn't mind being separated from each other once they were grown.

I thought of Camilo being digested within the entrails of the Viper, sharing his cell with an angel, watching the path of a fish moon as it swam across the sky. They'd been together more than half a year now, August to March, Camilo and the angel, fear and hope. I knew, from Marisol's smuggled letters, that political prisoners (all *balseros* fit this description) were rarely held more than one or two months in secret police headquarters, but were usually carted off to some distant prison for several years or to a hospital psychiatric ward where gruesome efforts could be made to alter their thoughts and desires. Because of our father's defiance, I imagined Camilo's case must be unusual. He had been in the Viper much longer than ordinary *balseros*. If he and the angel could wait, I told myself, so could I. I would not sell the Chronicle. We would wait for *los extremeños*, the Extreme Ones, for our cousins five centuries removed.

ALEC PREPARED AN IMPRESSIVE ARRAY OF SHELLFISH AND HOMEGROWN vegetables served with exotic sauces, some for dipping, others poured. We ate fried soft-shell crabs, and green mussels, raw giant clams, sliced and still twitching. We shared sauces flavored with plums, peanuts, and tamarind. For Rocky, Alec grilled a special treat of rattlesnake caught wild on the dunes. The diamond-patterned skin and row of excised rattles were already hanging from a beam on our patio next to my mother's red chilis and curative elephant garlic. They made our house look like the abode of ancient fetishists.

After dinner and homemade ginger ice cream, we pored over my family history. The genealogist showed me how my ancestors were all noted for one extremity of passion or another, for piracy, warrior-patriotism, or the fierce persistent plowing of a land where red soil yielded the world's finest tobacco, sweetest sugar, leanest, most feral cattle, and the most wistful poems imaginable. He showed me how during the seventeenth and eighteenth centuries some of Vicente's mixed-blood descendants had been enslaved on a large *encomienda*, a ranch granted as a reward to an Andalusian knight loyal to the rulers of Cuba, while other members of the Peregrín clan managed to become slave-owners themselves, receiving African and part-Indian slaves (sometimes their own mixed-blood cousins) as rewards for deeds of outrageous daring and valor in the many battles against British, French, and Dutch pirates. "They could have chosen a reward of gold in place of the slaves," said the genealogist, "but instead they chose land and human booty, knowing it would serve them profitably in their struggle to devour that frightening roadless wilderness of uncharted Cuban jungle.

"It was relatively easy," the genealogist continued, "to trace your ancestry forward, starting with Vicente Peregrín, whose records of birth and baptism are still found at the church parish of his native Extremaduran village.

"At first the priest of that parish refused to release Vicente's records, simple as they are, a date of birth, a date of baptism, the names of parents and siblings.

"I persisted. I demanded an explanation. The priest then falsified Vicente's records, and sent them to me with an apology for his initial refusal to be of assistance. I recognized these forgeries as fraudulent simply because the dates did not match what I'd read in the Chronicle of Antilia. There was something else. The paper was too new, and the ink was modern! I protested vehemently, threatening to take the man to court. Then I threatened the entire Catholic Church. Of course, I was bluffing, but our stumbling block crumbled. He called me and apologized, genuinely this time. Then he yielded. Here, look at this."

I scanned a series of loops and chains so complex that I couldn't imagine how anyone could tell whether these were fifteenth-century church records or the nonsense syllables of a child's playground verse. The genealogist went on, showing me how the native Cuban portion of my family tree was much more difficult, how churches had burned at various times or were carried away by hurricanes, how valuable documents were lost with each disaster and had been swiftly restored by conscientious priests through memory and by means of copies held in regal homes for their own reference, their personal reservoir of information about their ancestors and their slaves. In Vicente's adopted town of Trinidad, at the heart of the island, church fires had destroyed records in 1728 and 1793. Hurricanes had done the same in 1527, and again in 1825, and 1837, 1846, 1865, 1876, 1882, 1888, 1894, 1910, and 1926.

"You, Carmen"—the curator smiled—"descend from a region of terrible catastrophes. Acts of God. Wars, pirate attacks, slave rebellions. Vengeance. No wonder the language of your ancestor's chronicle is so flowery and sweet. A rebellion against the daily reality of violence and pain. In the original, of course. Your father's translation into modern Spanish has smoothed the fanciful wandering of Vicente's mind, the meandering, archaic phrases describing 'perfumes of the soul' and 'forests of enchantment.' Much of the lyricism has been lost, that intense and passionate praise for the beauty of a marvelous new land, for the color of its sky and shore, the height and grace of its trees, and most of all, for its newfound serenity, its peace beyond understanding, its illusion of a tropical paradise willed by God.

"Flamboyant words, as I see it, are natural to inheritors of frightful crimes, the Spanish Inquisition for instance. Why do you think the cruel and totally irrational Shining Path rebels are now growing so powerful in modern Peru? Surely it's not just because they have guns. Others before them have also possessed weapons. What the Shining Path owns, and uses as a lure, is a poetic label, a name which even after five centuries of disillusionment can still capture the hearts of people bred from a crossing of the lust for gold and a flight from burning flesh."

"Luckily," the genealogist interceded, "between your father's account of the family history—and it's a fascinating work, I might add, of great historical interest, unprecedented! At any rate, piecing together his notes and those of your ancestor Vicente, and the church records, we were able to work out the whole puzzle. It was quite a challenge," he added excitedly, "much more dynamic than counting tree rings, I suspect, and infinitely more significant." He winked at Alec, who merely smiled, shrugged, and offered him a glass of spiced rum mixed with whipping cream.

"What you have here in your possession, Carmen," the curator said, still trying to persuade me to sell, "is a missing link in Cuban letters. It covers a little bit of everything, early sixteenth-century cosmography, native Indian lore, even a few words of the extinct indigenous tongue of a cave dwelling tribe. Historical events, daily life in one of the very first villages established by the conquistadores, and most of all, world view. Back then, not every chronicler bothered with dreams, hopes, opinions. Most were too busy telling what they'd seen, not why. They listed locations of islands, shorelines, reefs, described native customs, battles, conquests, treasures found and seized. Few stopped to think about what they were doing. Discovering and exploring a new world was so dramatic, so exciting, that the daring horsemen of Extremadura simply crashed into life head-first. They must have been similar to modern daredevil stuntmen, only they carried real weapons. It must have felt like leaping off a cliff, or bungee jumping from a bridge into a river, or falling out of an airplane with no parachute. They didn't have any idea what they might find around the next corner: cannibals, headhunters, giants, sorcerers. Many knew they had opted for permanent exile and would never see their homes again, or their families. I can't begin to imagine their bravado, their acceptance of danger as a natural state.

"Of course, they were men skilled with the arquebus, crossbow, sword, and shield. They were dashing cavaliers, charging into battle behind their patron saint Santiago, who, although invisible on his black horse, they firmly believed to be leading their attacks, tossing sand into the eyes of the enemy.

"They were fearless, or at least, they were expected to be fearless. They were trained to live off whatever booty they could seize. These were men who were just emerging from nearly eight centuries of a defensive war against the conquering Moors. Can you imagine it, that many centuries of self-defense? Their Conquest of the Americas was a natural outgrowth of their experience as the conquered, their daily life in occupied territory. It's not so surprising, is it, that they raped, pillaged, enslaved, and demanded tribute? It only takes a small twist of the imagination for persecuted to become persecutor, to associate freedom with power.

"The product of such a birth was the overpowering dream of riches, leading to an irrational degree of courage. And secrets, even more intriguing than the dreams of wealth, because many who came to the New World came fleeing the Inquisition. They were condemned men, like Vicente, given a second chance, a last and only chance. Perhaps one of every three was a Jew, a Moor, or a forced convert, a New Christian. Or a child of mixed blood.

"Did you know that the list of the men who sailed with Columbus originally carried an X beside the name of each man accused of being a 'heretic' or a backsliding new convert, an imposter who was just pretending to convert, but was secretly continuing to practice some prohibited ancestral rite? The word 'criminal' was used by Spanish authorities to document the participation of these X-marked accused men in that first and most frightening of all expeditions, the one where they really didn't know whether they would fall off the end of the earth or sail into the mouth of a dragon.

"Later, the Duchess of Alba had all the marked names erased. This reduced the number of men who accompanied Columbus from one hundred and eleven to seventy-two. Thirty-nine men, in other words, were said to have never existed, at least not in any official capacity. In this way Spain could prove that the New World had been colonized entirely by men of respectable lineage. On paper, that is, but the real men, the men marked by an X on the original list, they still *did* exist, of course, in the Americas, on remote islands, in jungles and mountain hideouts. They'd made their escape, been wiped off the records, started over not only in a new land, but in a new form of existence, officially invisible, unaccountable. It was a sort of magic, like making someone disappear off a stage clouded by smoke."

After a studied silence, the genealogist mused, "Yet it's hard *really* to understand how men fleeing persecution could so swiftly become persecutors. As so many did. They made their own rules, established little invisible kingdoms, traced their own boundaries, imagined their new little worlds any way they wanted, any way at all! Just like your Cuba's Commander, I suppose, Carmen. He too began as a child scorned by church and state, a bastard, so to speak, the illegitimate son of a rancher's servant. Always seeking vengeance, like those Extreme Ones. Immense jungles filled with potential slaves. No restrictions. No one looking over their shoulders to check up on anyone else."

The genealogist fell silent. I could see he had offended the Spaniard, who moved away, grimacing. Now the curator grunted, to show how much he disagreed. "Noblemen," he said, "heroes, idealists, like Don Quixote, perhaps a little ridiculous, anachronous, but still clinging to lofty goals and enchanted visions. Dreamers. People wearied of the Inquisition. They grew tired and ended the spying. Not officially until 1834, it's true, but the real spying ended long before that. Everyone grew disgusted. No one likes to be spied on by neighbors. Ordinary people don't like to spy either, not after the first time, the first success, the first enemy burned alive."

For a long time we discussed my father's continuation of the Chronicle of Antilia, how he had managed to grasp and pursue its spirit of hope. In the introduction to his work my father had reached back into the distant past, far beyond Spain's hooded Inquisitors. He'd even suggested that Jesus spoke in parables to avoid being understood by the authorities who hoped to catch Him expressing forbidden sentiments. My father wrote, "The common people, our Lord knew, were accustomed to telling tales wound in a veil of similes and metaphors. They'd spent centuries learning how to avoid being understood."

My father recounted tales of a Roman Emperor who gave banquets and invited his critics, then repeated derogatory street jokes told at his own expense. The Emperor laughed, then abruptly ordered the beheading of any guests who laughed along with him.

I remembered a joke Camilo told me during the two hours I knew him before he set sail for Key West. I repeated it out loud now, to Alec and the curator and the genealogist. I felt very free, being able to repeat the jest without any fear of being beheaded. I couldn't stop thinking of Camilo, who, before telling me the illicit street joke, had locked the door, closed all the windows, and lowered his voice to a whisper:

"*El Comandante* went out for a walk along Embassy Row," Camilo had murmured. "As the Commander arrived in front of each foreign embassy, he noticed that huge crowds of would-be refugees suddenly went running off, shouting with delight.

"Curious and confused, the Commander grabbed an old man who couldn't run fast enough to get away and asked him what was going on. The Commander demanded to know why everyone was leaving Embassy Row just as their leader arrived. *'¿Por qué huyen todos?'*

"The old man answered, *'Bueno, Comandante,* if *you* are here to apply for permission to emigrate, then the rest of us can stay home, *en casa.'* "

Alec understood the joke, because he'd heard me repeat Camilo's Cuban street humor before, and the curator understood, because he'd studied the evasive humor of Spain's Age of Gold, but the genealogist, who was North American, and had never spent much time with refugees, had to have the punch line explained before he caught on.

"But that's not funny at all," he responded when he finally understood. "That's sad. It's bizarre, it's surrealistic." Thinking of Camilo and his flimsy raft, I agreed.

THE NEXT MORNING ALEC WAS FURIOUS WITH ME. HE RAGED SILENTLY AT first, refusing to say why he was so angry. Finally, he admitted that he was mad because I'd failed to sell the Chronicle for an amount of money that could have paid every single one of the many bribes needed to rescue Camilo.

"You don't even have to sell the legible translation," Alec pleaded. "All they want is the original, the old ripped pages full of stuff *you* can't even read, the Chronicle itself, not its contents. They want the five hundred years, not the story, not Vicente's words. If you keep those old pages they'll fall apart. You don't even know how to take care of them. They'll rot, you'll gradually lose them. You can have a replica made for yourself, and one for Camilo. Keep your father's modern translation, keep his analysis of Vicente's life, and his human-rights documents. Keep every-thing except Vicente's description of life in Antilia! Anyway, there *is* no Antilia. It was an illusion, he *didn't* find refuge in the Caribbean, he found pirates and gold but not safety. Admit that you need the money to help Camilo. Later, when he's free, your brother will understand. He would have done the same. He's educated, he wouldn't cling to a medieval dreamer's artifact."

WHENEVER WE ARGUED, I ACCUSED ALEC OF WITHDRAWING FROM OUR love, of hesitating, of threatening to walk away.

He hadn't threatened, but every time I saw him moving through my mother's garden, picking tomatoes and whistling to Rocky, I was afraid he'd just keep going, take her with him, past the golf course, the man-made lake and remnant dunes, over the horizon, vanishing into the brilliant white salt flats with their distant ghostly mirages of an ancient sea.

Then, a few minutes later, Alec would simply return to the house with an armload of prickly pear fruit and cherry tomatoes, and set about the business of cooking, just as if we hadn't been fighting at all. I skipped snacks, deciding to approach the dinner table hungry.

AT TIMES I FOUND IT HARD TO BELIEVE THAT I HAD MANAGED TO GET OUT of Cuba carrying my father's work, our ancestor's Chronicle, and even my brother's boldly defiant letters. Smuggling human-rights documents off the island was an offense punishable by unimagined horrors. I realized that I had been able to do it only because I had no idea what I was doing, because at the time I had not yet read the documents and didn't suspect that I might be carrying anything dangerous. Surely if I'd known, I would have retreated, surrendered before the Commander's first attack.

Camilo must have known that. He must have made me promise to carry the packet of documents out unopened precisely because he assumed that any sister born and raised in the calm and well-fed North would lack the desperation needed to challenge tyranny. That's why he'd made me wait awhile, to let the rats of time gnaw.

I wondered whether during that *rato* of waiting I had somehow been helped, whether an angel had accompanied me on the journey out of Cuba. I dreamed with my brother in his dungeon, with his angel hovering near the window, beneath a saber moon. I dreamed with long lines of people chained together, a *conga* line dancing into the sea. . . .

I wondered which choice I would have made in Camilo's place. If we'd been reversed, if he'd been born wild in the North, and I enslaved, in Cuba. If I'd been the one caught in his predicament. Would I have stayed on the Commander's island to suffer the silenced outrage of my father's assassination? Would I hide forever in a cave, like Sirena, or dance bravely into the sea, like Camilo?

"Somehow it's deeply disturbing to be born across the sea from a sibling," I mourned into Alec's ear one evening as we lolled in a hammock stretched between two smoke trees. "To claim a different nationality, different liberties, sorrows, rules-of-conduct, a different sense of humor. It's like dreaming that I have another self somewhere, a double or a mirror image, my reflection in a lake, altered by whirlpools and currents. Camilo is trapped in one of those glistening whirlpools. So is my other self."

"North Americans," Alec sympathized, "possess no framework for understanding what it's *really* like to be locked up inside secret police headquarters for any crime of any nature, but especially for one as innocuous as trying to float away from an island kingdom imagined by its ruler. We can't understand it, just as we can't really fathom Rocky's ability to recognize approaching visitors by their scent before they actually arrive."

"We're like different primitive tribes," I sighed, "Camilo and I. We're related, but separate. Our languages branch away from each other, with only a few words shared."

I FELT PREDESTINED, SELECTED TO HELP CAMILO. IT SEEMED TO BE MY ONLY assignment in life, along with learning to love. By witnessing Camilo's escape attempt, by observing its effects on Marisol, I had been condemned to let myself be tormented by the suffering of my double, that intangible mirror image, the reflection trapped in that whirlpool.

While Marisol and I roamed Old Havana together, waiting for Camilo's name to be beamed to us over Radio Martí, his mother told me mournfully that when Camilo was little he used to say he imagined freedom would be like a carnival, like the cheerful, lively scenes he'd watched on pirated Hollywood movies, the old black-and-white images of Coney Island, everyone buying and selling, laughing, celebrating, no one ever feeling sad or going hungry. She said she hoped that if his raft made it to Florida, he would not be disappointed by freedom. She hoped her son's liberty would be as exhilarating as he'd imagined, as delightfully lively and noisy and rambunctious, full of ferris wheels and cotton candy and shrieking children.

Now, gazing out across our desert at night, Alec and I agreed that Camilo would not find his endless carnival in the North. Liberty might seem dull, monotonous, an invisible component of daily life. Hardly anyone who possessed it ever noticed its presence or spoke of it. We certainly didn't bother to document it, as my father had documented his own gradual loss of freedom. But Camilo, I felt certain, would not be disappointed. I remembered his humor, his energy, his radiant eyes. He would find some way to make his freedom thrilling and precious.

A gust of wind swayed the hammock as if we were being rocked by some giant hand.

"We can learn from him if nothing else," Alec said. "Even if we can't set him free, we can keep this thing he craves protected, inside ourselves, you know, buried deep inside, so we can save it for him, maybe share it with him someday."

I smiled. Alec didn't sound like a scientist anymore. He'd absorbed the poetry of Martí.

"I used to imagine a childhood in which Camilo and I grew up together, under one roof, like an ordinary brother and sister. We invented a secret language and built fortresses of tarps and cardboard boxes. We chased butterflies with homemade nets and found hidden entrances and passageways leading to concealed hideouts where no adult could follow.

"In my real childhood, the one I spent traveling with my mother, there were always the smells of antiquities stashed in attics and basements, the feel of a tapestry taken from a castle wall, or the texture of stone on the paws of a carved Egyptian cat. We roamed thieves' bazaars in Morocco and Bombay. My childhood was not ordinary at all, but isolated, guarded, wary, dreamlike, even though I was always being dragged through crowds of robed strangers speaking unfamiliar tongues.

"I had the chance to experience every reality except my own. I was led through Mayan tombs and Aborigine songlines. I was expected to learn Maori dance steps and the lyrics to Guaraní harp melodies. There was only one thing I couldn't explore, and that was love."

*   *

ALEC'S FAMILY HAD TRAVELED EVEN MORE THAN MY MOTHER AND I. HIS father was a military career man, one of the Marine Corps guards stationed at U.S. Embassies overseas, those stoic guards required to remain behind in any crisis, always the last to leave after an explosion.

"We moved fourteen times in fifteen years," Alec said. "Then my parents were both killed by a terrorist bomb at an Embassy in the Middle East. I'm not even supposed to talk about it or tell anyone where it occurred. I can't name the country. Classified," he said quietly. "Classified information. Maybe that's why I'm always putting things in order, naming, measuring, classifying.

"So I was sent to live with my grandmother in Wyoming, where I was supposed to finish growing up. She lived in a big, quiet Victorian house. I listened to her rambling tales of pioneers and wagon trains. As a descendant of those pioneers, my grandmother grew up surrounded by her ancestors' possessions, Swiss clocks, farmers' almanacs, story quilts, walnut chests-of-drawers. When she grew up and got married she gave it all away to a thrift shop, and bought herself a suite of mirrored bedroom furniture with little gold flecks scattered across each surface. She bought imported wool plaid blankets, a twenty-six volume encyclopedia, and a battery-operated clock in the shape of a yellow daisy. Exultant, she claimed to be free of the past.

"But of course, she wasn't. She taught me to cook and garden. She also taught me how easily my surroundings could be weighed and measured, and how impossible it was to contain them within those boundaries once I'd marked them down on a garden calendar or recipe card. She taught me that I could make the same dish twice, and produce two completely different tastes and aromas. She told me the ingredients had a will of their own, and would mix if they wanted to, or stay separate, like oil and water.

"My grandmother used to point out angels as they passed through her garden. She said they came for the fragrance of lilac and rose. She told me that angels can't eat, but they can smell. She was always quoting a lot of famous thinkers and reciting poetry and ambiguous folk sayings. She taught me how to make home remedies for maladies of the flesh and to pray for the healing of any wounded spirit. She sang wistful hymns, and never turned away a stray dog.

"She taught me how to train our dogs to smile on command. That way they wouldn't scare the mail carrier and unexpected guests. Certain dogs can learn to smile easily, if they have floppy upper lips with a lot of flexibility.

"Some dogs smile only when they're embarrassed, like if you catch them in the act of chewing shoes or licking sandwiches, but others, like Rocky, are intelligent enough to use the smile as a greeting. Those are the dogs everybody loves, even total strangers love them, newspaper boys, door-to-door salesmen."

LISTENING TO ALEC, AND THINKING OF GHOST STORIES AND HOME remedies and prayers and folk sayings and stray dogs, I told him that his grandmother sounded a lot like my father's older relatives in Miami, except for the adopting of homeless dogs.

"Even though they're city people now, safe in Miami, they still recite tales of wild dog packs charging out of the Cuban jungle to snatch up reckless children, just like they talk about cannibals hiding in caves. Just as if time had never passed and no one had ever moved."

"Well, my grandma," Alec said proudly, "loved to cook for big crowds of friends and neighbors. And she also loved to dance.

So you and I must be two branches on the same big tree." An enormous, expanding tree.

"She's been dead a long time," Alec said, "and I still miss her. She died calmly, while pulling weeds out of the sweet pea patch."

I pressed my face against Alec's shoulder. We were huddled beneath a million stars, watching them float. "I guess I miss my mother too, in a way, now that I'm not so mad at her anymore, for believing she could fly away from home, from reality. I thought it was all pretend, make-believe, that flying stuff, but it wasn't, it was something just as real as those stars up there, and just as distant, just as mysterious. Sometimes I think I see her out here, she's a ghost floating through the garden inspecting your rows of blue corn, red peppers, and lemon-scented cucumbers."

Alec had planted a lot of fragrant things, geraniums that smelled like peppermint, basil with a pineapple fragrance, and tiny pink wild roses he brought down from the mountains whenever he went hiking with Rocky.

Alec planted things that brought butterflies and humming-birds to our garden, native desert shrubs with tubular crimson and magenta blossoms. He also planted things that glowed white in the black desert night, moonflowers and night-bloom-ing cereus.

My mother's garden was Alec's now. He loved it in her place, and in place of his grandmother. He loved it for himself and for me, saying he would try not to mind too much if I hardly ever got around to helping him with the weeds, as long as I enjoyed the flowers when their scents reached our window on hot evenings.

Maybe I would have missed my mother a lot more if Alec hadn't transformed her garden, if he hadn't come trekking out of the canyon right when he did, ready to take over my dog and my house and my inherited garden of cactus and herbs. I thought maybe it wasn't a coincidence, maybe it was intentional, organized, like Camilo's deliberate preparations for his departure from Cuba, his secret plans for my arrival. Maybe among the ghosts in the garden there were also angels assigned to push us along the paths of our lives.

"Maybe I would have mourned my mother more if I'd thought her death could have been prevented," I said, "if I'd believed I could have rescued her. But I knew it would have been impossible to protect her. She leaped off a cliff because she wanted to, because she had man-made wings attached to her body, and she said she wasn't afraid of shifting winds. She said she had studied wind and understood it. So she was beyond human hands when she died, beyond rescue. No one failed her, because she didn't ask anyone for help.

"But Camilo is different. He's within my reach. He *asked* for my help. And I know where he is, not flying, not wandering away, but locked up inside the Viper. It isn't so very far away from here, not really." I hoped we still had plenty of time left for helping my brother. I knew he might die inside the Viper if I misjudged time.

Yet rescue was a long and complicated path. Helping Camilo was like trying to follow a pirate's treasure map with coded symbols, unfamiliar landmarks, deliberately constructed false trails, and disguised traps.

OCCASIONAL CALLS FROM SPAIN AND MIAMI CONTINUED. BY PHONE WE kept track of our progress. Alina called me to say so-and-so was trying such-and-such, a new avenue of diplomatic string-pulling or boot-licking. If it failed we would all move on to the next plan, setting up another distant cousin as contact, another bureaucratic channel, a different set of bribes. And in my heart, another soaring raft of hope.

Gradually I grew tired of disappointments, weary, restless, lethargic. Something inside my throat was suffering defeat. I longed to separate my memory from Camilo's, to cut myself free from his chained dance.

Marisol sent ornate messages ending with excerpts from the poetry of Martí. Each, in a delicate filigree of letters, quoted the poet's ghost:

> *¡Eso es amor! Andar con pies desnudos,*
> *Por piedras, por espinas*

> ¡That is love! To walk barefoot,
> Over rocks, over spines.

So I WALKED OVER ROCKS AND SPINES, DREAMING OF CAMILO'S liberation. Alec helped me. He daydreamed at my side, taking time off now and then to cook a buffalo steak or to explain to Rocky why he'd taught her to smile.

Through his dungeon window, we mused, my brother could probably see a flower moon resting lightly on the angel's cupped hand. The angel would have many wings and many faces, all of them serene, white-hot, familiar. The angel would remind Camilo of home, a place we have never seen.

I perused and pronounced and treasured Camilo's notes. He wrote them especially for me, out of his past, imagining his future.

"P.S.

"¿Remember once you sent me a postcard from an ice cream factory, telling me it was your favorite food in the whole world? Well, here in Cuba we have a song about love being even better than the best ice cream, *mejor que el mantecado* (as if that extravagant praise is enough to explain everything) so perhaps you and I are not so different after all."

CAMILO, I IMAGINED, MUST DREAM WITH BIRD-EATING SPIDERS THE SIZE of his hand, with the courtship dances of scorpions, with corpses chopped up and hidden in cardboard boxes in the basements of ordinary families.

He would dream pictures sketched in the air, cartoons of one-eyed giants storming across a green land, bearded giants dragging jungle and rivers into the sea, hooded ogres burning minuscule fugitives at tiny wooden stakes the size of toothpicks.

Thieves, murderers, and cannibals must riot in those dungeons. They would recognize Camilo as a stranger, an outcast, a prisoner of conscience. They would recognize him by a swelling along the inner surface of one finger on his right hand, just below the fingernail. The brutes would know the meaning of this bruise, proof that he'd been busy scribbling secrets. The prisoners would call this bruise *"el callo intelectual,"* the "intellectual callus," but Camilo, always joking, would retort, "You mean *calloso*, not *callo*, el *calloso intelectual*, the 'intellectual callous,' a hardening of the heart, not of the skin." The criminals would trade objects they valued for the things Camilo needed, receiving from him cigarettes and sugar cubes, and giving him, in exchange, lumps of charcoal and pale shrouds stolen from the dead, allowing him to continue sketching his cartoons on the lacy surface of cloth. The charcoal, pressed against my brother's wounded finger, would make his flesh seem as dark and rough as broken wood. I would eventually receive those hieroglyphic scraps of shroud in dreams. They would be carried by the flaming wings of birds and by iridescent blue moths.

"P.S.

"You can't make the sea small by putting it into a basket. *El mar no se puede achicar con una canasta.*"

As my partner in love and in vigils, Alec had read through most of Camilo's letters and postscripts along with me, although he didn't enjoy re-reading them as I did, inhaling them, savoring their fury and hope.

Before reading Camilo's letters, Alec had never heard of José Martí. To me, not knowing the wistful poet Martí was like not knowing the story of David and Goliath. "He died a century ago, martyred for the cause of Cuban freedom from Spain," I had explained, "yet remaining alive in all our hearts, in our minds and songs." I said this as vehemently as if I had been raised in Cuba. The martyred poet had, after all, spent his entire adult life in exile. Martí had written that he had two homelands, Cuba and the night. "Night is everywhere," one of Camilo's notes proclaimed, "uniting us. *Nos une.*"

Martí, with his verse, had defeated Imperial Spain, weapons and troops. So why shouldn't Camilo, with his Chronicle, vanquish another giant?

April, then May . . . the heat grew torrid, overpowering, the sky such an intense blue that it hurt my eyes. The salt flats shimmered, and wavy lines were visible in the air. Mirages appeared and vanished. From cicadas hidden in the mesquite thickets came a constant high-pitched hum.

At night coyotes howled in the canyon. At dawn, as they finally caught and dismembered their prey, they yipped and yapped victory, sounding like monkeys shrieking in a jungle.

Every afternoon at exactly four o'clock (a time hot enough to roast ears of corn by lining them up on a red tile roof) an ice cream truck passed our house. Most of the affluent winter residents had already migrated north, like flocks of wild geese. Alec and Rocky and I were left behind to endure, along with the children of maids and gardeners, a summer that blazed and fumed. Together we all chased the ice cream truck, children racing behind Rocky, Alec following, my own weak legs trailing.

A few old couples also stayed. The men played golf at dawn and at dusk. The women formed bridge clubs and prayer chains and a tag patrol. They called each other up to share concerns about crises, dilemmas and heart attacks, asking for each other's prayers. They decided to include me, even though I told them I had never prayed out loud, not even when I saw the wind begin to shift as my mother leaped off her cliff, not even when Camilo was lost at sea and I was waiting with Marisol. Those, the Cuban prayers, had been silent ones, submerged, subconscious, instinctive, like the moans and grunts of wounded animals.

Now suddenly I was to be included in an old women's circle of gossip. Only it didn't feel like gossip, because nobody ever expressed disapproval of anyone else's disaster (the husband of one was recovering from a stroke, another had just found out she was in the early stages of lung cancer, others were losing granddaughters to crack cocaine, uncles to amnesia, sons to *ataques al corazón*, attacks against the heart). I was amazed when I realized that these frail old women didn't feel helpless. Their prayers were real, tangible, like life vests at sea. They kept us afloat. After asking the old folks to pray for Camilo in his Viper, I immediately felt overwhelmed by peace.

THE TAG PATROL STAYED UP ALL NIGHT CHASING AWAY THE YOUNG graffiti artists who'd begun migrating from distant urban neighborhoods to scrawl nicknames and cryptic symbols (shapes reminiscent of the footprints of seagulls and shorebirds, trailing in all directions across the sand of a waveswept beach at low tide) onto the walls surrounding ordinary houses. In retaliation, the tag patrol cruised along the perimeter of their walled city in golf carts, carrying walkie-talkies. Whenever they came across some young "scoundrel" spraying his name on a flat white surface, they called the Sheriff, who forced the teenagers to disguise their gang motifs. He gave them the choice of plain white paint or a mural.

The taggers were spice-hued sons of immigrants from tropical lands. They chose murals. Pretty soon the entire development looked like it had been dreamed up by a wild-eyed artist on some distant shore. The taggers produced tigers and strange birds, cinnamon faces peering out of green jungles, moons, suns, and constellations, children dangling like flowers from purple trees, serpents winding past rivers into the ruins of ancient cities. The Sheriff (son of a Yaqui Indian from Sonora) was satisfied. Secretly, I was delighted. The plain white golf course wall had left me feeling shut out or shut in, depending on where I happened to be standing at the moment. Now it was peopled by fantasies that looked very much like my own array of imagined feral memories.

*　　　　　*

THEN SOMEONE SPRAY-PAINTED THE SINGLE WORD "REALITY" IN BOLD black letters across one side of the ice cream truck. It was the side which always faced our adobe house as the truck passed along our street from east to west, following the flaming path of an incandescent sun.

Every afternoon when Rocky spotted the "Reality" truck and heard its cheerful bell-like song, she charged toward it, terrifying the driver until he learned to love her smile of greeting (at first he thought the smile was a silent snarl).

The ice cream vendor eventually covered up the word "Reality," trying to replace it with "World's Best Fudge Ripple," but the black letters of "Reality" still showed through the new paint, faintly, like a ghost under a sheet at Halloween, like the face of a frightened child in disguise.

Along with Rocky and Alec and the neighborhood children, I chased the Reality truck. It really did have the best fudge ripple I had ever tasted. Or maybe it was just the heat that inspired appreciation. I considered myself a connoisseur, an ice cream tasting expert. Sometimes I thought that if things didn't work out with Alec I would go someplace truly hot and open a World's Best Malt Shop, or land a job as taste-tester for Dove Bar, or sell quarts of homemade turtle pie, Mississippi mud, and triple chocolate passion. I could simply imagine love instead of experiencing it, and along the way, like Vicente Peregrín in his cave, I could take up the chains of mythology, merge the old and new, weave Greek images into a maze of medieval fantasy and indigenous Cuban dreams.

I thought about what I would do if Camilo was never released, if he died in the Viper or was transferred to one of the castle dungeons, or even if he was released from prison but never managed to get out of Cuba.

I was developing valuable skills, I reflected ruefully, even if I was doing most of it against my will: patience, prayer, love-which-is-better-than-ice-cream, feeling like part of an odd whimsical family and like part of a crazy, mixed-up community.

"There's not much else," Alec commented when I enumerated my doubts about the value of these skills. "You've just about named every accomplishment that matters, aside from tree-ring dating, of course, so we can understand our past, and the deciphering of medieval script, so we can make wild guesses about the continuation of that legacy."

We often hiked far up the canyon, where we made love outdoors, the only place either one of us had ever really felt at home. Love felt like cool water on a hot day, like shade on a sand dune, like untroubled sleep after a week of nightmares.

Rocky slept in the shade of a fan palm, and as a special gesture of love, when it was time to get dressed and head for our small whitewashed house, I called her "Jo" and I even called the house "home."

Wolfhounds are natural companions and hunting dogs, born to run ahead of a horse all day. Their long legs and easy lope carry them across hills without effort. Yet as soon as they have the chance, they seek out the coolness of shade, where they rest as easily as they run. They belong outdoors. As soon as they enter a house, their size makes them clumsy, their long fluffy tails knock down vases, their curiosity leads them into pantries and refrigerators. They push doors open, using their noses as prods. They lick things they aren't supposed to touch, and explore closets and shelves meant only for human treasures. Alec said our big dog was a lot like our love, rambunctious, unpredictable and enormous, impossible to ignore.

Alec finally confessed that he'd received Rocky ("Jo," he insisted) the same way I had. She'd just showed up on his porch in Tucson one day, moved into an empty crate he'd left lying around after unpacking a computer, and claimed it all as her own, everything, the crate and porch, Alec's food, his time, his heart. "She's like a giant Cupid," Alec said. Then he admitted he was afraid she might leave the same way, abandon us both and wander off to claim someone else, to bring some other couple together, choose two strangers and match them, transform them into a family. A big, furry gray Cupid smiling and aiming celestial arrowheads.

I harbored the same fear. We both knew we weren't really talking about a dog or an image of Cupid, but about the way love just shows up unexpectedly, giving the impression that it could also choose to leave, abruptly, without notice or warning, without signals, like the drifting of continents or the racing of stars across galaxies.

Could I ever stop loving Alec overnight? What about Camilo and Marisol? Somehow, through terror and anxiety, we had been pressed into a remotely linked three-cornered family, not our idea of a family, but a family nonetheless. It could just as easily be broken apart, a puzzle with discarded pieces, fragments of time and space forgotten.

But Alec and I hadn't been separated by arguments or restless dreams (I thought of returning to Cuba as a martyr; Alec spoke of spending a summer hunting and fishing on the Alaskan tundra, seeking out a total absence of trees, chasing salmon and bears) or unexplained moods of withdrawal and silence.

The sea hadn't separated my makeshift family. Prison walls and postal censors and the economic theories of military commanders hadn't managed to pry us apart. I felt safe.

In the evenings we watched shooting stars and recalled foreign myths. I told Alec and Rocky the legend of an old couple who lived in a marshy land inhabited mostly by birds and wild men. Angels came seeking refuge, but none of the savage, impious race of swamp dwellers would take them in. The old couple fed them and filled their wineglasses. No matter how much the angels drank, their glasses never emptied. That is how the old man and his wife knew they were in the presence of messengers of wind and fire.

The angels sent the old folks up to the top of a mountain to escape a flood. From the mountaintop they watched as their hut was destroyed. When the floodwater receded, the hut had become a mansion of marble. The angels offered the old couple a reward for their hospitality. The man and his wife said all they wanted was to die at the same time, so that neither would be left behind on this earth, lonely. So the angels turned them into two trees, an oak tree and a lime. "The two trees," I concluded, "still grow very close together, their branches touching, beside the ruins of a marble wall far across the sea."

I remembered seeing the two trees and the white wall in Phrygia, many years earlier, when I was just a child and still thought of love as a spirited horse with pale wings. I remembered hearing the legend, originally a pagan tale, converted to its Christian version later, the immortal visitors no longer supermen, but simply gentle messengers of a loving God.

Alec counted half a dozen meteors that night, as we wondered why no one had bothered to modernize the constellations, changing Orion into a robot and calling the Big Dipper a laser gun.

"I wonder," Alec said, watching the sky, "exactly when people suddenly decided to give up telling stories about the past, and replace them with futuristic tales instead, science fiction, space travel, life in cities beneath the sea. That crossroads in time," he speculated, "must have been very recent. We must be one of the first generations to abandon our ancestors." He said it exactly the way he would report a tree-ring count.

Wistfully, I grinned and confessed, "I can't name the day when I finally realized I would never turn into Pegasus, or even find him grazing at the edge of a quiet pool. But somewhere along the way I had to accept it, reluctantly. It's called growing up, but maybe it should be called growing down instead, growing smaller inside, less expectant. But you know, I still can't help imagining that somehow, if I run fast enough, I might find myself in the sky, up there above clouds, flying. It's not a nightdream or a daydream, but a craving, like realizing that you want a milkshake for breakfast instead of eggs or cereal."

With Alec close by, I didn't attempt to fly, but simply hovered close to reality, waiting, watching the desert shimmer and flash. May passed, and June was devoured by a bewildering shower of decisions.

Once God decided to make us capable of love, He started sending opportunities to prove it. Without warning, we were asked to absorb into our home a refugee who was not Camilo, a stranger who needed help. We found ourselves overwhelmed by need.

"He's making us practice, isn't He?" I asked Alec.

He said he didn't know why God behaved the way He did, but forcing us to practice did seem a likely motive. "After all, no musician would go on stage without rehearsals. Maybe we're supposed to treat love like music, sharpen our skills, exercise our voices."

The refugee was a Peruvian Indian girl who, while fleeing the Shining Path rebels on a remote Andean peak, had been caught by one of the notorious predatory "slave cats" who roam the region, and was sold into twentieth-century bondage. She was purchased by a group of brutal men who dragged her across five thousand miles of wilderness, through strangled jungle and rocky canyons, across a dozen borders. In the North she was sold again and again, each time for a hefty profit. She ended up working as a maid in one of the condominiums facing our panoramic golf course wall.

She cried all day and all night, until eventually her new employer took her to the prayer chain in dismay. Startled, the prayer ladies brought her to my door at midnight, saying, "You speak Spanish, talk to her, find out what's wrong with her, why is she so sad?" They said her employer thought she'd come to the U.S. of her own free will, looking for work.

The girl could barely speak Spanish. Her phrases were sprinkled with the Quechua of her Inca ancestors. She spoke mostly in the present tense and in infinitives. As an expression of wonder, she would repeat, "*¡Saber! ¡*To know!" after nearly everything she said about her life. Alec said it made her sound like a philosopher, like a Socrates in disguise.

She couldn't read or write. She couldn't count, weigh, or measure. She didn't know how old she was or how many brothers she had. She had never seen a calendar or a map.

She loved flowers, and she moved about Alec's garden collecting seeds in the palm of her hand, then wrapping them in scraps of paper. She was hoarding the seeds for her journey home, she said, swearing that if she found a way to get home she would never leave again without her brothers and sisters. She said she had been unbearably lonely living in a house where no one understood anything she said.

She thought Rocky was a small horse, a pony with deer eyes,

or some sort of gray woolly llama without the usual strong humped back.

She was terrified of men, even Alec, who always treated her kindly.

She was baffled by gadgets. She had never seen a vacuum cleaner or garbage disposal. She didn't know how to use a telephone, but held it up and spoke into the wrong end, trying to call her church in Cuzco to ask the priests for advice on how to get home.

"I to see the whole world," she exclaimed when we asked her what she planned to do next. *"Yo ver el mundo entero."*

She said her home was a stone shack near a lake in the mountains. She said she couldn't understand a home with more than one room and with no guinea pigs caged in the corners where they could be fed shoots of barley so they could grow fat and be eaten on feast days.

"To miss the singing of my sisters," she mourned, *"extrañar a las canciones de mis hermanas.* And the flutes of my brothers, *mis hermanos."*

I could hear their songs emerging from potato fields at the rim of a mountain lake, the wistful strains of flutes coming down from high meadows, where brothers guarded their small flocks of sheep and llamas.

Our new friend told ghost stories, and believed them vehemently. She also believed her dreams. Angels who spoke to her in dreams, she said, were always obeyed.

She listened patiently to my tale of Camilo, saying it was a familiar dilemma, it happened every day, this disappearing of brothers. She advised me to pretend I'd never had a brother, especially if anyone asked. She said, "To tell them you don't know, you not to remember. *No acordarse."*

She said she had some brothers who were rebels, *rebeldes*, and others who were government soldiers, *soldados* instructed to destroy the uprising. She said she had watched them try to kill each other at a gathering of her family on a feast day. She said some of them had succeeded in killing each other, she didn't know how many. "¡If anyone to ask, I to say I never to have any brothers at all, just sisters! Brothers," she insisted, "are to be dangerous, *peligrosos*, you never to tell which one to be in trouble with the police or the drug lords or the Shining Path, *el Sendero Luminoso*. Brothers," she added, "*Los hermanos siempre esconderse*, they are always to hide, always to tell you not to say you know them."

ALEC SERVED HER A MEAL OF DEEP-FRIED CATFISH, HUSH PUPPIES, AND mustard greens with bacon. She said she felt right at home. She said we could be her family now. She said Alec could even be her brother. She said she had noticed that in the North women weren't secretive about having brothers.

The prayer chain ladies came for their Peruvian waif. They asked me what she had said, why was she always crying, always afraid.

I answered, "She's sad because she's lonely, and she's afraid of slavery. She wants to sing with her sisters."

They left the girl with us, waving their hands in confusion, saying, "No, she must be lying, it's impossible to be held as a slave these days, it just doesn't happen." They insisted their friend had hired her from a temporary agency, the same way everyone always hired maids.

THE GIRL STAYED WITH US WHILE WE WAITED FOR CAMILO. SHE HELPED ME imagine his dungeon, his window, his angel. She helped me wait for letters from Marisol. She said she was good at waiting. She said every time anyone in her family climbed a mountain pass, they add one more stone to a pile of rocks perched at the summit. She explained that as far as anyone can remember this has always been done, so that some of the piles are very tall and very wide at the base, like small man-made mountains resting on top of the big God-made ones. She described this small gesture of moving one small stone as a reverent and significant action, an act of faith and gratitude, a reminder to be thankful for one more survival, one more journey from potato field to market, or back.

Our new friend longed to return home. Her face grew horrified when she described the condos to us in the same way she planned to describe them someday to her sisters. Too big, too empty, too many windows, too much silence. She showed no signs of recovering from her homesickness. The Shining Path, she insisted, couldn't keep her away from her sisters, even if it had succeeded in separating her brothers from each other and from her and from their herds and their flutes.

We drove her to Los Angeles and put her on an airplane to Lima. She left with a suitcase full of hand-me-down clothes and flower seeds, relieved to be going home, both heartbroken (for her past) and ecstatic (for her imagined future) at the same time.

At the airport she asked Alec to buy her a magazine from one of the stands. She leafed through its shiny pages, promising that next time we saw her she would know how to read.

"I to stand on the street in Cuzco," she told us in her childlike version of present-tense Spanish, "and I to watch television through the window of a store, *por la ventana.* Cartoons, bright colors, dogs to chase cats, cats to chase yellow birds. Children to play tricks on their parents and neighbors, *los vecinos.*

"Someday to return to *Estados Unidos,*" she vowed, "to come with all my sisters and as many of my brothers as . . ." She paused. "The same sun," she vowed, "to shine on all of us, the same rain, everyone wet. *El mismo sol, la misma lluvia. Se mojan todos.*"

"People should not be lonely," Alec agreed. "We can tolerate just about anything, but not that. When I was little I wanted a pet, but it wasn't allowed. We were always moving, always packing. So I ran around outside wherever we were, catching any little creature I could find. I kept tiny poisonous frogs in my room, and bug-eyed chameleons, and shiny green beetles, and once, in India, I caught a wounded bird and kept it until it was healed. All of this secretly, in boxes under beds, or behind dressers, or on shelves in the hidden parts of dark closets."

Suddenly I was overcome by a fleeting realization that my obsessions (Cuba, Camilo, our father's unquiet ghost, the wistfully rhymed dreams of Martí, my ancestors' Chronicle) were difficult for Alec to endure. We spent much of our time together analyzing an island he'd never seen, people he'd never met, a helplessness neither of us could deny, and a hope that, alone, we outsiders, despite our wealth of freedom, could not fulfill.

"I wanted a pet too," I told our Peruvian friend right before she got on her airplane. "Only I wanted a friendship even more, *un amistad,* so I took my imaginary half brother with me wherever we went. I never had the chance to find any other kind of friend than the kind you imagine. Instead, I received objects and stories, other people's legends." Carved ostrich eggs, an old ivory row of sculptured elephants linked trunk to tail, a Hupa basketry cap, a Sioux buffalo robe, stories about flying horses and old people who turn into trees.

I thought of all the objects I had received in Peru while my mother was collecting mummies for sale. A wooden flask the Incas used for drinking llama blood during sacrificial rituals. A rug woven from the longest, softest hair of an alpaca. A tiny silver figurine in the shape of a *vicuña*.

The girl repeated that she would soon learn to read. She said it in English, the way Alec had taught her the night before, in the present tense, in the infinitive: "I to learn to read." It sounded like a lament, the English "I" when spoken with passion becoming the universal Spanish-language word of anguish, "*¡Ay!*"

She stood in the airport lounge, between a candy machine and a drinking fountain, promising herself that soon she would have children, and that they would go to school. "I to learn to drive a car," she uttered, a pledge so daring, so strange, so bold, that we all stood together laughing at the thought of a car winding its way through the high narrow footpaths of her mountain stronghold.

"I to send you a mountain herb which to make you happy," she told me.

I answered, "No, don't send herbs. Here we can't find happiness in leaves chewed or swallowed," but she insisted, "If only to find my leaf here, to be happy."

Then she warned me, "If your father's ghost to speak in to dream, you to obey, but not to answer. To answer a ghost is to die, to accept death."

I LEFT THE AIRPORT WITH ALEC, CONFUSED BY THE PERUVIAN GIRL'S advice, confused about time, space, love. No answering ghosts in dreams, no happiness without a magical leaf from a certain tree. When we arrived home, after passing monstrous sprawling cities, life-size statues of dinosaurs, and fields of wind machines perched on barren slopes (looking so much like Don Quixote's windmills that I would not have been surprised to see lean helmeted knights galloping on bony steeds), I set about the task of reading and re-reading every word Camilo ever wrote, feeling certain that if I listened to my paper half brother long enough and often enough, he would come to life, and all confusion would be dispelled:

"P.S.

"*Hace mucho tiempo,* long ago, *El Comandante* discovered that our father had been quietly and surreptitiously investigating human rights violations. So he arranged the assassination of our father, threatened your mother, frightening her into fleeing (because your mother was, after all, not a Cuban citizen, so the Commander knew he could never own her completely, and this made her unfamiliar, unpredictable, dangerous) and he bribed my mother, although she never knew she was being purchased, not until much later. In this land of scarcity my mother received houses, cars, privileges, a Sugar Ministry position, respect. The Commander found it easy to convince my mother that her husband's mysterious death was accidental, an unfortunate tragedy, perhaps even a martyrdom of sorts, a loss for the sake of the revolution. No, she was not the Commander's courtesan, do not misunderstand me. He did not touch her flesh, only her spirit. He enslaved her by capturing her belief. You know what George Bernard Shaw said about Don Quixote: 'Reading made Don Quixote a gentleman, but believing what he read made him mad.'

"Of course, in exchange for her belief, my mother received houses and cars (now they mean nothing to her, she doesn't want them, doesn't need more than one house, more than one car, but the Commander won't take them back, he won't give them to someone who has nothing. All rewards go to the Old Guard, to the Inner Circle, the Nomenklatura, those who believe. By accepting the Commander's dream she lost both her family and her awareness of that loss, her sense of family. She became a collaborator, the Commander's inadvertent accomplice. She meant no harm. In fact, her intentions were honorable, the feeding of children born to strangers, the offering of medicine to suffering peasants. Was it not your northern poet Robert Frost who said: '¿Why abandon a belief merely because it ceases to be true?' And remember the warning of Dante, who swore that the hottest places in hell are reserved for those who in time of great moral crisis maintain their neutrality. And so the chain of my thought continues, as I strive to forgive our parents' generation. . . ."

FORGIVING OUR ANCESTORS WAS THE LAST THING ON MY MIND. THE chain of Camilo's thought bound me in a different way. I was worried about him, and about Marisol, Alina, even the Peruvian *andariega*, the wanderer. I fretted over my perplexity when faced with chances to love.

Interruptions came one after the other, swallowing the month of June. Immersion in Camilo's dilemma had to wait. Two of the prayer chain ladies came searching for me as I roamed Alec's garden, a stack of Camilo's letters clutched in my hand. I imagined that if I held them up to the sun, additional messages might appear, notes penned with invisible ink would take form.

The two neighbors said that a local crisis was in progress. An old man from one of the condos had built a contraption secretly, in his garage, and now he was taking it out, and preparing to leave his wife of fifty-three years behind, desolate, abandoned. "We must pray for him," came their faithful chorus.

With an irritated sigh, I folded Camilo's letters and went with my new friends to watch as the old man flew away in a golf cart he'd fitted with a helicopter propeller and an assortment of other odd-shaped metallic appendages. His flying golf cart had the appearance of an enormous shiny insect as it vanished into the sky over the distant salt flats, one more mirage absorbed into the heat. His wife, standing next to us, was weeping and saying, "He calls himself Icarus."

We climbed into my jeep and followed him out to the salt flats, bumping our way across dunes and dry washes. Icarus had landed on the flat white bed of the ancient sea, unharmed. He said he knew enough to stay low, far away from the sun.

He left his invention where it landed and returned home with his wife. That night the two of them came to our house at Alec's request, for a meal of tandoori lamb and curried cheese. Rocky licked the old man's fingers. His wife had already forgiven him. We watched the stars and consumed Alec's best ice cream pie, a homemade coffee-flavored pie, decorated with slivers of toasted hazelnut arranged along layers of fudge and caramel. Being surrounded by neighbors, I reflected, was not so frightening after all.

SUMMER GREW LIKE A TYPHOON, PREDICTABLE, YET DEFYING PREPARATIONS for its power. We drooped beneath its weight. I could barely find the energy to pray for Camilo. The smoke trees bloomed a brilliant purple against a cornflower-blue sky. The petals, shedding onto the desert sand, formed little abstract patterns reminiscent of Navajo sand paintings.

Alina finally called from Spain. Her voice, reaching me across oceans and time zones, was distant, delicate, hopeful. She said that if she kept trying to communicate with Camilo he would be persecuted more fiercely than ever, because she was a defector, and therefore branded as a traitor to the revolution, a deserter. She said she would write to me, I would find ways to smuggle letters to Camilo, we would certainly have the cooperation of the Spanish cousins and plenty of money from their ancestral reserves of gold, and together, by coordinating all this, by writing in code (she would send me a key) we would surely succeed in setting Camilo free.

Her enthusiasm was contagious. I found myself shivering despite the afternoon heat. We chatted for awhile, shared phrases of optimism and reassurance, exchanged wishes, then said good-bye, until later, until soon.

I hung up, losing my connection to her hope, then went outside, still shivering. A glance at the giant thermometer Alec had hung (he said it was to "let us know how miserable we are") on the patio told me the air surrounding my skin had reached one hundred and eighteen degrees Fahrenheit in the shade. Rocky lay panting and dozing beneath the enormous numbers of the thermometer, shaped like a canary-yellow sun with little blazes of orange fire emerging all around the perimeter. I walked out into the garden, beneath a blaze of real flame, remembering that angels were not cool and icy white like our statues of them, but fiery and translucent, like hot gusts of wind.

MARISOL SENT TWO VERSIONS OF THE SAME LETTER. ONE WAS A SIMPLE version mailed from the house of a cousin in Miami, the other a complex rendition of the same anxieties, the same sentences only in their ornate forms, embroidered with borders of sentiment and verse.

In the clear form I saw that she had no idea what was going on anywhere. She hadn't received any of my letters. She hadn't heard from Alina or anyone in Spain. She felt cut off from the world. She had taken to hiding in one of her more remote houses, traveling into Havana only to check the mail or to beg for a chance to visit Camilo.

She wrote: "As bad as it is for him, it could have been even worse. He could have been a *married* rafter, *un balsero casado*, like so many of these young men who throw themselves into the sea. Then his arrest would have brought not only his own despair, *desesperación*, and my agony, *agonía*, but the pain, *el dolor*, of a deserted wife as well. It would have ended in divorce. Very few wives can survive the dual burden of a husband who flees the homeland promising to find some way to rescue her later, from afar, and at the same time the burden of persecution and harassment by the police for alleged collaboration, for keeping the flight secret, for making plans, scheming, etc. Already the strains on our families are so great, without all this. Already the women feel they serve double duty, working at their government jobs all day, then having to wait for hours in the ration lines, and for what, a handful of rice, a few grains per day at most, one meal a day, while the husband waits for his dinner, expects miracles to emerge from these empty kitchens, some blame the wife instead of the tyranny, some get angry when the wife is tired after such a day. And to make it worse, the young couples have no homes, no new houses are being constructed. They have to divide rooms and share with in-laws or siblings. Some of the women don't want to bring children into Option Zero. ¡If you think our situation was bad when you were here last summer, imagine, *imagínate,* how much worse it is now, every day a little worse, a little more impossible to bear!"

I TRIED TO ANSWER MARISOL'S PLEAS FOR INFORMATION ON THE PROGRESS of our negotiations. It was all so complicated, involving so many people, me, Alec, Alina, the Miamense and Spanish cousins, the Viper officials, all controlled by the anonymous whim of a single censor, and ultimately, by the circuitous route outlined by *El Comandante* and his capricious moods.

I tried to keep Marisol updated, but I myself knew so little! Each of us could see only a small portion of the truth. We were like the blind men touching an elephant, each feeling and describing a different form, each version truthful, yet none accurate. Alina was directing the entire process, but even she knew only what she could learn from across oceans and centuries.

When I wrote to Marisol I had to speak in circles. I had to take myself out of my real body and say, "Plans for my trip to Spain are underway," when I was actually trying to say, "Plans for Camilo's trip . . ."

I felt forced to become a divided person, half there in the desert and half in Cuba. But it was not the Cuba inhabited by Marisol and Camilo. It was some other Cuba, a Cuba where one could take refuge from attack, Vicente's imaginary island of Antilia.

I needed to forgive, but instead I hated. I hated the censor. I hated him more than the Commander. I hated him (or her) because throughout this storm of emotions, only the censor could remain anonymous, remote, intact. And I was ashamed of my hatred, knowing that on some other island of time or space, I might have hired myself out, proudly, as a censor or prison guard.

*   *

WHILE WE WAITED FOR CAMILO, ALEC DISCOVERED THAT THE NEWLY elected government of our freshly sprouted desert community was using tax dollars to sunbathe on the Seychelles Islands. Alec had been contracted by the Arid Lands Research Institute to collect samples of acacia wood in drought-stricken regions of Kenya. On his way home, he spotted our new mayor and his entire city council (a conglomeration of ambitious local small businessmen with no experience or qualifications for governing: one was a plumber, another ran a hamburger stand, another labeled himself "consultant" but had never done anything beyond hire himself out to get ordinary people excited about expensive projects they could never afford to complete) in Madagascar, boarding a cruise for the Seychelles.

Alec conducted a little flurry of swift investigations, a few questions here and there, until he concluded, correctly as it turned out after a brief series of scandalous local hearings, that the mayor and city council of our newborn golf course community had billed the trip to their constituents as a "research" project, ostensibly to prepare themselves for the onslaught of tourism expected to strike our windswept desert at any moment. They claimed to be studying the architecture of resort communities.

Their corruption gave us just a taste of the bitterness Camilo must have felt when, as a young boy, he explored the cave beneath our ancestral home at the heart of Cuba, and learned the details of our father's murder. Suddenly we saw that the dreaded things of Cuba were not unique. "Could it happen here?" Alec asked, aghast.

*   *

SUCCESS CAME IN FLASHES, LIKE BURSTS OF LIGHTNING IN A DARK SKY. Marisol sent a smuggled letter. On the first of July, Alina called from a tiny village in southern Spain, not far from the Portuguese border: After nearly a year of captivity, my brother was finally out of the Viper, although he was not yet out of Cuba. We were all one step closer to the light shed by love.

9
¿to Love?

¿Amar? ¡Eso es un voto! Es un espíritu
Que a otro se libra

To love? That is a vote! It's a spirit
That sets someone else free

JOSÉ MARTÍ

A FTER HEARING AND READING THE MIRACULOUS NEWS, I PULLED AN atlas off the shelf of my mother's library, and found a map of Extremadura, the names landing like feathery leaves resting against my tongue: *Fuente de Cantos*, Fountain of Songs, *Jerez de la Frontera*, Sherry of the Horsemen, *Granja de Torrehermosa*, Ranch of the Beautiful Tower, *Arroyo de la Luz*, Stream of Light. From deep within the heart of the Caribbean, Camilo's triumphant message had reached me through a Mediterranean village haunted by the ghosts of Inquisitors, *conquistadores*, and poets.

Exultant, I felt compelled to race all over our nascent desert town, through a heat that approached the fervor of madness, a heat that attained, on that marvelous blue day, at high noon, a full one hundred and twenty-five degrees Fahrenheit, in the shade, as measured by Alec's cheerful sun-shaped thermometer. July, in our hometown, was a month designed for a solar version of lunacy.

Rocky raced with me. We chased down every prayer-chain link we could find, begging each to call the others and help me say thanks to God for Camilo's partial and tentative release.

SOME MIRACLES ARE INSTANTANEOUS TRANSFORMATIONS. OTHERS ARE gradual metamorphoses. Many require a vigil, a ripening, gestation. These, like Camilo's path to freedom, emerge slowly and painfully, passing from hidden darkness to astounding light the way a subterranean creature burrows toward the surface, earth filling its eyes, gravel clogging its throat.

Immediately, I began to receive a shower of detailed letters from my brother, letters written after his release, then smuggled, swiftly, from Cuba to Spain, then back to the *Américas*, to my scalding hot, raging mad corner of a vast, incomprehensible desert:

> "Dear Sister Carmen,
>
> "At first I thought you were arrogant, flaunting your freedom-by-birth, your total, perhaps excessive liberty, your permission to think, speak, write, shout, sing anything you please.
>
> "Now I see that your obscure gestures toward my freedom (I learned of these efforts from my mother and Alina and from some of the Spanish cousins, five centuries removed, who finally came to pay both their respects and their money to the Commander himself, for old times' sake, in memory of *La Edad de Oro*, the conquerors' Age of Gold, our shared inheritance, the

Conquest, in memory of victory which is always
accompanied by defeat), yes, your efforts were tiny but
eventually fruitful, seeds from which the remainder grew,
mustard seeds, if we are to believe the parables (¿do we?)
of our true Lord.

"I imagine you have continued on with your daily life
during all of this, seldom thinking of us, of your brief
foray into this netherworld you glimpsed but did not
experience.

"I imagine you have been happy this year, with your
liberty and your true-love Alec, and that immense puppy
you wrote to my mother about, and all the rest, the
garden, the silk birds and floating demon, the fevers, tree
rings, luxurious exotic foods, everything you described so
fully for my entertainment in the Viper (no, that was not
your purpose in writing, but my mother always found a
way to get the letters in to me, so that I could enjoy
distant images of unfamiliar ways; for this I thank you
even more than for your conscious efforts; for this I
lived, for the inadvertent moments of awareness of a
world outside my cell) and I must tell you that both my
mother and I have treasured and resented every luminous
word you helped transfer into our perpetual gloom.

"Soon, if God wills, I am to arrive in Spain and be
reunited with Alina, my heart's desire. The Spanish
cousins have offered to help me get started in my second
career. I will need the Chronicle. I hope it has served
you well, taught you, as it taught my father, I'm sorry, I
mean *our* father, about the innate perseverance of love.

"When my training in Spain is complete, I will send

for you from Miami. You were, after all, my witness at
the onset of this journey, and soon you will be my
witness at its conclusion, ¿no?"

As usual, there was no signature, no return address, no date, as
if Camilo had grown so accustomed to secrecy that even outside
the Viper, he could no longer reveal his surroundings.

The long, searching monologue continued:

"This is how it was the day I discovered our ancestors'
Chronicle and their bones, along with our father's
documents:

"We traveled from Havana to the heart of the island
to visit cousins (¡the Peregrín family has an unlimited
supply of distant relatives!) Vicente's house was empty,
too old and ruined for modern human habitation. The
revolutionary government had left it standing because it
was a vestige of the Age of Gold and might eventually fit
into some museum designed to expose the horrors of the
Conquest and colonialism.

"Horrors, yes, but as a child I saw our ancestral home
not as a symbol, but as an enchanted castle or a tent in
the woods. I was happy exploring its crumbling walls.
Suddenly I fell into the dark cave entrance, tumbling
down through a broken tile in the floor. I landed there,
in that world without light, and quickly, I climbed back
out, then secretly, cautiously, fetched a lantern from my
cousins' house a few kilometers away.

"If you cannot imagine a house built over a cave, just
think of the conveniences: the outhouse emptied into an

underground stream, washing all filth out to sea. Fleeing
during any emergency was easy in a house underlain by
secret passageways. Hiding was a part of daily life,
whether from hurricanes, fires, pirates, wars, or the
Inquisition.

"I went back down, determined to discover any
treasures hidden there. Perhaps if you were Cuban you
could understand islands. Here we grow up immersed in
tales of pirate gold, even now, despite the Commander,
despite *Comunismo*. Whatever else Cuba has become, it is
still the Caribbean, still hovering at the edge of the map.

"I found two skeletons in an embrace, between them
the Chronicle, carefully wrapped and bound. I didn't
read it right away. First I searched for gold doubloons,
for pieces-of-eight, for gold-handled swords embedded
with Colombian emeralds, with pearls from the palaces
of mermaids.

"There are many other skeletons in that cavern, if you
look around (someday you will). Vicente and Sirena must
have noticed them. I believe they were Sirena's ancestors,
buried there ceremonially or accidentally, while hiding.
Some of the corpses died face down, as if executed,
others face up, hands crossed over the chest in a gesture
of tranquillity.

"I found beads, ceramic jars, astronomical charts
scratched into rock walls (native constellations, pathways
of the sun and moon) but I left everything intact, the
skeletons untouched, the artifacts in place. It is all there
for you to rediscover on your own. All I took was the
Chronicle, along with its thick stack of modern pages,

the laments and accusations added by our father right
before his death.

"Sirena was wearing a necklace when she died, stone
beads with a green frog-shaped pendant. Vicente
clutched a sword (not gold-handled) and a shield. An
empty wooden chest stood open nearby, robbed of its
contents centuries before I found it (gold, as we know
from the Chronicle, Inca gold, and silver, emeralds,
pearls). I kept my discovery secret for a long time.
Eventually, after reading our father's painstakingly
deciphered modern version of Vicente's script, and after
reading the new documents, our father's work, I told my
mother.

"Naturally, she didn't believe me. ¿Who would? So I
sneaked the whole package of documents to Havana,
where we were well-known as loyal, hard-line
Communists. The Neighborhood Committee rarely
questioned us. We were never searched by the secret
police. As my revolutionary mother's son, I was treated
with respect. We always attended every rally, every
parade, every interminable speech. We always stayed
until the end, no matter how long the harangue, and you
know our Commander, a speaker of Guinness-record-
book proportions, to him ten hours are as nothing, even
in hot sun or pouring rain; hurricane winds barely elicit a
pause in his train of thought. We always stayed to the
end, cheering slogans, smiling, shouting louder than
anyone else, and we held up banners and praised the
Commander's brilliance. My mother said he was lit from
within, you could see him glowing, he was a man on fire

(as I got older I saw that you could also smell the smoke, taste the ash) so we believed we were safe, and for a long time we were. . . ."

THESE LONG, SINUOUS LETTERS SEEMED SO CALM NOW THAT THE REAL-life drama was half finished. Out of the Viper, but still in Cuba, my brother had become a historian. As if we had all the time in the world, no limits, no calendars, no gnawing *ratos*, my bilingual "rats of time."

NEWS OF CAMILO'S RELEASE FROM THE VIPER ARRIVED JUST IN TIME FOR our little desert town's first official Fourth of July chili cook-off. Alec won by a long shot. We celebrated with as many of the neighbors as we could find (more and more were fleeing the searing heat of summer, flying north) and when we learned that July was also National Ice Cream month, Alec hastily whipped up a few batches of tin roof, peanut butter 'n fudge brownie, and cookies 'n cream, and he offered prizes (simple things, T-shirts, balloons, baseball caps) at a "Heat Wave Ice Cream Eating Con-test." Most of the contestants were adults, but all of the winners were children. Alec said that aside from adopting Rocky and me, dreaming up the contest was the third best thing he'd ever done. The second best, he added, was helping me dream with Camilo's freedom.

Of course, even though Camilo was now half free (in the first and most basic sense of the word, that is, no longer imprisoned between dungeon walls) I still continued dreaming with him and his angel in their cell, and I dreamed with Camilo drowning. In the dream, all around us others were gliding contentedly along the slick shiny surfaces of massive waves. They skated on the sea, surfing, skiing, waltzing, moon-walking. Only my brother and I were sucked into the ominous depths between a fiercely swirling whirlpool . . . I dreamed with exotic birds, hornbills, kingfishers, lorikeets, macaws, bee-eaters, golden-breasted mynahs, fruit doves, citron-crested cockatoos, tanagers, green Cuban parrots, monkey-eating eagles.

The birds could speak. They conversed in the extinct tongue of Sirena's cave-dwelling tribe. They were telling each other my secrets. Then the creatures switched easily to Spanish, followed by Arabic, Yoruba, English, Russian . . . I dreamed with winged beasts of every sort, flying squirrels, gliding geckos, flying fish, dragonflies. Peregrine falcons . . . I dreamed with the Peregrín family in flight, Vicente, Sirena, then slaves and masters, then rebels, Camilo, Alina, Marisol, Vicente and Sirena, all soaring away into blue space . . .

SUDDENLY, AS I RACED ALL OVER THE DESERT SHARING MY GOOD NEWS and inviting children to Alec's Fourth of July Heat Wave Ice Cream Eating Contest, it occurred to me that someday when I grew old, everything I dreamed while young would return to me: flying horses, birds, waves, my imaginary half brother accompanying me on expeditions to faraway places as my mother collects the artifacts of ghostly strangers.

I REMEMBERED BEING DRAGGED THROUGH TOMBS IN GUANAJUATO, WHILE my mother bargained with a skeleton-vendor for the artifacts found with posed skulls. That night I was visited by a floating demon-skull that spoke to me in a language I couldn't understand. I thought I had no one to tell except my imaginary half brother (in my fear I'd forgotten, momentarily, about talking to God).

I remembered climbing a volcano on horseback. Beneath the

lava traversed by my horse's hoofs, the remains of a buried village could be made out, roasted walls, broken bricks, a church steeple protruding from a cleft between black boulders. The horse spooked and ran away with me, threatening to topple me over a crusted lava cliff. But my imaginary half brother was at my side, and he grabbed the bridle and hung on, pulling the horse to a reluctant halt, leaving me staring out over the brink of the precipice, gazing into blue.

I remembered lying deathly ill, feverish and trembling, in an isolated cabin on the shores of Lake Atitlán in the Guatemalan Highlands. My mother left me alone while she floated away on a small boat, across the lake, to the foot of one of the beautifully symmetrical twin volcanic peaks, where she planned to buy blouses from a village where the women covered every inch of their cloth with embroidered birds of every size, form, and hue.

My mother was always taking me to places where strange fevers attacked us, never the same fever twice. She would recover swiftly and easily, while I, too young and small, lingered between reality and dream.

That day, while my mother was gone, I would have died, but a young Maya boy came to the door of the cabin and peered in. Seeing me so weak and scalded by fever, he brought me soup and a brew of herbs. He held my head and made me drink the heat. He plastered wet leaves all over my forehead, and said, in broken Spanish, that their fragrance would cure me.

Then he backed out of the door, smiling and speaking a language I couldn't understand. I knew he was an angel. I turned to my imaginary half brother and asked him what the angel had said. My brother said he'd only heard a melody, like birdsong, without words.

When my mother returned to the cabin with her purchased

mountain of embroidered birds, she was surprised to find me well. She gave me a blouse overwhelmed by birds, and I wore it for years, until the threads fell away from the seams.

NOW, WITH CAMILO HALF FREE, I FELT JUST AS I HAD WHEN I SAW THAT blouse. Camilo was on his way out of Cuba, and all I could see was an expanse of multicolored wings bursting away in every direction.

AT FIRST I FELT BURDENED BY QUESTIONS. THEN, GRADUALLY, I REALIZED that many of the answers were already in his original packet of letters to me, many of them had been there all along, neatly stacked postscripts explaining everything.

Now, after a Fourth of July unlike any other in my memory (one filled with true thoughts of independence) I went back over these postscripts with a different eye, an eye cleansed of its wounds:

"P.S.

"If you are truly going to understand your own brother (or any Cuban, for that matter) then you must learn the life of Martí. If it is a life you already know, and a verse you have already treasured, then try to see these notes as just one more dream shared together, leaping across the sea:

"José Martí was that most delicate of romantic creatures, the poet, a man unlikely to risk his flesh for any cause other than freedom. He was neither big nor strong. When he was just a boy he was arrested by Imperial Spain for promoting Cuban independence, a

movement lagging many decades behind the
independence wars of Mexico and South America.

"Spain still saw Cuba as her last stronghold, her most
loyal subject. Here she had launched her Age of Gold.
Here her treasure fleets had stopped on their way to the
royal treasuries of Castile. Here, in Havana Harbor, and
even in Vicente's little town of Trinidad, Spain had
fought off the British, Dutch, and French pirates. Here
she held her island key to the world she persisted in
calling 'New.'

"She called us, the Cuban people, her 'ever-faithful
isle.' Spain believed she could hold on to Cuba forever.
We were the last of her treasures, her sugar barrel, her
slave, her source of wealth. We were taxed so heavily
that only a few wealthy native-born *criollos* could afford
the poll tax, while Spanish-born *peninsulares* flocked to the
polls to choose their Ruling Council.

"Instead of salaries, the local magistrates depended for
their incomes on a percentage of the fines they obtained
by trying and condemning Cubans for a thousand
insignificant violations of absurd decrees.

"Naturally, the people rebelled. This only intensified
their persecution. Suddenly they were supposed to fly
white flags from their roofs, or risk destruction of their
homes. Men over fifteen years of age were prohibited
from leaving their farms for any reason unless they had
permission. Unmarried women were ordered to live in
assigned locations.

"The rebellion took many years, several wars, many
forms. From 1868 to 1878 we fought the Ten Years War,
concentrated largely in sporadic campaigns in the eastern

mountains. A restless pause, then the Little War, barely eleven months long. But the people were tired, fearful; they lacked the spirit for another prolonged siege (¡always, on an island, when we face a war we know that we will be killing not enemies, but brothers, cousins!) Then fifteen years of unquiet peace, and then finally, the widespread revolution of the 1890's. That is when the entire isle, *la isla entera,* went up in smoke, with Havana starving, and soldiers trying to choke us by stretching chains of forts across the width of the island from north to south, like necklaces, like collars and belts, hundreds of thousands of enemy soldiers stationed in rows, all neatly lined up, standing less than two meters apart. The forts were built so close together that guards could see from one to the next, and between the forts there were barricades of toppled jungle.

"Somehow the Cuban rebels were continually able to cross back and forth across these lines at night, by making themselves silent and invisible (as we do now, surrounded by secret police and their informers) or by hiding beneath tropical shrubs and towering grasses that spring up so rapidly that the Spaniards, accustomed to their arid climate, could not clear the vegetation as fast as it grew.

"Through all those wars the voice of José Martí burst upon this land, his poetry of love alternating with his eloquent, troubled (he longed to be a man of peace) call to arms. He had been sent into exile, he'd lived in every country except his own, traveled all over Spain and Latin America, taught at a high school in New York. He wrote from afar, sending his lonely verses home surreptitiously, weeping and causing tears to fall from every eye in Cuba.

"I am told that there in the North your heroes are never poets, but here we can hardly think of a hero who started as anything other than a master of soothing words. It is as if our hearts have long been aflame (still burning at wooden stakes) and we need these pleasing verses to calm them.

"Our people loved, and still love, José Martí, more than any living hero, certainly more than any poet before or since.

"Soon after the onset of the last of our three wars against Spain, the poet returned to his homeland and took up arms. He died at a place called Dos Ríos (not far from the mountain where our own father's airplane crashed) when he charged into battle *alone*, on a white horse (or so the legend goes) perhaps so excited he forgot to wait for the rest of his battalion, perhaps a deliberate sacrifice designed to inspire others, or a penance offered for the uncounted deaths already inspired by his poetic call to arms.

"Some think the Cuban people fought for the memory of Martí as much as for themselves and their future generations. The island was torn limb from limb, and still it seemed this third war could not be won.

"That is when your North Americans came. Teddy Roosevelt charged our hills with his Rough Riders, and the war ended swiftly, easily, as if it had all been a child's game, as if our own Generals had not led the *guajiros*, the peasants, along with their children and mothers, through three decades, on and off, of a struggle

fueled by such boldness, such passion, such madness,
that no one could believe it was suddenly over.

"We were more deeply wounded by Roosevelt's
victory than by our own defeat. Imagine the outrage of
our Cuban Generals as the Spanish flag came down, only
to be replaced by your Northern flag instead of by our
own, the one with a triangle of blood and a single star,
the one we'd been sewing in secret, keeping the cloth
hidden in our palm-thatched huts, looking forward to
the day when it would be brought out into the open
blue sky.

"Our Generals were not present at the signing of the
treaty or the raising of another foreign flag. They had
become invisible. They rode with ghosts.

"¡The Americans may have been practical and efficient,
but they didn't see what they had done! They forgot to
think of our centuries of colonization, our decades of
rebellion. It was as if we had never existed at all. We had
been dreamed.

"We hated them. We still do. Our Commander still
demands an apology. I picture the ghost of Teddy
Roosevelt apologizing to the ghost of José Martí. Then, I
add, it will be the Commander's turn to apologize too,
for turning the dream of Martí into a mockery of prisons
resembling, in every respect, the Spanish dungeon where
Martí, as a teenager, was imprisoned as punishment for
his dream.

"Great dilemmas emerge from that era of rebellion.
We simultaneously love and hate Spain (just as we also
detest and revere your North, your Fountain of Youth,
the destination of our brittle rafts). ¡And the father of

José Martí was himself born in Spain! The poet
composed loving verses about his father's homeland,
even while demanding liberty from that same precious
Iberia:

Amo la tierra florida

I love the flowering earth

And of course Martí described your North as well, the
place where he found the freedom to write as he pleased;
yet he wrote that he'd lived in the 'belly of the beast.'
He'd felt himself swallowed by the North, consumed by
refuge, by safety, by a land so vast that it yearned to
swallow all of Cuba as well.

"After the Spanish flag came down, many thousands of
the colonial soldiers remained in Cuba, married Cuban
women, became completely (except by birth) Cuban.
The enemy was now, once again, family. All was forgiven, all became fused, joined, united. That is the dilemma I find fascinating, the pathway I find enchanting:
After the decades of war, individuals looked at each
other and asked themselves, '¿To love, or to hate?' ¡And
of course, with the horrors of battle still fresh in their
minds, the choice was easy!"

THE LIFE OF MARTÍ WAS ALREADY SO FAMILIAR TO ME THAT THESE
descriptions simply reminded me how much I loved the poet's
own struggle to decide between love and hate. Camilo, I imagined, must now be making those choices himself, choosing between bitterness and hope.

I found myself faced with the same decision. During my desert vigil, I'd repeatedly thought of the Commander, his secret police, the prison guards, and Cuba's postal censors, always with deliberate rage. I'd felt myself capable of murder.

Now, Camilo's notes, re-read with new hope for his safety, were making me aware of swift changes taking place in the forms of my reality.

I noticed every word, the way he wrote *ser*, "to be," when referring to innate characteristics like strength and intelligence. The way he used *estar*, another, more fleeting "to be" when describing locations of houses capable of being picked up and carried away by hurricane winds. I noticed that fear and death were always referred to with the temporary form, *estar*. "I have fear, *tengo miedo*," Camilo would muse, as if *miedo* was something solid, something he could set down or give away, a burden he could easily dispose of whenever the notion struck him.

"He is dead" became *"está muerto,"* he is temporarily dead. In Spanish, my brother's descriptions of death carried the implication of an eventual return to life.

Now, re-reading camilo's postscripts, I suddenly saw cuba in a different light, as if viewed from the air, from a dizzying height. The island seemed full of pilgrims, people wandering through cities and jungles, longing to go home. They were all seeking a promised land, had been seeking it for centuries, imagining triumph as a dream called home. And I was one of them.

I was glad Camilo had trusted me with his packet of pain and hope. I loved to ruffle through the pages, finding postscripts I had not yet read attentively enough to catch every detail, the ones I had scanned too quickly the first time through, when I was still too numb to understand.

From the entrails of the Viper, my brother had written one particularly disturbing, arduously smuggled query on a scrap of soft pale cloth:

"¿When you were in Havana, did you notice the walls, the words? *¿Las paredes, las palabras?*

"¿Did you see how we have secretly scrawled, across every blank space, the single word, '¡NO!' We chose this as our only protest, because it is short, we can spray-paint it swiftly, then run away before the police notice. This humble word appears on all our walls during this time of our transition from loss to hope. We chose it because it gives the people hope, when they see that someone is bold enough to shout in the Commander's face: '¡NO! ¡NO! ¡NO! No, *Comandante,* this we will not accept, no, you cannot treat us this way, we do not agree. *No estamos de acuerdo.'* "

NO ESTAMOS DE ACUERDO. NO, WE DO NOT AGREE TO HATE YOU AND fear you. You can't trick us anymore. I absorbed that ¡NO! from Camilo's pain, and kept it with me, permanently, part of myself, my past, my memory.

Along with the pain and hate, we set aside fear, all of us did. We set the burden down. Camilo and Marisol in Cuba. Alina in Spain. Alec and I, simmering in our desert.

ALEC WAS OFFERED A PERMANENT POSITION AT THE UNIVERSITY OF Arizona during the end of that flaming summer. September, the start of the school year, a time for learning. Choosing love, I moved with him.

I felt myself melting and growing fluid. Every time I thought of love, I remembered Vicente and Sirena. No two lovers could have faced greater obstacles.

Two months had passed since Camilo's release. Two months of immersion in his letters, the Chronicle, his future. Alec assumed the whole terrible vigil would soon be over. I assumed nothing.

We sold my adobe home, packed Rocky into the jeep, and drove all over the foothills surrounding Tucson, until we found another old adobe on a wild, boulder-strewn site where our dog could be left to roam unfenced and untied.

She chased coyotes and rabbits, and when she came into heat, she ran wild, and eventually gave birth to giant puppies.

Whenever there was a wolf's moon, I thought of the Chronicle, of Camilo and Alina, and of Marisol, of her name meaning sea-and-sun, of her explosive past and her future foreshadowed by Greek tragedies and the memory of Martí, a memory he'd described as a basket of flames, *"un cesto de llamas."*

ALEC WENT TO WORK TEACHING AND COUNTING TREE RINGS, AND I enrolled in the university's folklore program, where I could study the fine, nearly indistinguishable line between fact and myth, between act and belief, creation and conjuring.

I studied nymphs and satyrs, Native American coyote legends, African spider tales, Australian dream songs, golden apples and golden fleeces, El Dorado in his golden city, and La Llorona, that frightful bereaved mother who mourns all over Latin America, searching for her lost child. Giants, elves, sirens, and mermen came swimming through my investigations.

Camilo wrote to me faithfully, every single week, first from

Cuba, then later, triumphantly, from Madrid, Miami, Geneva, New York, Washington, D.C. He wrote that he was making progress with the continuation of our father's work.

Months passed, another warm desert autumn, the pleasant winter. Another ardent spring, and suddenly, miraculously, Camilo's name was everywhere, printed on every newspaper, floating across every television screen. My brother had finally taken his accumulated sea of documents to a meeting of the United Nations Human Rights Commission. Everything, all the details of our father's assassination, all the swiftly dissolving stored-up secrets.

The details, he told me excitedly, in his letters, had been gathered in fragments from the air traffic controller who'd been ordered to falsify navigational signals to the small plane that had carried our doomed father, so many years before, into that tropical storm, slamming him against a mountain at the wild eastern end of the island.

The plane had been taking our father, by order of the Commander, to a secret meeting in the mountains of Oriente Province, to the Sierra Maestra, the Teacher Mountains. The meeting was to be a chance to discuss our father's work, negotiate, sign an emotional treaty, reach a compromise. Our father was the only passenger.

The plane vanished, along with (or so the Commander believed) a packet containing what was, at the time, the most comprehensive existing documentation of human rights violations in the Commander's Cuba: tortures, executions without trial, false imprisonments, threats, castigations, terror imposed upon the innocent relatives of condemned dissidents.

Of course, the precious documents were not enclosed in that plane as it carried our father to his death. Before agreeing to meet with *El Comandante*, our father hid all his papers deep in the cave beneath our ancestral home at the heart of the island, so that Camilo, unborn at the time, could rediscover them during his childhood visits to that neglected home. ¡We did, after all, have our secret language, our tongue of clicks and sibilance and visions!

NOW ALL THE UNWRITTEN CODES OF SILENCE HAD FINALLY BEEN BROKEN. Camilo spoke to everyone who agreed to listen. The air traffic controller confided in him. He was an old man by then. He'd floated to the Key of Bones on a raft of inner tubes and palm logs, eventually settling in New Jersey, where he drove a taxi and kept his guilt hidden, until Camilo tracked him down and scratched at the crusts of wounded memory. The old man, testifying in Geneva, confirmed that our father had died on a feral, explosive night, and that he had watched it happen, had caused it to happen, a glowing pinpoint flaring on the flat surface of his square tracking screen.

IN MIAMI, CAMILO MANAGED TO FIND THE WIDOW OF THE PILOT WHO'D flown our father to his fiery death. She testified that on the night of the airborne assassination, the Commander had warned her husband that unless he helped out with a top secret "special assignment," there could be trouble for his children the next day at school: a fire, poison, some unexplained disturbance . . .

From one of his houses in Cuba, the Commander, watching Camilo's entire televised presentation on CNN, cried outrage. He cried falsification of documents. He demanded apologies, retractions. He said his honor was at stake ("burning at the stake," Camilo corrected, at a press conference in Paris) and would be verified by history ("vilified by history," Camilo told reporters, chuckling, "or verified by myth").

By then, over eighteen months had passed since the buoyance of Camilo's frail raft of inner tubes and hope had carried him on a journey that moved him much farther than either of us had ever dared imagine.

They had been months of cyclones and monsoons, of solar flares, tsunamis, and rivers escaping their earthen banks. All over the world, villages were buried under rubble, and farms drowned beneath floodwaters.

The Commander's captive daughter escaped from Cuba disguised as a foreigner. More and more rafts left the island each day.

The Peregrín documents were all published, even Vicente's ancient tale of love, which proved to be the most popular segment of the massive volume, the "Chronicle of Antilia." My brother had originally titled his masterpiece "The Dream of Martí," but the publisher changed it in order to emphasize the mythical nature of the poet's island.

Throughout his work, Camilo used the poetry of the martyr to illustrate Cuba's centuries-old longing for a refuge from tyranny. For several months, the volumes could be seen prominently displayed in the window of every bookstore in the developed world, their covers wrapped in green jungle vines, fragrant orchids, and swooping birds.

Camilo's appendix to the Chronicle documented not only our father's murder and numerous other acts of force, but even offered proof of the black-marketing of human flesh by sorcerers during the Commander's final plunge toward Option Zero, when everyone in Cuba was so hungry that no one asked the source of meat, but simply grasped it, cooked and ate.

In the foreword, Camilo explained that *"Como lo soñó Martí"* meant "As dreamed by Martí," a Cuban colloquialism used to describe anything that turns out wonderfully, like the martyred poet's vision of love, flowers, freedom, justice, and music on the island homeland he'd loved so passionately. They were old dreams, ancient dreams, universal ones. The poet had borrowed them from myth, from legend, from truth, from hope, from the Bible, and set them all to rhyme.

In Camilo's published version of our family history, one description struck me as particularly portentous. It was the story of his own arrest, a description of the night when my brother had launched his raft of hope:

"Even in darkness, even at night, I knew that everything was hot and wide, a glorious, vibrant wild blue, that same rich, deep blue seen on the robes of El Greco's painted saints. I was happy, more than ever before, more happy than scared. Then I heard a voice. At sea you are not expecting to hear voices. You know that when you do, it will either be God or the authorities.

"They pulled me up off the raft, my eyes tightly shut to avoid accepting these men as real, to make them into a dream. I refused to see their faces. To me, they became men who'd lost their faces, men who became soldiers and gave up their eyes and mouths and ears. No nostrils either, or smiles, no tear ducts, no tongues. No human language that could be understood. Like creatures who had never learned to speak. Like those imagined by the Apostle Paul: 'If I speak with the tongues of men and of angels, but do not have love, I have become a noisy gong or a clanging cymbal.' "

LOVE, I THOUGHT, LOVE. SCRIPTURES DESCRIBED IT AS SOMETHING THAT "believes all things, hopes all things, endures all things."

God had promised that "love never fails." I sighed, and wept, sensing that my end of that chain of love would always fail, knowing I wouldn't do for a stranger what I'd done for my half brother. And what had I actually done? I'd kept a vigil, waited, struggled to communicate through censored mail. It was not so much to do, yet when I asked myself the question I'd managed to avoid until now, I knew that I wouldn't be able to keep that same vigil for someone else's half brother, for some cousin or uncle of some distant link at the far end of a prayer chain. I would lack the endurance, the patience.

I wasn't a Rescue Sister. I wouldn't know how to patrol the Caribbean *searching* for people to save from the sharks. I wasn't like my father, or Camilo, or Marisol. I was nearsighted. I had a hard time seeing anyone who wasn't standing right in front of me. I wouldn't be the type to go digging up human rights violations for investigation, or fighting in a jungle because I hoped that someday the children of strangers might receive shoes. The violations and bare feet would have to slap me in the face and shake me before I would notice them. Maybe it had something to do with being a native-born North American, with feeling immune from danger, protected by the dark, gold-embossed rectangle of my passport. Maybe I was selfish. Perhaps I lacked the vision of Martí, the wistfulness, the passion, the galloping charge toward martyrdom. Maybe courage came only as an afterthought to fear.

10

As Dreamed by Martí

Yo sueño con los ojos
Abiertos, y de día
Y noche siempre sueño.
Y sobre las espumas
Del ancho mar revuelto,
Y por entre las crespas
Arenas del desierto . . .

I dream with my eyes
Open, and by day
And at night I always dream.
And over the foam
Of the wide turbulent sea,
And among the crisp
Sands of the desert . . .

JOSÉ MARTÍ

ONCE THE NIGHTMARE HAD ENDED, I WAS ABLE TO LOOK BACK without flinching. My year of waiting for Camilo's release had encompassed a cycle of flash floods and searing heat. There were forty-eight wars on earth that year, but none of them gripped me as fiercely as the spiritual battle my brother fought while encased in the entrails of the Viper.

It was the year that Cubans began secretly celebrating a holiday they named Day of the Rafters. On this day, people toss white flowers into the sea in memory of all the lost *balseros*. It is a holiday we still celebrate in my family, on both sides of the

Florida Straits. I like to imagine that sooner or later the petals drifting north will meet those drifting south and be united. Each year, as we toss our petals onto the waves, Camilo and I recite a verse of peace and forgiveness, a poem dreamed long ago by José Martí. It is a lyrical verse in which the rebel cultivates white roses, *la rosa blanca,* for his enemies as well as his friends.

It was also the year that on Mother's Day a young Cuban woman died on her raft so that her small son could survive. All the men on the raft had been swept overboard by waves. Only the mother and child remained, clinging to ropes. Giving their last swallow of fresh water to her son, the woman then drank from the sea. The salt inflamed her brain, but the boy survived. To me, with the possibility of motherhood reserved inside my embryonic future, this minuscule everyday event seemed significant.

It was the year I received a complex censored note from Marisol, in which she told me of the wistful joys and fears of motherhood, by reciting, with the twisted loops of medieval script: "Female sea turtles weep big salty tears whenever they emerge from the depths to lay their eggs in hot sand."

That vigilant year preceded a summer of riots in Havana, followed by the mass exodus of more rafters than the Commander could stop, more than Florida would accept. It was a year when the *balseros* who survived their ordeal at sea could still hope to be granted political asylum in the U.S., when the eyes, hearts and doors of *los Estados Unidos* had not yet slammed shut, when *balseros* did not yet fear the barbed wire of foreign detention camps but only the Viper's entrails. It was a year when Camilo and I did not yet feel betrayed by *América,* a refuge that had not yet become as mythical as Antilia.

           *   *

As soon as Camilo was truly free, we began planning a double wedding. Camilo and Alina, Alec and I, we would all be married, like two sets of twins, in an exuberant dual ceremony under the scintillating Caribbean sky. Camilo and I communicated openly now, no codes, no metaphors. We called each other by phone, talked for hours, wrote long speculative letters expressing wonder about distances in space and the chronology of geological time. Our letters were full of words like Cretaceous and light-seconds, velocities, luminosity, and exosphere. We were still weighing and measuring.

We wondered about the future of our cousins, less fortunate than Camilo, how many others were desperate to flee on rafts. Some were *guajiro* peasants at the heart of the island, others "volunteered" in the tunnels beneath Havana. Marisol smuggled a note suggesting that the tunnels might be intended as burial sites for mass graves, in case of a rebellion.

We wondered about Marisol. We would always wonder about her, how she had survived, how deeply she had suffered, and how long.

We couldn't help her. She was like a shadow-image snapped by a polaroid camera. She would not take form until exposed to sunlight.

I thought of my own mother, fixed in my memory now, a helpless fledgling bird tossed by wind. "She was just learning to fly," I thought, whenever anyone offered condolences, whenever I heard, "She was so young" or "She was just entering her prime."

She had first gone to Cuba as a friend of Hemingway, but later had entertained herself by collecting *santería* figurines and talismans from cults in the scattered slums surrounding Havana. Perhaps that is why, as a child, I always dreaded dolls, found them menacing, buried them in the closet beneath blankets and sleeping bags, so they couldn't spring to life with their hollow limbs and ritualistic eyes.

My mother dabbled in the realm of spirits. It was her fatal error. She had been initiated into *santero* rites, becoming a "horse" of Yemayá. She claimed she'd been ridden by the spirit of a female sea. She sacrificed animals and fed fruits and flowers into the mouths of statues. Then she met my father and swiftly traded idolatry for ideology, switching her blood rituals and occult Yoruba phrases for the memorized promises of the revolution.

Perhaps the wind that carried her into that cliff was not an ordinary wind after all. . . . I dreamed with the purging of poets banished into gardens.

NOW THAT HE WAS FREE, I COULD FINALLY TELL CAMILO, WHEN HE called long distance from Miami or Geneva, that while he was still in the Viper I had never allowed myself to think of Cuba as only one tiny suffering nation among so many. I'd had to put the warring tribes of Bosnia out of my mind, and the starving children of Somalia. I told Camilo that until he was free I couldn't concern myself with the turmoil in Haiti or Peru. I didn't allow myself to continue wondering about the enslaved Andean girl who'd once turned to us for help, telling me her ghost stories and pleading for a way home.

"People are changed," I shout-whispered into the phone, "by knowing that a relative (no matter how distant or tenuous or previously insignificant the relationship) is the one experiencing, at a precise moment, pain or terror. The pain and terror become real, tangible, audible, possible. You realize it could happen to anyone, to you, or your husband, or (a despair unimaginable until that moment) to a child, your own child who so faithfully depends on you for protection. You become paralyzed, entranced."

IN TUCSON, AFTER THAT BREATHLESS YEAR OF WAITING, I COULD FINALLY face my feelings about Camilo's release. My emotions had been "on hold," like a telephone playing pre-recorded music. I had been a hostage of the family reunion we'd never finished. My two hours with Camilo in Old Havana had grown to the size of a hideous monster, a ravenous brute.

Alec had agonized at my side. Now he could admit his own relief and his secret envy. He said he felt like I was giving up a second love.

Even Rocky noticed the difference. We paid more attention to her now. We relaxed, invited neighbors to barbeques along with their dogs. Alec fed the dogs tidbits of lamb and pronghorn antelope.

A few months after the move, I wrote a letter of thanks to the prayer chain ladies near my old home in the California desert. They answered with descriptions of their joy at seeing Camilo's image on TV, reading his statements in *Newsweek* and *Time*. They said that of all their prayer requests over many years in many different prayer chains all over the U.S., the pleas on Camilo's behalf had been their most abstract, the most distant, their empathy for him the most difficult to reach. They said they had often been faced with debilitating physical ailments, with terrible natural disasters, dreadful accidents, explosive family secrets, betrayals, children in comas, mothers in suicidal depressions, grandfathers facing the amputation of limbs. But they found it even harder to understand rafts pushed away from distant shores, a sea patrolled with machine guns, monasteries converted into dungeons. They said they'd found it so frightening that just to avoid thinking of Camilo in his cell, they would sometimes forget to pray at all. They said they'd given up trying to understand, left it entirely up to God. They said it reminded them too much of sons and brothers and husbands lost in the jungles of Vietnam, the frost of Korea, the shores of Normandy or Guadalcanal. They said it was too hard to find room in their hearts for refugees while the North was finally at peace.

MARISOL, WHO FOUND NO WAY TO FLEE HER ISLAND, REMAINED TRAPPED. Her feelings about Camilo's release remained hidden. The censors still controlled her. She was never free to reveal her emotions, not even in the clarity and simplicity of her smuggled notes, but her former panic was now suppressed. The notes were brief now, only a veiled, surreptitious glow seeping through the words, as if the ink had been scented or the paper soaked in perfume.

Camilo was out of her territory. She no longer had any power to help him. Motherhood was distilled, a memory. Yet we knew she was satisfied, gratified, content. We sensed that her anxiety was now replaced by longing, her terror by nostalgia.

GRADUALLY WE LEARNED HOW MANY CORNERS OF THE EARTH HAD BEEN touched by my brother's plight. Behind-the-scenes advocates of Camilo emerged from secrecy. The genealogist and curator turned out to have taken an active part in securing his release, both of them having offered advice and encouragement to Alina and the Spanish cousins. The curator had even traveled to Cuba to have his say. He was received politely by one of the Commander's top aides, but he never knew whether anyone had listened to his testimony of words piled on top of histories.

Camilo and I received congratulations from even the most

unexpected quarters, from friends of the prayer chain ladies (let-ters came from Minnesota, South Carolina, Vancouver, Chi-cago) and from distant relatives in other countries. It turned out that the Peregrín clan had been spreading gradually, century by century, across all of Latin America and Europe; we had cousins in Argentina, Denmark, Guatemala, Portugal, Toronto.

Our Peruvian friend sent a carefully lettered note that seemed to have been written by a child. She'd heard about Camilo while watching the news through the window of an electronics store on a cobblestone street in Cuzco. She said she was proudly learning to read. She added that, having accepted me as part of her own family, she now knew Camilo was one brother she would never have to hide.

CAMILO'S OWN VOLCANIC FEELINGS CAME THROUGH IN EVERY LETTER, every phone call, even when he might have wished to keep them secret. We even learned the Commander's reaction. After he finally calmed down, he expressed regret of an unusual sort. In an interview with a German journalist, he admitted that Camilo's release had inspired the perseverance of thousands of other dissi-dents (he called them names like complainers, *majaderos*, and ingrates, *malagradecidos*) resulting in the launching of unprece-dented numbers of flimsy rafts from the beaches of Cuba, so many that the authorities could not possibly capture all of them, but had to let many go unrestrained, knowing that, in three out of four cases, the waves and sharks would finish their job for them.

IF THE PRISON CENSOR WAS MOVED IN ANY WAY BY CAMILO'S ESCAPE, WE never knew. Only this role remained completely anonymous, thoroughly detached. I liked to imagine that on quiet evenings the censor was tormented by doubt, wondering just how much agony he (or she) had caused, wondering whether a page or line or word removed from any one of a hundred letters had made the difference between hope and despair. I liked to imagine that eventually the censor grew restless, fearful, disillusioned, and eventually sailed away, landing on the Key of Bones, settling in Miami, where someday we would all meet each other and discuss the humorous past, laughing at a remembered thought cut from a note with ridiculous scissors, as if that dissection could have stopped the process that by then would be recognized as inevitable.

WE HELD A WILD, RAUCOUS ENORMOUS DOUBLE WEDDING ON AN isolated key in the Caribbean. We pitched tents on a palm-studded beach and flew in mountains of rice and black beans, roast pork and guava paste, and rum made fragrant by dagger-shaped slivers of tropical lime.

A flotilla of small boats brought so many distant cousins to our wedding from Miami that when we danced, our *conga* line was so long I thought the island was threatening to sink beneath our swaying weight.

Old ladies followed us around, the four of us, Camilo and Alina, Alec and me, offering congratulations and folk sayings and ghost stories and jests. Rocky chased sand crabs and seagulls.

Alec had made our cake himself, inventing the recipe as he went along, alternating layers of freshly grated coconut cream, milk chocolate, rum, caramel, and pineapple.

YEARS LATER, I WOULD LOOK BACK AT OUR WEDDING, WHICH SEEMED LIKE something permanent, a floating island of celebration still crisscrossing the sea at its own speed, like a boat that never runs aground. I would look back and think, gratefully, how I gradually discovered that Alec hated to argue, how we continued settling most disputes before sitting down to dinner, how as a concession to love I learned to discipline my appetite, although often I cheated between meals, seizing cookies, stray bites of fruit, slices of smoked cheese.

I would look back and think how my love for Alec had grown expansive, how I reached a point where I couldn't imagine life without his bouquets of homegrown flowers arrayed, like miniature rainbows, along the ledge of the kitchen window. Love had become as necessary as food or water or air, as essential as solid earth to walk on instead of waves.

I would look back, glad that we'd continued making (finding) love outdoors (it was like a fragrance already present, waiting to be inhaled) while our children were at school, glad that we'd been surrounded by sun, thorns, boulders, and a desert sky so vivid, so wide and intensely blue that we felt like we were flying.

I would look back with few regrets, remembering how, as we entered our thirties, both Alec and I began to gain weight, how we had to cut back on our ice cream, although Rocky could devour as many mice and gophers as she pleased.

I recalled our speculations about floating in outer space, how we daydreamed weightless days filled with soaring love and creamy malted-milk crunch. I would remember the day we realized that our children were growing up in a new millennium, and would probably end up riding space-shuttle buses to Venus or Mars on holidays. How glad we were that we'd seen a few mountains and forests before that happened, how amazed that we still didn't know our own world, our own family. It seemed too soon to move on.

Something had happened to time. It had become distorted, foreshortened, altered. The earth was only a few billion years old, and already it was fading. Only a few thousand years earlier, biblical sages had survived seven hundred years, eight hundred, nine hundred. Now we could barely hope for seventy, or eighty, or ninety, just a few dozen journeys around the sun.

NONE OF IT HAD EVER BEEN PERFECT. ALEC AND I CAME VERY CLOSE TO losing our love (it can float away, if you're not holding on) because sometimes, especially after the birth of each child, I would imagine that he was turning out like my father, that by now he would have secretly found another wife or planned some incredible act of courage that would result in a Commander's vengeance, another mysterious disappearance in midair.

It took us years to make (discover) friends in Tucson. We were so busy with children and careers that we even neglected each other occasionally, and others often.

We named the children after Camilo, Alina, Marisol, Sirena, and Vicente. They grew up so quickly that sometimes I would open my eyes in the morning, and think perhaps I had dreamed their infancies, imagined their adolescence.

For years at a time I forgot about Camilo and Alina, postponed visits to Miami, settled for nothing more than brief, sporadic friendly notes lacking the passion of more difficult times, the intense, detonated communications of our previous selves, when Camilo had truly been captive in a life-and-death situation, the letters that had been hurled like hand grenades across the sea of our fears.

Eventually, as Alec and I aged, and as our children left us, we were reminded that this was our only time on earth. We slowed our careers. Alec joined a garden club and started inviting friends over for meals of wistful pre-revolutionary Cuban recipes he'd learned from my father's cousins during our occasional visits to Miami. He served spiced beef roasts stuffed with sausage and olives, manioc drenched in garlic sauce, and the burnt milk candy concocted by immersing a can of condensed milk in a pot of boiling water for one hour. Alec even took up golf. He said he didn't care what he was doing, as long as he was outdoors and accompanied by friends.

I joined a prayer chain and attended dog obedience shows (Alec said you can tell a lot about a man by the tricks he teaches his dog) and genealogy workshops, where I learned how to trace my mother's lineage. I discovered that she descended on one side from a family of Greek olive growers, and on the other from the fifteenth-century marriage of a notorious British pirate and the daughter of a half-Chinese slave he'd purchased in India.

I even traced the genealogy of Irish wolfhounds, finding fourth-century references to their arrival as gifts in Rome, where a senator wrote to his brother in Britain thanking him for a gift of seven Irish hounds, saying "All Rome viewed them with wonder." This note made me think how easy it is to be deceived by visible traits, to think that just because something is big it will also be dangerous, that just because the wolfhound is enormous it will be vicious, even with dark gentle eyes and a sweet disposition. Wolfhounds, I decided, were much like love, terrifying to view from a distance, and wonderful to possess. Alec said his grandma had taught him that God gives us dogs to practice caring for children (to practice accepting that wild streak we can never control) and then, when we are old, He gets us accustomed to the idea of death by allowing us to remember how many generations of pets we have outlived.

*　　　　　*

I WOULD LOOK BACK, IN OLD AGE, FROM THAT JOYFUL ACCEPTANCE OF love, and remember our ebullient wedding on that isolated key in the Caribbean. I wore a blue silk dress overwhelmed by multicolored flocks of embroidered birds. Alina wore white.

Camilo, at the wedding, after the ceremony, while everyone else was dancing and eating, told me he had been taking flying lessons, and had not only obtained his license, but had gone far beyond, had accumulated three hundred hours of stunt flying experience, all paid for willingly by our cousins five centuries removed, who'd asked, in exchange (politely, Camilo added) for nothing more than a signed and notarized affidavit forfeiting all claim to the Inca gold seized from pirates by Vicente Peregrín, the gold later stolen from our ancestor in that cave beneath his home, stolen by his own brother, who victoriously carried it back to Extremadura, and never, for the duration of his long and pleasurable life, mentioned Vicente or Cuba again.

Camilo, at our double wedding, explained to me, proudly, vehemently, passionately, that he was now one of the Rescue Brothers who flew out of Miami every day, searching the Caribbean waves for raft people, peering down against the glare of reflected sun, seeking refugees who needed deliverance from the sharks and thirst and exhaustion that pursued them all the way from Cuba to the Key of Bones, or into the sky.

"I never fly solo," Camilo added. Then he stretched his arm across the winged shoulder of an invisible angel and invited me into the sky.

WE WENT UP (THE THREE OF US) IN AN OLD CESSNA. THE SKY WAS HOT, clear, tropical blue. On the ground, Camilo and the angel had carefully completed their walk-around, checking the metal for cracks, feeling the rivets, bolts, and hinges with their fingertips, testing the fuel by smell, looking for invasive birds' nests and insects that could damage the movements of flight.

Then we shared the wide sound of the engine starting up. I nestled into my seat beside the angel, cocooned within my seatbelt. The hard surface of the island's landing strip passed below, as if in a dream. Then came our miraculous lift into blue space, the reality of distance and height, the sensation of unlimited time, a view of sand and coconut palms, our giant *conga* line, the people waving up at us, Alec, Alina, Rocky, the old women, everyone dancing, shaking, running . . .

Then waves, sky, and behind us, a trail of looping white smoke signals, as Camilo perfumed the exhaust with oil.

"¡Como lo soñó Martí!" my brother shouted as we flipped upside-down. I shrieked. The angel laughed. It was a pleasant sound, like the ringing of a thousand tiny bells. Behind us a strand of symbols had emerged, letters, an upside-down exclamation mark, then NO and another, right-side-up exclamation mark.

Below us, a raft was floating toward the small key where we'd left our double-wedding party in full swing. Seven pairs of hands were raised to the sky, waving. I counted one woman, two small children, and four men, all as gaunt as skeletons wrapped in leather, skin blistered by sun.

We swooped low. Camilo was speaking, the angel humming. I heard a position reported, then a reply over the radio, the U.S. Coast Guard answering.

No, nothing defeats love, no, I was thinking, taking words from the angel's soft instrumental hum.

WE POUNCED DOWN TO REASSURE THE LONE *BALSEROS* THAT THEIR rescue was on its way. Above us, breaking up into small white puffs of defiance, I could still make out Camilo's answer to the

Commander's imagined plans for our ancestors' homeland. My brother's vehement, smoky "¡NO!" was breaking up, floating away, ready to resume its shape (this we knew because the angel shout-whispered it into our ears) as the puffs of oiled smoke traveled toward Cuba and eventually reached Havana Harbor. Camilo's single syllable would be seen from the sea wall, from the medieval castles of Old Havana, from Marisol's window, from the Commander's office . . .

YES, CAMILO HAD, AFTER ALL, FOUND A WAY TO MAKE FREEDOM exciting. He would not be disappointed. Flames rose from the angel's wings. Our imaginations were on fire, a white-hot blaze, leaping across the sea, across time.

For me, that moment of skywriting became euphoria. I carry its memory with me, always, just in case . . . I hold onto the faces of those rafters as they gazed up at the layered blue and saw, encased within that Cessna's rigid, opaque metal wings, those other softer wings, the translucent ones made of fire and wind.

11

Postscript

Empieza el hombre en fuego y para en ala

Man begins in fire and ends in wings

JOSÉ MARTÍ

F OR SOME YEARS AFTER OUR MARVELOUS DOUBLE WEDDING AND CELES-
tial Rescue Brothers flight, I felt haunted by our inability to
help Marisol. From her I had learned the most important lesson
of my life: we . . . must . . . have . . . faith . . . *hay* . . .
que . . . *tener* . . . *fe.*

I learned that slow, grueling lesson with gritted teeth and
clenched fists. I learned it while Marisol sang at the concert,
while she waited with a bronzed image of Doña Inés, while she
desperately smuggled one hopeful message after another. How
could I forget Marisol?

Long before her death, and long after (she died peacefully
after eighty-three journeys around the sun, during a day-care
center field trip to the beach, surrounded by wind, small chil-

dren, and angels) I was haunted by Marisol. I couldn't stop wondering what it had been like to be a mother struggling for the liberty of her son, knowing that as soon as he was free, she might never see him again. Her only hope was to outlive the bearded giant, a nebulous goal, which, through patience and courage, she eventually succeeded in reaching.

At the time of Camilo's release from the Viper and from Cuba, Marisol knew that as punishment for her efforts to free him, she would be held as a perpetual hostage of the Commander. It was a personal castigation, vehement and bitter, but it was not meant for her. The torment was intended for Camilo, and perhaps for our father's ghost as well. The Commander must have thought of this punishment himself, deliberately, receiving from its tangled implications some malevolent aura of satisfaction.

It was to be Camilo's affliction for the duration of his life, even after he was free, even after Marisol was dead. It would pursue my brother wherever he went, no matter how warm his welcome, how fervent his followers, how lively his jokes and *conga* lines. He could never escape the tentacles and tendrils of this, the Commander's condemnation: My brother had been freed in exchange for his mother's captivity. She could never leave; he could never return. They could never talk on the phone or meet over a dining room table or join hands to celebrate our true Lord's birth at Christmas, or to eat twelve grapes at midnight on New Year's Eve, or to commemorate anniversaries, birthdays, and graduations. They would not cry together at funerals.

ALTHOUGH I SUSPECTED THIS CRUEL LACERATION, I DID NOT HAVE IT confirmed until many years later, when I was finally able to visit Marisol in the same odd chimney-shaped house where she and

Camilo had first greeted me during that hurricane season of 1992.

Marisol had her own little business by then, just as she had sworn she would. It was a home day-care center. She was perennially surrounded by a dozen small children who shouted and squealed at her side, making her smile.

She said the years of waiting had made her old. Now the children were once again making her young. She said she had discovered the Fountain of Youth, and it was not in Florida, but in open sky. Marisol explained that she was making up for the years she had not spent playing with Camilo when he was little.

"I lived only for the revolution then," she confessed. "Only for the Commander's words and for my husband's ghost as he struggled to convince me that the words were just illusions. I thought the revolution would put shoes on the peasants' feet, food in their mouths. I didn't know it would shred the design of our lives, toss our scraps onto distant shores.

"I had not yet allowed myself to believe that my husband had been murdered, assassinated, executed without trial. At first I would not even admit that it was true he was a bigamist, that he had another wife in another country, your mother, *tu mamá.*"

Marisol said Camilo, although just a child, was the one who had gradually convinced her of the Commander's betrayal, and of her husband's secret. " 'A betrayal of faith,' he said, this when he was only twelve years old and was beginning to understand our inheritance of layered deceptions, *nuestra herencia de engaños.*"

MARISOL ASKED ME HOW I HAD MANAGED TO KEEP LOVING HER ACROSS that wild sea, those turbulent waves and fiendish winds of the Caribbean, how, when we never really knew each other at all, except for a few days spent together in crisis, in anguish, days of waiting, days strung together like beads, each one round and whole and finite, ending with the Radio Martí broadcast at seven o'clock each evening. Now she embraced me. We wept. I knew she wasn't really asking me "¿how?" She was asking herself. We had been writing to each other for many years by then, complex, cryptic symbols at first, and then finally, after the Commander's inevitable fall (a tumble through time and space) the ordinary clear and simple letters most people write to each other across seas and continents, inquiries about health, news of journeys, rites of passage, victories, and disappointments.

"¿How?" SHE REPEATED A FEW YEARS LATER. *"¿CÓMO?"* SHE WONDERED, still surrounded by small, excited children with their big, round, Fountain-of-Youth eyes. Camilo and Alina were at our side this time, with their daughters, and Alec, with our sons, who, despite all our sensible parental arguments, had insisted on bringing along, on this pilgrimage to Cuba, our matriarchal Rocky (a centenarian, as measured in dog years) and two of her many enormous descendants. The dogs, much taller than most of the children, were busy licking faces and bare toes and the rims of coffee cups.

"¿How?" CAMILO ECHOED. HE HAD OFTEN TOLD ME THAT HIS daughters, born in Miami, were so free they might never choose to believe that their father had been peered at by one-eyed giants through slits in a metal door, in a converted vine-clad monastery, in that quiet Havana suburb called the Viper.

"¿How?" he exhaled. *"¿Cómo?* By sending smoke signals, forbidden jokes, poetic metaphors, parables, tales of small everyday events, which, when sent across the sea, become significant, like omens or oracles, the prophecy of ordinary people speaking in tongues. ¡Skywriting! *¡La escritura aérea!"*

I thought of his emotions floating across the sky, a reflex of the tortured human spirit. I imagined typhoons, siroccos, trade winds, harmattans, chinooks, monsoons, twisters, mistrals, mare's tails, Zephyrs, Aeolus, wind tunnels, bellows, howls, whistles, gusts, squalls, gales, tempests . . . I thought of these winds as any student of folklore would, with a mixture of surprise, delight, and the fervent desire for some sort of belief.

This happened at a time when all the statues on the island had already been toppled. They'd been smashed and beheaded during that panic following the Commander's death, when mobs inverted Lenin and broke Don Quixote, and even sent Doña Inés sailing down from her perch. Of course, they left José Martí standing. In fact they polished his surface and brought him bouquets of white roses, and recited into his marble ear their own bubbling fountains of verse. They left the angels standing, and Cristo, arms outstretched, face tranquil, eyes gazing beyond land and sea.

BY THEN CAMILO AND ALINA WERE BOTH PROFESSIONAL SIMULTANEOUS translators in Miami, performing acrobatics of the mind, providing the alchemy for international negotiations and corporate bargaining. "We work in a medieval Moorish bazaar," Camilo liked to jest (his humor returned with a vengeance once he was free—nothing was spared, not even his childhood carnival of capitalism brought to life as a thieves' bazaar, not even freedom of speech, or of the press, or the liberties of satirical cartoonists). "We wear silk veils draped across our faces," Camilo said, describing his work. "We traverse dark alleyways, using secret hand signals, evading evil wizards, seeking magic lanterns." I could see how satisfied he was with his freedom to say these things.

CAMILO CONFIDED THAT HE OFTEN DREAMED WITH HIS ANGEL. HE SAID the angel was no longer just his, but was shared with someone else, someone anonymous, crouched in some cave or cell, awaiting rescue.

Marisol said her husband's ghost had appeared to her in a vision, commanding her to raise many children and go on with her life as if she had never borne a son and lost him, as if there had never been any separations.

I took my turn to speak, when the time seemed right, when there was a brief moment of flashing lightning and tropical silence, heat curling into the room in waves, Marisol spreading and waving an old peacock-shaped fan of blue Chinese silk to cool the wet faces of dogs and children.

I told about the bearded demon who still occasionally floated through my kitchen and patio in Tucson. I said I kept love and wolfhounds to chase it away, out into the desert, into a sparse forest of saguaro cactus and howling coyotes.

I said that I had dreamed with the censor, not the ordinary Cuban postal censor, but the prison censor, the one who decided whether Camilo would know when relatives were trying to contact him through the walls of the Viper. I said in the dream I had forgiven that censor, who then moved on, glided away, to some other island, some other time.

WE SHOULD HAVE BEEN ENJOYING AN ORDINARY FAMILY REUNION, children shrieking, pastries vanishing from carefully planned mounds, grandmothers dancing with tiny cautious barefoot steps.

With the Commander's fall, the era of exile had truly ended, but we, the Peregríns, had never finished our first reunion so many years earlier, the one interrupted by Camilo's departure. Now we needed to dissect the hardened tissues of our wounds, to count the rings of our wood, measure their width, the droughts and floods.

Camilo told me the Viper was much as I'd imagined, only without windows. From the outside, he said, Villa Marista was the most placid structure imaginable, a confiscated monastery, blossoms, vines, hibiscus and jasmine.

Inside, he revealed, it was still truly medieval, like my imagined castle dungeon, a labyrinth of corridors and stairways, rows of cells lined up along dark hallways.

"The rooms where they search and interrogate," Camilo said softly, his memory threatening to spring back to life, "are brightly lit. Green vinyl chairs. Desks. They give you documents to sign, confessions. They take you to a gymnasium where you become the living ball in a bizarre ritual game, tossed, batted, kicked. They keep score. You can't distinguish between their goal and yours. Everyone is wearing a uniform of one sort or another.

"They tell you the Viper is just a doorway into a long dark tunnel leading to other, more insidious, permanent prisons. You realize you have been living during a reign of demons. It is something you already knew very well, from the tales you have heard, but now you understand the meaning of terror. Before, you knew, you heard, you saw, but you escaped, inside yourself, into the sky, the sea. Now, you feel it, breathe it, a toxin in the air, fumes, something exhaled by a dragon emerging from its cavern, green fire. They threaten your family. They say they will make further accusations, friends, cousins, uncles, your mother.

They say they wish you had children, then they could *really*
teach you. They splash cold water on your face.

"You sign the documents. Without reading them."

Camilo sighed. None of this was flowing easily from his
mouth or heart. It was coming in stiff, gasping bursts, in blasts
from a cave of wind. His children were listening. My children
were listening. Even the wolfhounds seemed attentive.

"The Commander comes to your cell to visit. He lectures. You
agree with everything he says. You have been ungrateful. He is
magnanimous, a giant of history, a father figure, your benefactor,
an altruist, unappreciated.

"Your cell is dark. The only light enters through a series of
very small narrow slits high in the wall. Yes, it is your daydreamed window, Carmen, yes, there is a window just as you
imagined, but this real window is far too small for a view of
flamingos and pale moths. No scent of the sea. You are inland,
far from any shore. No breeze. Never a glimpse of the howling
wolf's moon.

"Light filters in from the hallway through those high slits. The
angel you imagined is with you, the angel is real, not a fantasy.
Your only visible companion. You have long conversations with
the angel in many languages, including some that don't exist,
never existed, until that moment. The angel has many wings and
many faces. The wings are not cold and white, but fiery, translucent, luminous, attached to their own source of light.

"Interrogations begin in the morning. You don't know what
time it is when they return you to your cell, your slit of light,
your glowing, loquacious angel.

"Your ears ring. The vibration is like music, because you know
it means you are still alive, still hearing. Blood flows from your
entrails. Urine is red, sky is black. The air is like a mist in the

jungle, thick with visions and the dreams of ghosts. You see poems written on the walls by prisoners who preceded you, and after awhile you give up wondering where those souls dwell now.

"Guards watch you through a peephole. They shine flashlights at your eyes. They whistle to each other, some sort of code.

"Your bed is a wooden board. It hangs from the ceiling. The cell door is metal. It creaks when the giants enter or leave.

"Yes, Carmen, you were right. They are very big, standing up, towering over you. You are very small, reclining or crouching, a child, a newborn baby, waiting for food, for water, for voices, waiting to be picked up and comforted."

"No, I did not keep my sense of humor. There were no cartoons written on air, only prayers, only pleas.

"If you had companions, perhaps together you would secretly joke about the guards, make fun of them, challenge your friends to a duel of wit. Find medicine in the laughter. But no, you are alone with the angel, in darkness, and the angel speaks of things that are no longer funny, of light, music, manna, rivers flowing from hidden springs in vast deserts.

"Yes, sometimes the angel picks you up, places you in the sky, on God's shoulder. You look down, dizzy from the height. Everything below is small but not comical. A world of stinging ants and swarming bees. You float back down, saddened, yet relieved.

"You dream, and your dreams glide out through the high slits, down the dark hallways, up the stairs, out the guarded doors, to people you love who are far away, farther than you ever imagined a place on earth can be. You have not been taught to measure that kind of distance. Later, years later, your loved ones will tell you how they saw your dreams floating in the air, how you dreamed together, ignoring the walls and waves that separated you from each other.

"Then you are free, not only out of the Viper, but off the island, flying away, leaping the sea. You look down and see clouds. You learn, in a foreign land, where nobody understands you even though they speak the same language, you learn that others have been working to free you, dreaming of your freedom, praying for your release, sending pleas and arguments and testimonies and dollars, all of it hurtling into a deep well, all vanishing, except the prayers. Then the Commander decides you can go. He has not experienced a change of heart. He has not been moved by the pleas of your loved ones. He has not finished with you or with them. He has seen a way to keep you bound, even when you are across the sea. But of course, the decision is not his. He is not in charge, by now he must be starting to realize that. Someday it will be the final blow, but not yet.

"Out there, in that open world, you will find you are still afraid to speak, to take your documents to Geneva or New York, to the United Nations or Amnesty International or Americas Watch or Freedom House. You are afraid the Commander might hurt those left behind. You know he can put your friends in the Viper as retribution for your offense. He can take your cousins, your mother. They will be assigned to work brigades digging tunnels under the old city or to chop sugarcane in the torrid green countryside. They will be referred to as volunteers.

"Yes, you are disappointed by freedom, but only because it does not protect your loved ones from the Commander, only because you cannot share it; it does not stretch across the sea. You long for a liberty made of elastic, new, improved manufactured freedom, one that expands beyond its natural boundaries.

"The Commander is still with you, inside of you, a parasite. He chews on your guts, he spits at your eyes, a cobra. You can never escape him. He follows you.

"So you stop writing to the ones you love who are not yet free. You speak out in public, show the documents, hold press conferences, appear on talk shows, answer questions. You never ask yourself whether anyone on the island is being punished for your boldness. You already know the answer.

"Then, years later, when finally the Commander is gone, dead, forgotten by most, you are reunited at home. You see that yes, those who stayed must have suffered. This you see by their eyes, by their silence. You plan a dinner together, a party, a family reunion. There are many children, a new generation, delightfully ignorant, free of memories. You finally see what you have done. You know your skywriting was seen from below. You hope it was all you could do, the triumph, exultation, the shouts.

"Yet yes, you see how the others have suffered from your actions, how they were accused, tortured, confined, enslaved.

"Yet *you* did not create this inferno. You are only a witness, a bystander. You have done nothing cruel or savage, you just sailed away on a raft, so innocent, so dreamlike, almost pleasing, when viewed in retrospect, an adventure, a youthful act of defiance against a man who never really controlled you at all, never really controlled anything at all, a man who created illusions, a conjurer.

"You have floated, you have soared, leaving the others behind to be accused. They are like tiny figures in a whimsical medieval portrait of hell, something sketched by Bosch."

*   *

CAMILO SAID HE THOUGHT ABOUT THE CHRONICLE OF ANTILIA EVERY DAY, about that refuge of the imagination. "How Vicente and Sirena loved each other so much that they perished together, hidden in a cave, rather than allow themselves to be separated, even though they'd hurt each other so often, loved each other so imperfectly, understood each other so incompletely.

"I think we're all just like them," Camilo added. "We have our home above a cave, our darkness, our secrecy. We keep treasure, or a memory of it, an image of it, knowing it never belonged to us, never belonged to anyone, but was captured and traded repeatedly, stolen, seized, stolen again.

"We have our unfinished Chronicle, layers of mysterious chained script scrawled across space, waiting to be deciphered. And from it we learn only that trust, *confianza*, is as close to God as we can be on this earth, and betrayal, *engaño*, as close to the inferno." Camilo sighed when he'd finished this confession. It was the longest, deepest sigh I'd ever heard. It carried with it shrouds and winds and feathers and leaves. I knew I would never hear a sigh like that again. My brother was finally on his way home.

DECADES AFTER THAT LONG-AWAITED FAMILY REUNION WITH CAMILO AND Marisol, Alec and I retired from the University of Arizona (he from the Tree-Ring Laboratory and I from the Folklore Program, where I had, for many years, been studying legends about Titans, nereids, ogres, jinni, and sylphs). We crossed the sea and moved into my crumbling ancestral home at the heart of the island.

We rebuilt it the way we thought Vicente Peregrín and Sirena would have liked, with fragrant vines and flowering herbs draped across every archway.

*　　　　　　　*

WE LIVE ABOVE THE CAVE NOW. WE RAISE A FEW CATTLE AND A SMALL
field of sugarcane (¡not enough to require slaves!) at the edge of
this wilderness of jungle and flaming wings.

I NEVER MADE ANY CLAIM TO MY SPANISH COUSINS' INCA GOLD, BUT
dozens of Miami and Havana cousins did, as well as a few unre-
lated Peregríns from Colombia, Uruguay, and the Canary Islands. Both the Peruvian government and the Shining Path
rebels filed claims to what they believed must be their rightful
portions of the gold. An Amazonian drug lord did the same.

The Spanish cousins were so tied up with lawsuits and public-
ity that they hardly ever had a chance to visit, but when they did
come to Cuba, we held joyful family reunions of unprecedented
proportions. "Mammoth, gargantuan, colossal," were a few of the
adjectives used by *Newsweek* and *People* magazine (for many years
reporters followed Camilo wherever he went) to describe our
long sinuous wildly boisterous *conga* lines of cousins, angels, and
wolfhounds.

One of our sons (the one named Vicente) has moved to Extremadura, that remote, starkly poetic region of Spain, where he
barters wine and harvests cork, a partner of the cousins five
centuries removed. He chuckles when he tells us that the priest
who helped us find the Spanish cousins left the church soon
after, to marry the daughter of one of our Peregrín cousins, and
that together the newlyweds made a barefoot pilgrimage to the
Holy Land, by way of a freighter across the Mediterranean to
Morocco, followed by a long, dangerous trek by camel caravan
through the markets and sand dunes of the ancient world.

*　　　　　　　*

OUR NORTHERN LIFE HAS NOT LEFT US COMPLETELY BEHIND. I STILL GET Christmas cards from prayer chain friends in Tucson and California. We still send each other prayer requests, and we pass the exchange of pleas and thanks along many invisible links to God.

I am, however, still attacked by monstrous tropical fevers, and my curiosity about the strange dreams of those around me continues. For instance, during the winter of 1998 I learned that the old man who called himself Icarus had finally patented his flying golf cart, creating an era of traffic jams in the skies above Palm Springs.

And the Peruvian waif learned to read and write beautiful poetry, Andean legends, paper daydreams. Camilo was the one who helped her get started in her craft. He even used a portion of his own book royalties to educate her children in Miami (she arrived unannounced after reading the Chronicle, carrying a suitcase full of Andean wildflower seeds, accompanied by a husband, half a dozen daughters, and as many of her brothers and sisters as she could find after the Peruvian mountains finally settled into an unquiet peace). Camilo writes to me, with glee, that every time our Inca friend takes an elevator to his penthouse office, she brings along a stone to place at the top of a pile she has created on the soil surrounding a potted palm.

ALEC STUDIES MAHOGANY TREES IN THE JUNGLE AT THE HEART OF THIS island we both love so passionately, and I gather fragments of legends once told and re-told in the now-extinct language of the Hidden Ones. I learned, from an old woman who heard it from her grandmother, that once, on a ranch near Trinidad, there was a girl who was kidnapped by pirates three times in a row. Three times the girl was taken to the same camp in the Tortugas to await her ransom. When she was finally returned to her home for the last time (she was an old woman by then) a priest sat outside her house and watched as her anger grew. Within a few hours he had counted more than 50,000 devils entering and leaving through a gourd that hung from her ceiling, and that's how he understood the depth of a young hostage's aging fury.

I am slowly compiling an as-told-to volume of these obscure (yet significant) Cuban tales.

ON QUIET EVENINGS, ALEC LIGHTS SCENTED CANDLES AND SERVES luxurious meals of udders fried in a sauce of olive oil, fragrant lemongrass, and wild Malabar almonds. He has planted a forest of cinnamon trees. Together we enjoy abundant and unexpected splashes of an outdoors love that now, in old age, falls upon us in dense curtains along with the hot tropical rain of the island's heart.

During *siesta* hour I embroider silk birds with poised wings, perched above pale soaring horses. An angel floats in and out of our rooms chasing bearded demons. I have noticed that time moves in slow circles, on endless waves, like rafts set adrift.

We keep wolfhounds in the patio. Alec trains them to smile on command. He tells our grandchildren how his own pioneer grandmother used to claim (vehemently) that once upon a time in some ancient Ethiopian kingdom, the people chose a dog as their ruler, because they knew the dog would be able to sniff out the difference between good and evil, and would find no fear in evil, but would growl and attack it, while licking the fingers of good. Rocky, of course, is gone, but her memory has taken on legendary proportions. My grandchildren often recall the stories they have heard about her size and the sweetness of her smile, her taste for lizards and tidbits of ice cream, and the way she could spot a bearded demon miles away, and chase it so far that it wouldn't come back for months. Rocky is, in other words, a mythical dog now, dead but larger than life.

My brother's escape from Cuba is similar. His grandchildren grow nostalgic imagining the danger they missed by being born too late. They think of Camilo as some sort of antiquated gun-slinging television hero, a comic-book supercharacter brought to life. Camilo says he denies all claims to heroism, but of course no one believes him (¡how could we, remembering that lonely raft at sea!).

ALEC IMPORTS A SUPPLY OF EXTRA FLASHLIGHT BATTERIES FOR OUR expeditions into the cave, which can be reached through a secret compartment beneath the floor where Vicente and Sirena once vanished into their love, and where, on occasion, we still dis-cover (and leave untouched) the skeletons of those who died while hiding.

On festive occasions we invite all the neighbors (mostly dis-tant cousins on my father's side) and Alec cooks goat stew with saffron rice. We concoct immense tubs of our own fresh ice cream in jungle flavors: mocha, wild cashew, purple *níspero*, or-ange *mamey*.

In my spare time I research Alec's Dutch, French, and German ancestry. I have already carried his family tree back to the early 1500s, to that daring and tragic Age of Gold. I am discovering that Alec's lineage, like my own, descends from a long chain of fugitives, pirates, slaves, sailors, and cosmographers.

WHEN OUR GREAT-GRANDCHILDREN COME TO VISIT US FROM TUCSON, Miami, and the cork forests of Extremadura, they play in the jungle, chasing butterflies and unicorns. Knowing they are in good company (the angel floats beside them) we allow them their freedom to romp and dream (of course, the decision is not ours; we couldn't stop them if we tried).

From Miami, where Camilo and Alina make their permanent home, my brother writes to me quite often. His letters are long, elaborate, lyrical, self-revealing testimonies, never ambiguous or hypocritical. That unchained script, he claims, is his way of infusing his aging freedom with the reclaimed thrill of youth.

Camilo and I are finally getting to know each other. We're old now, and we are just beginning to have the time and sense for long visits, quiet conversations and leisurely meals followed by hot, lethargic afternoons spent in my verdant patio among the wolfhounds, where we sit swaying in hammocks, dozing, singing, or exchanging tall tales.

Usually we like each other. Sometimes he frustrates me with his way of saying "you" when he means "I" and with his disdain for ice cream–tasting contests and expansive silk fields of embroidered birds. I, in turn, exasperate him because I continue imagining his feelings instead of asking him what they really are. Camilo accuses me of censoring my speech even when we are alone and free with no need to disguise our emotions. He says I get sidetracked too easily (he calls this a tendency to place parentheses around large chunks of my life). I defend myself stubbornly, insisting that since ancient times, life has always followed zigzag pathways. Then we both laugh, knowing how old-fashioned and impractical I sound. Camilo says I am just like Vicente Peregrín, incapable of learning the art of celestial navigation. I remind my brother that in Vicente's day, it was called *navegar por fantasía*, to navigate by fantasy, and that I, if nothing else, am an expert at that.

I believe that like most siblings, Camilo and I have loved each other all along, thanks to the angel, that fiery messenger who followed us around reminding us how little we know and how soon we will have to stop pretending.

CAMILO IS STILL VERY MUCH IN LOVE WITH ALINA, ALTHOUGH HE DOES repeat to her, on occasion, how much she wounded him by defecting at a time when he had not yet resolved to hurt Marisol by doing the same. Alina responds by reminding her husband that she was injured when he allowed her to defect alone. It should have all been over long ago, but we modern Peregríns still find ourselves dreaming, nearly every night, with stranded rafts and skywritten phrases. We continue to feel helpless even when we are not.

CAMILO STILL FLIES. HE STILL SKYWRITES, PATROLLING THE CARIBBEAN FOR raft people, warning, with an exaggerated ominous grin, "just in case." Occasionally I see his smoke signals drifting past my tall open windows at the heart of the island. By the time these messages reach me the smoke has broken into puffs of fragrant white, and usually I can't read a word of it, but somehow I find the shapes comforting because I know it means Camilo and so many others are constantly reinventing our freedom.

Camilo has willed the original manuscript of the Chronicle, along with all our father's papers, and his own, to a small private library dedicated recently in Trinidad, on a cobblestone street not far from our ancestral ranch. The library was dedicated by the genealogist and the Sevillan curator, both invited to Cuba by Camilo as a gesture of gratitude for their small but critical roles in freeing him from the Viper.

Camilo has asked me to document my own version of all the events surrounding his attempt to escape from the Commander's Cuba on a raft (hence this naïve and simplified narration, a mere seed when compared with Camilo's eloquent forest of revelations). He says it is important to remember that the era of Cuban raft people affected tens of thousands of ordinary families who were forced to wait anxiously on both sides of the Caribbean for news from Radio Martí, news that would bring them either torment or joy. He said the library commemorating *balseros* should include at least one North American female point of view, my own. He asked me to write this history with the heart of a mother, from my refuge of imagined Northern safety.

He said, "Tell whatever comes to your mind, whatever struck you as significant, and also what you felt about the experience, the layers of emotion, fear piled on top of hope, rage on top of joy, anxiety, dread, uncertainty." He instructed me, very specifically, to compare his tropical island to my daily life in the Northern desert, so that eventually someone reading it from a vantage point of the distant future could look back and see exactly where these two drifting currents might meet. Camilo says it is essential to view each sliver of history from many sides, as if the past were a hologram, or a fire opal or star sapphire, reflecting different shapes and hues when viewed from different angles. On quiet days I go to Camilo's library and leaf through the testimonies of rafters who survived, and of the parents, siblings, and cousins who waited to find out whether the wind and waves had carried them to the Key of Bones or into the sky.

NOW AND THEN ONE COUSIN OR ANOTHER MENTIONS CASUALLY THAT during the flurry of interrogations surrounding Camilo's arrest, accusations of collaboration were hurled like bottles at a riot, and a period of imprisonment in the Viper usually followed. Several cousins have now documented, for Camilo's library, the odd and terrifying experience of being punished for someone else's secret embarkation from home on a raft. Alina has written her testimony as well, and Alec is working on his. Only Marisol never had a chance to open her receptacle of memories.

Marisol never told anyone the details of her punishment. We never *really* knew whether she was arrested, interrogated, tortured, threatened . . . but, quite naturally (like seedlings or moss) legends grew up around her memory, and I have often heard it said that she was tied up with barbed wire and dragged across the thorns of a toppled rose bush, then left naked on an ant hill to be stung by angry insects. Dismayed, I know that no matter what else I hear, this must always be the version I will secretly continue to believe.

I miss Marisol, even though she lived far away and I never really knew her. I dream with seeing her at our next big family reunion, the one where we all go home and dance on clouds and shout from the sky, surrounded by light.

I worry (even though our true Lord, for two millennia, has been telling us we don't have to worry about anything) that when I enter that realm of light and song, my father will also be there, waiting, but since we've never met, we might not recognize each other. I plan to ask an angel to point him out. I also hope to meet Alec's grandma, and his parents, and Vicente Peregrín and Sirena, five centuries dead, speaking their two separate languages, still (inadvertently) teaching others about love.

But there is more to this chronicle, of course: on the evening of my father's airborne assassination he hastily jotted the following appendix to the documentation of his plight:

"Tonight I will be killed, not because I don't know how to avoid this secret execution, but because I have been warned that if I do rescue myself, my dear wife Marisol, who is with child, will be killed in my place, as a way of forcing me to comply with the Commander's wishes.

"I confess that I do have another wife, but she is safe now, off the island, and therefore out of the orbit of our tropical lives, which can never really continue anywhere but here. I, unlike so many others, cannot become an exile, because my work is here, and to my unborn child I do hereby will its hidden pages, along with those of our ancestors Vicente and Sirena, who, without meaning to, taught me about love. Unfortunately, in my case the lesson was learned too late, and was received at one of those explosive moments in history when love does not seem to be an ordinary possibility, but appears dreamlike and otherworldly, like something viewed through a telescope, across light years, from a distant, unknown galaxy of heat and light."

THIS APPENDIX HAD ITS OWN RESONANCE. IN THE YEAR 2015, A FORMER United Nations delegate commented, in his memoirs, that the moving account of our father's murder, delivered with passion and courage by Camilo Peregrín in Geneva so many years earlier, was instrumental in triggering the process of thought that gradually altered international opinion regarding the Commander, who, until that time, had still been viewed by so many Third-World nations as a "savior and culture-hero of mythic proportions."

A noted Valencian historian wrote that intellectuals in the developed world had failed to acknowledge and protest the widespread repression and corruption of the Cuban Commander's reign of terror, particularly its propensity to punish family members along with, or instead of, dissidents, a tradition inherited, the historian lamented, not only from other totalitarian communist tyrannies, but from the medieval Inquisition as well, an institution that, like so many others, revered itself as the champion of freedom and justice.

On a more personal level, during a *Playboy* interview some time around the year 2000, a famous Brazilian actress mentioned that after reading the Chronicle of Antilia and playing the part of Sirena in a television mini-series released during the summer of 1999, she was so moved by the passion and regrets of Vicente and Sirena that she felt inspired to spend less time on the road and more time with her family.

THE COMMANDER HAS BEEN DEAD FOR MANY YEARS, AN EVIL MYTH, HIS name pronounced only as a curse. Perhaps his dreaded memory could have been expected to control our actions, but in reality, we have acted just as we would have if he had never lived at all.

Before moving to Cuba, Alec and I briefly debated the wisdom of our fanciful wish, our nostalgic daydream, this recalling, through borrowed memories, the lives of others.

What if another Commander should suddenly rise up, pulling onto his feet enormous steel-toed boots? What if it all happens again, the horror, the silence, the desperation?

Then we remembered (the angel quietly reminded us) that a Commander could loom anywhere, at any moment, under any pretext of economic reform or political restructuring or ethnic purity or unanimity of belief, veiled by any guise of morality or responsibility or equanimity or nobility of thought.

SO HERE WE ARE, ALEC AND I, LIVING ABOVE THE CAVE OF MY ANCESTORS, knowing that we are just as safe, and just as vulnerable, as any-one in Tucson or Miami, Geneva or the cork forests of Extrema-dura. Camilo, when he flies down from Miami to visit, whispers that in the North there are now sudden rumblings of censorship and tyranny, and Alina confides that she is sometimes afraid for the safety of her great-grandchildren. So we are beginning to devise a secret language, the five of us, Alec and I along with my brother, my sister-in-law and this fiery sibilant angel (heat fills the room where we work, flames spill out of the windows).

We are busy collaborating, struggling to devise an indecipherable code, borrowing words from the Hidden Ones and images from ancient fables.

"¡Just in case!" Camilo explains. "Just in case the people of the North, impatient for perfection, decide to turn their problems over to some attractive human leader who promises homemade earthly miracles. We are evolving away from our rulers," he adds, "or else they are swimming away from us in this sea of confusion."

OUR SECRET PEREGRÍN LANGUAGE IS VERY EASY TO UNDERSTAND IN SOME ways. The words simply sound like birds and insects. Phrases float and drift. We have our collection of silent hand signals, grunts, groans, hisses and barely perceptible movements of the eyebrow and lip. By putting together whole sentences we can tell each other things that appear to be nothing more than harmless jungle tales, but of course they are not really stories at all. They are solid packets of memory bundled up and hidden next to our hearts, where they feel so much like soft, round weapons that when we dance, the coded memories bounce around our lungs and make us laugh.

Even that circular laughter has fitted itself into the disguised syntax of our new language. And of course, in Miami, under his elegant antique matrimonial bed, my brother has stashed enough rope and inner tubes to carry his entire family away from the

North, just in case one of those ominous new potentates suddenly decides to censor the smoky, coded shapes Camilo so lovingly inserts into each rolling dance of natural cloud.

> Carmen Peregrín Larue
> Ranch of Antilia
> Trinidad, Cuba
>
> Hurricane Season
> Year of Our Lord, 2033

ACKNOWLEDGMENTS

I am deeply grateful for the patience, love, and support of my husband, Curtis, and my children, Victor and Nicole.

For their parts in our family's real-life rafter drama, I am especially thankful to Héctor Peña Fernández, my parents Eloísa and Martin, *mi abuelita* Fefa, José and Diznarda Ferrer, Mercedes and Tomás Burcet, Lelis and Ernesto Montoto, Anita Suárez, Fefita and Fabio Díaz, Maritza Alvarez, Igor Pérez Uría, Amy and Jonas Back, Radio Martí, and *Los Hermanos al Rescate.*

For prayers, I am thankful to the prayer chains, J.G., D.G., R.B., P.B., Eileen Schnarr, Connie Boyd, and Pat Herrell.

For the precious gift of encouragement, I thank my agent Julie Castiglia, author Joaquín Fraxedas, and bookseller Kathy Gluesenkamp.

For unusual empathy and brilliant editing, I am deeply grateful to Leslie Meredith.

For their love and faith, I thank many relatives in Cuba, who for their own safety cannot be named. To my *balsero* cousins Marvin Pérez Uría and Julio Pérez Uría, I wish to express the utmost gratitude for their trust and hope, and to Lupe, Alaín, Arlene, Ivelise, and the Alonso family, I offer thanks for sharing the vigil.

I am indebted to Marvin Pérez Uría for a copy of our extensive family tree, which provided inspiration for the dream of Antilia, and to Mayra Sánchez-Johnson, President of the Cuban Genealogical Society, for helping me explore additional branches.

Above all, for the persistence of love I thank God.

ABOUT THE AUTHOR

Margarita Engle is the daughter of a Cuban mother and American father. Born and raised in Los Angeles, she grew to love Cuba during extended childhood visits and continues to travel there whenever travel restrictions allow.

Her first novel, *Singing to Cuba* (Arte Público Press, 1993), chronicles the sorrows and hopes of a Cuban peasant family uprooted by the revolution. Her short stories, nonfiction and award-winning haiku have appeared in various literary journals, national Hispanic magazines and in anthologies such as *Short Fiction by Hispanic Writers of the United States* (Arte Público Press, 1993), *In Other Words: Literature of Latinas of the U.S.* (Arte Público Press, 1994), *New Worlds of Literature* (W.W. Norton, 1994), *A Haiku Moment* (Charles E. Tuttle, 1993), *A Haiku Path* (Haiku Society of America, 1994), *Hispanic, Female and Young: An Anthology* (Pinata Books, 1994), and *Four Seasons* (Ko Poetry Association, Japan, 1991).

Engle's editorial columns on Hispanic culture are nationally syndicated by Hispanic Link News Service in Washington, D.C., and she has written many technical articles for agricultural and gardening magazines. Trained as an agronomist and botanist, she also studied creative writing with award-winning bilingual novelist and University of California Chancellor Tomás

Rivera, author of *Y No Se Lo Tragó la Tierra,* And The Earth Did Not Part.

Engle is the recipient of the prestigious Cintas Fellowship for 1994–95. She lives in California with her husband and children.